TARAN MATHARU

CONTENDER

THE CHAMPION

Hodder
Children's
Books

HODDER CHILDREN'S BOOKS

First published in Great Britain in 2021 by Hodder & Stoughton
This paperback edition published in 2022

1 3 5 7 9 10 8 6 4 2

Text copyright © Taran Matharu, 2021

The moral rights of the author have been asserted.

A CIP catalogue record for this book is available from the British Library.

ISBN: 978 1 444 93905 7

Typeset in Garamond by Avon DataSet Ltd, Arden Court, Alcester, Warwickshire

Printed and bound by Clays Ltd, Elcograf S.p.A.

The paper and board used in this book are made from wood from responsible sources.

Hodder Children's Books
An imprint of Hachette Children's Group
Part of Hodder & Stoughton
Carmelite House
50 Victoria Embankment
London EC4Y 0DZ

An Hachette UK Company
www.hachette.co.uk

www.hachettechildrens.co.uk

CONTENDER

THE CHAMPION

Also by Taran Matharu

SUMMONER
The Novice
The Inquisition
The Battlemage
The Outcast (*The Prequel*)
The Summoner's Handbook

CONTENDER
The Chosen
The Challenger
The Champion

To my readers, for all your support.
This book could not have been written without you.

PROLOGUE

'You're a murderer, Cade.'

Finch's voice drifted from the darkness. Cade could not see him. He floated in a black oblivion.

He knew this was not real. That somewhere he lay in bed, tossing and turning from fever. He had a memory of it. Saw it in his mind's eye.

Quintus, fussing over the infection in his leg. Unpicking the rough stitching with his gladius. Draining and cleaning the infection that had set deep into his leg.

Amber, bathing his head with a wet rag. Blessedly cool as his brow burned and he tossed from the pain.

But the fever dream did not abate, even as he clawed at consciousness. He could not wake, no matter how hard he tried.

More memories flashed across Cade's psyche. The slavers, taking him to New Rome in chains. The emperor, trading armour and freedom for victory in the arena. His return, and the battle with the alpha. Amber kissing him. He clung to

1

that single, happy memory, but it melted away like snow.

'Murderer!'

Cade walked in the sands of the arena now. It was almost empty. No cheering crowds. No emperor watching from his box.

But there were men standing in front of him. Pale as corpses, eyes wide and staring. Finch. The Chinese soldier. The Confederate Colonel.

Three men he had killed, for the entertainment of thousands.

'I had no choice,' Cade whispered. 'Abaddon made me do it.'

'There's always a choice, Cade,' Finch's voice rasped across the sand. 'Abaddon picked you for a reason. Because deep down, he knew what you were. A killer.'

He laughed, a choking, wheezing laugh. And as Cade spun away, seeking the oblivion of unconsciousness, Finch's voice morphed into the cruel voice of Abaddon's avatar.

'What's the matter, Cade?' she giggled. 'Don't you like my game?'

But then there was another voice. It was distant. But kind.

'. . . gonna be OK,' it said. 'You can do this.'

He saw his mother. His father. Going about their lives, cooking together in their home's kitchen, like they always did. His home. And he would return someday. One way or another.

He half-opened his eyes.

Amber looked down at him, her brown eyes filled with concern.

2

'Your fever's breaking, Cade,' she whispered. 'I don't know if you can hear me. Just keep fighting. Just a little longer.'

It was hard to keep his eyes open. He closed them, and felt her fingers smooth his sweat-slick hair.

Fight a little longer.

He could do that.

ONE

Two months later

Cade pressed his face into the soil, praying he would remain unseen. He stilled his breath and listened to the throaty rumbles of the giant beasts ahead of him.

Not yet.

The rushing sounds of the river beyond accompanied the sound, and the wind moaned through the leaves of the trees above. But only one sound broke through the tempest of his thoughts. Thudding. Footsteps that shook the very ground.

Branches crackled as they neared, snapping beneath an enormous weight. Cade clenched his fists, forcing himself to remain motionless.

Just a little closer.

One breath. Two.

They were right on top of him.

'Now!' he roared, leaping to his feet.

Without looking to see if his friends had joined him, he

charged towards the herd that had halted no more than a stone's throw ahead of them.

A pair of shouts joined his own as Cade waved his arms at the startled animals; a dozen long-necked sauropods seemed to blot out the sky. More than he had expected.

Twenty feet. Ten. *Five*.

Cade's scream choked in his throat. He halted in the shadow of the nearest beast. For a moment their eyes met, and he saw the dull cow-like eyes roll back in their sockets.

Amber and Quintus came to a stop on either side of him, their yells fading, in awe of the elephantine beasts before them.

'Move,' Amber screamed hoarsely. 'Come on!'

For a long, hanging second, the beasts only stared. And then, as if by some unknown signal, the herd turned and ran.

'Go!' Quintus yelled.

The very air thundered from the stampede. The chase had begun, and now Bea, Trix and Yoshi emerged from the trees nearby, crowding in from the side, screaming like banshees and forcing the lumbering giants to hug the riverbank.

As they followed the path of least resistance between the tree line and the flowing water, Cade watched the largest of the beasts slow, though whether due to exhaustion or the realisation that the small humans chasing them were no danger, Cade could not guess.

'Just a little further!' Cade panted.

But the beasts had come to a halt, the nearest creature even turning to face them. It was a large specimen, its neck and flanks pitted with scars from attacks by far more formidable predators.

It took a step forwards, its long tail lashing behind. And then, a final outcry, as two more figures emerged from the trees. Scott and Grace.

They waved a giant banner, hollering at the top of their lungs. The flag, no more than a stretched sackcloth between two poles, looked puny. But at its centre, painted in ash, charcoal and river clay, was a giant eye.

The sight was enough to startle the beasts once more, and the ground reverberated as they took a further few steps back from the new arrivals.

It was enough. The great matriarch that led them fell away from the front of the herd, braying with panic. And then the moan turned into a single scream, cut short almost immediately.

At the loss of their leader, the beasts scattered into the woods, barreling by Bea, Trix and Yoshi as they dived for cover behind the trees.

Cade staggered, panting, to where the great sauropod had fallen: a pit that had been covered with branches, and then a thin screen of mud and leaves.

He crouched and peered over the crumbling edge. It was a cruel sight. The great beast had been spitted by sharpened stakes embedded at the bottom, fire hardened and sharpened to pierce the thick hide and flesh that had fallen upon them.

Even in his moment of triumph, Cade could not help but feel a tinge of regret for having killed the gentle giant. The sauropod breathed a last shuddering breath before its head fell to the ground.

'It worked!' Scott cried. He scrambled up beside Cade and

stared down. The look of elation on his face soon faded at the grisly sight below.

The others joined them, equally in awe of what they had done.

'I didn't think we'd . . . manage it,' Amber said.

Cade shook his head. 'Native Americans used to do something similar for thousands of years. We just used a pit instead of a cliff.'

That hole in the ground had been their personal hell for longer than he cared to remember. It had taken weeks to dig. In fact, it would have been impossible had there not been a natural depression there already, likely carved by a now defunct tributary of the river.

The gathering of their 'bait' had also been tricky, for the sauropods would only be tempted by the tender shoots and buds from the tall branches that even they could not reach. Luckily, Quintus could climb like a monkey, cutting free the branches and gathering the bitter fruits that the great beasts seemed to love. They had left these near a natural bush trail, and had taken turns to camp out there, waiting for the herd to come.

As for the eye banner, Cade hadn't been sure it would work. But Amber had come up with it when she saw the same markings on a butterfly's wing, designed no doubt to scare other animals too.

'Now what?' Yoshi interrupted Cade's thoughts.

'Fetch Amber's axe,' Cade said. 'And Scott, you go up ahead to watch for predators. We won't have long before they come to scavenge.'

He gripped the knotted rope set in the pit's side and began to descend. It was going to be a bloody evening.

TWO

As the sun slowly began its descent towards the horizon, the team got to work.

The hunt had been one of desperation. Fish, once plentiful, had become scarce, with their stretch of river empty of the small silver shoals that Yoshi had once caught in his nets. They had been forced to make an attempt at big game.

But it had been worth the risk. The giant they had felled was a treasure-trove of food. Cade's only regret was that they had not planned better for harvesting the great bounty. He now realised that their work had only just begun.

First, they had to breach the tough hide on the outside – thicker than a rhino's and twice as tough, with a layer of yellowed fat beneath. It took almost an hour of hacking with Amber's axe to cut a hole in its belly. Another to pull forth the folds of intestine and get to the nutritious organs within. There was no hope of cutting through the great bones and sinews of the legs, though Scott succeeded in cutting free a tail tip the length of a forearm. He dry heaved when he was done.

Regardless, it was the fatted offal within that they needed in the first place. In the modern world, humanity had turned their noses up at anything but the muscles. Yet their ancestors would have fought for the nutritious organs within. The starving teens were no different.

Quintus had some experience in the butchering of meat, having rustled sheep from the Picts he had fought in Scotland. But he had never come close to processing an animal this size. Yet, to Cade's surprise, the nimble boy crawled into the belly of the beast itself, gladius in hand.

Soon enough, Quintus shoved out the wobbling lump of purple flesh that was its liver, so heavy it took two of them to lift it. Next came the football-sized kidneys, and the heart so large that Cade could put his fist through the arteries. More organs followed, ones Cade could not recognise, but he trusted Quintus to know what he was doing.

As for Grace, she busied herself with attacking one of the giant legs, cutting away at the knee joint with Amber's axe. All the while, the others worked at carving gobs of grainy yellow fat from around the belly's slit . . . And then the pterosaurs came. Circling overhead like vultures.

Once these flying scavengers arrived, Cade knew their time was almost up. Their arrival was the first sign carnivores looked for, if the smell of blood did not attract them first. When Grace finally succeeded in cutting free the leg, he accepted it was time to load up.

It was painful to leave before a carnivore was actually seen,

11

but Cade knew by the time they were warned of one's approach, it would be too late to take the meat with them. So he called it, wiping the blood and sweat from his brow, ignoring the disappointed groans of the others.

Exhausted, they succeeded in transferring their prize out of the pit and back to the keep in a single trip, hauling it up in makeshift wooden cages they had made specially for the occasion, and then dragged in sleds of sackcloth and sapling logs. It was a mountain of meat.

But they could not feast yet. Only a snack, to give them strength for what was to come next.

Having passed through the tunnel back to the keep, they lit their firepit and flash roasted select slices from the tail tip. Soon, they were sitting around the fire, hungry chewing precluding any conversation. The only noise was the soft groans of relief as they filled their bellies. It had been their first taste of meat in a long time.

'You sure this is going to work?' Yoshi finally said, mumbling through a mouthful of sauropod flesh.

He nodded to the structure that they had spent almost as long building as they had digging the trap. A wooden shed, rough and ready as a shed could be, with walls of logs and mud, and a roof of branches, sealed with woven palm leaves and sackcloth from their bedding. Who would have known just how important Amber's axe would end up being? None of this would have been possible without it.

The smokehouse was smaller than Cade would have liked. But it would have to do.

'Let's get cutting,' Cade said.

Now the most gruelling work of all began. Freshly sharpened swords hacked at the steaming meat, slicing strips to be hung on the horizontal poles affixed within their rickety shed.

Cade himself worked on the great, clawed foot that Grace had succeeded in detaching. He was careful not to nick his blade on the enormous leg bones within. To hold up such weight, they must have been strong as steel.

It looked for all the world like an elephant's foot, with the same leathery skin and longer claws. Cade was just glad that the herd of sauropods that had stumbled across their path was of the smaller variety.

They worked into the night. Fat was transferred to buckets, to be kept in the cool of the baths below the keep. It was to be rendered later, and their main source of energy – without carbohydrates to fuel them, they were in sore need of it. It would be their cooking oil, their butter, their soup and sauce.

Only when they were done did they light a fire within the shed itself, using green leaves to produce the most smoke, and stop the fire from spreading to the shed itself.

Cade knew only the theory of what they were doing – that the smoke would dehydrate the meat to the point of preservation, making a dinosaur jerky that would last for months.

When the fire was lit, and the smoke billowed into the shed, the group fell where they lay. But not Cade. He sat and stared at the sputtering flames, his face blackened, arms bloodied to the elbows.

13

Survival was one thing. But he knew that soon, the Codex would speak again. And the game . . . would start once more.

THREE

The Codex had been silent since the battle with the alpha. But the timer . . . it ticked away, just as it had before. Two months had passed already, with no sign of the drone waking.

There was a week to go. Cade had decided to focus on survival and ignore the dark cloud of dread that filled his nightmares.

'Mind if I join you?'

Amber's voice broke through his thoughts, startling him from the nodding doze that he had become used to over the past month. Their fear of a return from the slavers of New Rome meant that one of them kept watch each night, keeping an eye out for any ships coming up the river, or dark figures emerging from the tree line.

Cade nodded and scooted aside, and Amber collapsed beside him. It was cool at the top of the mountain, and though he had yet to bathe away the grime of yesterday's hunt, it was a welcome relief from the hot work below.

'How's the fire?' he asked.

15

She shrugged. 'Yoshi's keeping an eye on it.'

Her fingers intertwined with his, an unconscious affection that still set his heart aflame. He clasped them back, and the two stared out across the valley. It was beautiful this time of night. The twin moons of red and white cast a warm glow across the expanse of trees, tinged with the first rays of the sun blushing the horizon.

'It's nice up here,' she said. 'Romantic.'

She lay her head on his shoulder, and he smiled. The food they had gathered today had lifted a great weight from those shoulders.

'Who knew you could still be romantic while covered in dinosaur guts?' he said.

She kicked him gently, but he heard her snort. 'Way to ruin the moment.'

Their romance, hardly begun before his battle with the alpha, had been interrupted by his long recovery. But it was Amber who had sat by his bed as he had tossed and turned from the pain. Amber who had tended to his legs, and bathed his forehead as it blazed hot with fever.

Despite it all, Cade had recovered well, though he was left with a few scars. Thankfully, there was no permanent damage.

'We don't need to keep watch tonight,' Amber said, shifting closer.

Even now, Cade couldn't tell if it was the cold or affection. But he smiled nonetheless.

'Oh yeah?' he asked. 'How do you figure that?'

'Look at the pit.'

Cade squinted through the red light of the moons, his eyes

following the reflection of the river. At first, he could see only shadows. But as his eyes adjusted, he could see the shifting shapes, a darker black against the gloom. And as the breeze changed, he could almost hear the snarls and snap of teeth as the predators of the jungle fought over the carcass.

'You think any slavers are gonna come for us with every predator in the vicinity hanging around?'

Cade pressed his lips to her forehead. 'I think it's worth the risk if I get to spend the evening with you.'

Amber chuckled. 'That was just the right amount of cheesy. What did you have planned for me?'

'Dinner and a movie?' he asked.

'Classic,' she mumbled, lifting her head and stretching. 'Can you get hold of some *Terminator* movies for me? You said they made a few more.'

Cade shook his head. 'Trust me. Once you've seen the second, you don't want to watch the rest.'

Amber sighed.

'So . . . dino meat and Le Prince's projector?' he asked.

That earned him a grin.

'It'll have to do,' she said, feigning disappointment. 'Although I don't think I'd like to look at another Hydra as long as I live.'

'You're telling me.' Cade shuddered. 'I'm just glad I only had to fight one of their alphas. The last contenders fought hundreds of them . . . and won.'

The pair linked arms and began the long journey back down the mountain. At the top of the trail they gazed out over the red-sand expanse that stretched as far as the eye could see.

'You ever wonder what happened to the Romans who were here before us?' Amber asked. 'Quintus's legion, and the ones that came before?'

Cade bit his lip. He had pondered that very thing. The soldiers, Earth's prior contenders, had marched away to attack another species in one of Abaddon's rounds. An attempt to move up the leaderboard, and away from the red line that would mean Earth's destruction if they dropped beneath it. But then they vanished. At least, Cade and his friends hadn't come across them yet.

Was there another caldera somewhere in the distance? One populated by the primeval beasts of that rival species' past?

There was still a lot they did not know. Cade wasn't even sure if they would be defending an attack from a species below their leaderboard, as they had in the last round, or attacking a species above them to move up the leaderboard, as the Romans had.

'Cade?'

He hesitated, unwilling to turn their happy evening sour. 'Abaddon brought us here to replace them. That means they're . . . not here any more. Let's leave it at that.'

Amber gave him a half-smile. 'I like to think they're still out there.'

Cade doubted it. It had been years by now.

'You never know,' he said. 'Let's hope so.'

He took her hand. It was time for their first official date.

FOUR

Food. It had been the contenders' obsession for months, as inescapable as the hunger that had clawed at their bellies every waking moment.

Cade had dreamed of food most nights. Of his mother's pakoras, fresh from the pan. Sweet jalebis, pretzel-shaped and dripping orange syrup, ready to dissolve in his mouth.

But that night, with his first full belly in months, it was not food that occupied his dreams. No, only the giggling laughter of Abaddon, as claws and teeth reached for him from the recesses of his mind.

Cade jolted awake, cold sweat pooled on his chest. It was still dark; the red of the moon through the cracks in the shutters was all that lit the commander's room, which he still shared with the other boys.

He sat up and shook himself like a dog, as if he could rid himself of the nightmare. There was no such luck though. Even the soft snores of the others did not turn the oppressive darkness into anything less scary, the primordial part of his brain keeping his heart beating fast.

'You're awake.'

Amber's voice called out from the doorway, and Cade looked up to see her figure silhouetted against the flickering light of the Codex and its timer. He wondered if he had been crying out in his sleep and she had heard him from the girls' room across the hall.

'Come on, might as well check on the smokehouse. It'll be light soon.'

Cade groaned and rolled from the bed, careful not to tread on the snoring form of Quintus. The other boys had brought bunk beds from below up to the room – still too afraid to sleep in the ground floor barracks.

But the young legionary was more comfortable on the floor with a straw-filled mattress. He had taken to sleeping there while Cade recovered, to attend him if he needed water or help reaching the toilets far below. The arrangement had just stuck. Not that Cade minded.

Cade tiptoed over, and Amber led him to the round stone table in the room between the girls' and the boys' rooms.

'We need to talk,' she said, sitting down and motioning to the next chair over.

'Oh?' Cade said.

He sat on the stone chair, and only now did he see her clearly in the flickering blue light of the ticking timer. Her face was drawn and grim, stark contrast to the smile and soft kiss she had given him the night before.

'After our night together . . . I . . . I don't think we should be together any more.'

Cade's heart twisted in his chest.

'I don't understand,' he choked, the cold shock of disappointment chasing the sleep-drunk fog from his mind.

'I just . . . you're not a good match.'

Amber tossed her hair and leaned back in the chair.

'The whole night, all I could think of was . . . how fragile you are.'

She motioned at him, summing him up with a dismissive wave of her hand. Cade felt his throat close up, and a hint of tears prick the edges of his eyes.

'Amber . . .'

But he could not think of anything else to say. It was so sudden. Had he read their date so wrong? They had talked through the night, watching the sunset, even as their heads nodded in sleep. A soft kiss goodbye, heartfelt and tender. It had all been so perfect.

'I need to think of my future here,' Amber said, seemingly ignorant of the abject misery her words were causing him. 'I need someone who's going to look after me. You know?'

Amber had never needed, nor wanted a protector. She was as independent as any girl he'd met.

'This isn't like you, Amber,' Cade said. 'Why are you saying this?'

She smiled, but in the ethereal glow it seemed to have a cruel twist to it. It was familiar somehow.

'I just can't be with someone as pathetic as you are.'

Cade reached for her hand, and as his fingers brushed her own, he felt a static shock. Amber's smile turned into a shark-like grin, even as her face shrank and morphed, and

21

her figure shrank before his eyes.

Within moments, he was looking down at a cherubic little girl, her chubby legs dangling from the chair.

Abaddon's avatar.

'Your face!' Abaddon giggled. 'My my, you *do* care about that silly girl.'

Cade stared, speechless.

Abaddon jumped to the ground, her face contorted with malicious pleasure.

'You must forgive my little joke,' Abaddon said, pointing a dainty finger at his distraught face. 'Or rather, forget it swiftly, and listen well. I will only instruct you once.'

Cade's heart, already racing, seemed to rattle in his chest in anticipation of the cruel god's news. Their time of rest was over. From this moment until the timer reset . . . they would live in terror.

'My little crew of contenders has matured well,' Abaddon said. 'But watching you battle here bores me. It is time for you to fly the nest, little bird. To succeed where those before you failed. It is time to attack.'

The girl motioned behind Cade, where the Codex's flickering timer was replaced by the leaderboard – that pyramid of symbols that denoted where each of the Pantheon's contenders sat within the game.

As before, mankind was represented by a human skull. The red line under the third row delineated where humans and the other species above them would have their home planet destroyed, should they fall beneath it.

'You only have one path to attack upwards – this species, here.'

The block above the human skull flashed, and a symbol appeared there. To Cade's surprise, the symbol was not dissimilar to their own – humanlike but for the enormous eyeholes, non-existent teeth, and an upper skull that was distended like a football. It was, in a word . . . alien.

Abaddon paused, as if waiting for Cade to speak.

'What happens if we fail?' Cade managed.

Abaddon giggled.

'I will abandon you in their territory to fend for yourselves. Perhaps you can scratch out some form of existence in their lands. But that is not the real consequence. If you lose, I will not be bringing new contenders to the keep. It will be left undefended, and the next attack from below will find no resistance. Your planet will fall beneath the red line and . . . poof.'

Abaddon clapped her hands, wiggling her dainty fingers.

'Who are they?' Cade asked. 'Are they sentient? Do they have weapons?'

Abaddon tapped her button nose. 'Your Roman counterparts garnered little knowledge of this species before failing in their attack.' She chuckled. 'It has to be written down for the Codex to record it. Why, they did not even have time to give it a name before they were defeated! But you have the skull as a clue. Be glad you have that, at least.'

'Where will we go?' Cade asked. 'And what are the rules?'

Abaddon tossed her golden curls.

'There are no rules, other than that there cannot be a single enemy left alive in their headquarters before the timer runs out. As for where, you will find out soon enough.'

Cade shuddered involuntarily as the little girl's sweet voice spoke of death. It was sickening.

Abaddon giggled again. 'But you have not asked the most important question.'

Cade drew a blank.

'You must leave in exactly two hours, or the round is forfeit,' Abaddon said. 'Gather in the desert, and follow the rising sun.'

And with that . . . she was gone.

FIVE

'How long now?'

Cade did not even have time to register who had spoken, instead shouting over his shoulder as he poured the well's bucketful of water into his amphora. 'Ten minutes!'

The keep was a mess of activity, as the newly woken contenders hurried to ready themselves for the attack.

Yet, in the cold light of the early morning, Cade took comfort in the preparations they had made before Abaddon had spoken.

In a way, the threat of the slavers' return had been a blessing in disguise. What little food they had was packed in sackcloths, ready to be moved in case they had to abandon their home.

Their weapons were kept sharp and by their bedsides, as was the linen armour of those who had fought in the arena. Bedding and sackcloth tents had been prepared to take with them, and the sleds they had used to transport the sauropod meat to the smokehouse were ready to go as well, one for each of them.

But there was still so much to do. Amphorae had to be filled with water, and Bea and Trix had volunteered to run to the graveyard in the desert to gather spare jugs to refill for their journey. Even now, he kicked himself for not doing so before.

The meat, now smoked, was being packed to take with them, and an amphora of rendered fat was brought too. The rods and nets they used to catch fish, rare though that was, needed to be taken from their place beside the river.

Fruit they had left on the trees – to stop it rotting – had to be picked from the mountaintop and brought along. There was another week left on the timer, and they needed enough food to last them.

And with each moment, they remembered other things they needed. Utensils to eat with. Spare sackcloth for crafting. Sticks to hold up their tents, should the place they were going have none – certainly the desert would not yield any.

Moreover, the sun would bake them to a crisp if they had to march across the desert without cover. So makeshift parasols were under construction, made by the deft fingers of Quintus and Yoshi. By some good fortune, Quintus had built one before, to shade him as he fished along the riverbank.

A shatter of crockery followed by a scream of frustration sounded from behind him. Bea and Trix were back, and one of the amphorae they had brought from the desert had smashed on the cobbles.

Ignoring their annoyance, Cade tugged one from their arms and uncorked it, then began to fill it as he had done with the others.

'Well done,' was all he managed. 'You take over now.'

He dropped the empty bucket back in the well and turned to survey the others. Their sleds were lined up in front of the door in the keep's wall, almost all fully packed.

Drake's armour, that which Cade had worn in the battle against the alpha, was too heavy and hot to wear through the trek in the desert. It lay packed atop his own sled, the one at the very front.

To his surprise, everyone but the twins was waiting for him beside their sleds. Quintus and Yoshi had only managed four rudimentary parasols, but they were big enough to be shared between two people if they walked beside each other.

All in all, they were as ready as they could be. He stood beside the well, staring at the Codex, which had begun following him again.

There was a smaller timer below the first, denoting their time to prepare.

00:00:01:11
00:00:01:10
00:00:01:09

'Come on,' he called over to Bea and Trix as they filled another batch of amphorae and lowered the bucket once more.

00:00:00:57
00:00:00:56
00:00:00:55

'That's the last one.' He tapped Bea on the shoulder. 'Leave it. We can't risk it.'

He picked up two full amphorae and stumbled over to his sled, loading them as carefully as he could amid the morass of sacking, sticks and rope.

The twins followed, taking up their stations beside their sleds and looking mournfully at the pile of empty amphorae they had left behind.

'Move out,' Cade bellowed. 'We have to get to the desert, now!'

They pulled, the runners of the sleds scraping against the ground. The wood screeched along the cobblestones, then began to judder over the bones in the muddy field beyond the keep.

Ribs scattered beneath Cade's feet as the Codex hovered in front of him, the count dropping slowly.

00:00:00:19
00:00:00:18
00:00:00:17

'Come on!' Cade yelled, heaving on the rope as the desert sand shone ahead, just beyond the shade of the cliffs on either side.

He felt the crunch of sand and salt beneath his feet as the timer ticked down to zero. He dropped the rope and staggered, turning to see the others grind to a halt beside him.

His eyes turned to the Codex, waiting. For three juddering breaths, he waited. But if they had missed it, there was no indication. Only the flicker as the smaller timer disappeared, and the larger one continued its inexorable count.

'Did we make it?' Amber panted.

Cade turned towards her, and his eyes widened. Just behind them, a giant, opaque forcefield had bisected the canyon, blocking their return to the keep.

'There's our answer,' he said, feeling a twinge of annoyance. Part of him had hoped they'd be able to bend the rules and sneak back to the keep for more water. He should have known better.

'So what now?' Scott wheezed, flat on his back behind them.

Cade turned to the blazing sun, already feeling his skin burning under its glare.

'We walk,' he said.

SIX

The walk was hell. One that was made harder by their flimsy parasols, which could only cover four pairs. Every ten minutes, two of them would switch places, for there were eight of them walking the desert.

And even with this paltry shade, there was little to protect them from the reflection of the salt crust in the desert. The fair-skinned Bea and Trix, as well as the freckled Scott, were struggling the most.

They had stopped to make headscarves from the spare sackcloth they had brought. But after a day's walk, their water stores were already beginning to empty. If they did not see their destination within a day, they would die in this desert.

'How much further?' Bea asked.

Cade, leading the train of sleds alongside Amber, gazed once more at the horizon. But it was devoid of all life. Just an endless glaring white.

'There's nothing,' Cade called. 'We should take a break.'

He waited for the others to catch up, and they gathered

in a circle, sitting on their sleds with their parasols held high.

'Maybe we should travel at night,' Amber said after the group had caught their breath and gulped down more water.

'Then we can't follow the sun,' Grace replied.

'Is that what we're following?' Yoshi kicked the sand in frustration. 'Then we're on a wild goose chase.'

Cade furrowed his brow. There hadn't been time to tell everyone the full scope of Abaddon's instructions.

'Well, it's what Abaddon told us to do. Why do you say that?'

'Because the sun moves. We'll be curving from left to right. Basically a meandering circle, depending on how this planet is positioned.'

Yoshi illustrated his point with a sweeping finger.

'Well, what should we do instead?' Cade asked.

Yoshi shrugged. 'We're at Abaddon's mercy. His little toys to move as he likes. I'm just saying he's set us a pointless task. At the very least the Codex could be leading us instead of this sun crap.'

Scott chuckled bitterly. 'Well, maybe he just wants us all tanned for when we go into battle. You know, we gotta look good for the show.'

Grace rolled her eyes, though Cade saw the edges of her lips twitch.

He looked to Quintus. The young legionary was not the most talkative, but Cade had hardly heard a word from him since they had set off.

'Quintus . . . what do you think?' he said loudly, for Quintus was not watching their lips, but rather staring at the ground.

31

His friend looked up, and only now did Cade see the dejection in his eyes.

'My legion was three thousand, and . . . there were a few hundred others. They did this before us. Walked into the desert. They had weapons. Food. Much more than we.' He bit his lip. 'We are eight. Hungry. Little armour. How can we win where they . . . did not?'

His words echoed the heat-fuddled thoughts that Cade himself had been having. He'd been trying to ignore them; they were a bridge to be crossed later.

No one spoke, but he saw their eyes turn to him.

'Abaddon would not put us in a situation we had no hope of winning,' Cade muttered.

'Wouldn't he though?' Grace demanded. 'Maybe he's bored of us. Wants to wipe the slate clean. When we attack, we don't drop below the red line. That only happens if we get attacked from below and lose.'

'So he might throw us away on a suicide mission and get new contenders to replace us?' Amber asked.

'Why not?' Grace asked. 'He's done it before.'

Cade let out a long breath. 'He did mention there would be new contenders, didn't he?' He tried to remember. 'Right before my battle with the alpha – something about getting help?'

'So . . . we're going to meet them before the attack?' Scott asked.

'Or maybe they're the ones who will replace us,' Grace retorted.

Cade wished he could remember the exact wording of

what Abaddon had said. But it had *felt* like they would be given help.

'Look,' he said, holding up his hands. 'I can't read Abaddon's mind. Who knows what sick motivations he has. But what I can tell you is he doesn't lie.'

'Yeah, right . . .' Grace muttered.

'If he said we'll be getting help, then I believe him,' Cade went on. 'Quintus, do you know if there are any missing legions that he might place in the keep? We know he has a thing for Romans.'

But Quintus wasn't listening. He was standing on his sled, staring out across the plains.

'Quintus?'

The young legionary turned, and Cade saw the hint of a smile upon his friend's face.

'I see something.'

He beckoned Cade to jump up, and Cade did, blinking as he left their makeshift shade. Quintus pointed.

At first, Cade could not see anything, his eyes yet to adjust to the glare. But then, as he focused, he saw it, just to the right of the sun's place above the horizon.

It was small, almost a stain on the white of the salt flats. But the more he looked, the more he could make out. A structure. Alone in the sea of sand.

'Well, at least we're not going on a wild goose chase,' Cade announced. 'Come on . . . if we hurry we can get there before nightfall.'

They approached as the sun set, the structure casting a long shadow towards them as they staggered the last hundred feet of their day's journey.

It was a ruin. It was made of stone, though the outsides were blackened with the fire that had destroyed what must have once been a fort.

A crumbling tower at its front dominated their view, with a ring wall in varying states of disrepair behind it. Strangely, there was a wide space open beneath the tower, with large iron gates rusted off their hinges lying in the sand in front of it.

It was, as far as Cade could tell, human in origin. But then . . . who knew what their enemy was capable of.

'What is it?' Scott called out.

The Codex zoomed off, though the question was not necessarily addressed to it. In a flash of blue, it scanned the fort, before returning to its original position.

'*The harbour settlement of Jomsborg was completed in 965 in northwestern Poland, by order of the Danish king Harold Bluetooth, as recorded in the Viking sagas of Knytlinga and Fagrskinna.*'

Cade stared at the fort, realising that it must contain an entire village within, and that the wide space beneath the tower may well have been the harbour entrance for ships. Excitement, and even a tinge of hope, fluttered through his chest, but with an equal measure of disappointment. The fire damage on the outside told him that much of what was once there would have been burned to a crisp.

'Did he say *bluetooth*?' Scott asked.

'*Yes,*' the Codex replied in its robotic voice.

34

'That's what Bluetooth was named after,' Cade said, remembering that bit of trivia from the long historical documentaries he once watched with his father. 'The inventor was a fan of Viking history.'

He grabbed the rope and moved forwards.

'Come on. If it's a trap, there's not much we can do about it.'

SEVEN

Cade hurried ahead, dragging the sled behind him, new strength coming to him with the anticipation of rest. The temperature had dropped dramatically, and his sweat-soaked clothes were beginning to chill. There was not much hope of finding wood for them to burn, but if it was to be their final destination, they could burn the sleds.

He staggered through the entryway with trepidation, for the stone above seemed to be held up by dust alone. Yet, once they emerged from beneath, they found themselves in a space far larger than he had expected.

It was a village, that was for sure, made up of a series of stone shells that had no roofs at all. But strangely, there was a wide, open basin in front of where the houses stood, with wooden platforms built into the air.

Cade realised that they were standing in the harbour itself – now devoid of water. The wooden platforms must have been the jetties, surviving the fire thanks to the water they had once sat upon.

Not so the houses, which were more blackened and decrepit than he had thought they would be. Many had fallen to rubble, but the tower itself was made entirely of stone, and was the only building in the vicinity that might afford proper shelter. He only hoped it would not collapse when they entered.

'I wonder how long this has been here,' Yoshi said.

Cade was wondering the same thing, but since it had never been scanned, there was no way of knowing. His only clue was the yellowing grass that remained – suggesting it had been here in the desert only a few years.

It might have lain in ruin on Earth for centuries before Abaddon teleported it into stasis, ready to be dropped on Acies at a moment's notice. One thing was for sure: this was no coincidence.

'Codex, do we continue following the sun tomorrow?' Cade asked.

The Codex floated silently, and ignored his question.

'Great,' he groaned before turning to the group.

'I know we're all tired. But we have to take advantage of the light before it gets dark. Let's split into two groups – Amber, Grace, Scott, you circle left. Bea, Trix, Yoshi, circle right. Anything we can burn, any tools, anything at all, bring it back here. Quintus and I will watch the sleds, see if we can't get the Codex to tell us what's going on.'

'Aye aye, Captain,' Scott said, throwing an exaggerated salute.

This earned him a good-natured shove from Grace, and the two groups trudged away.

When their footsteps had receded, Cade sat down heavily beside Quintus on the legionary's sled.

'You think your legion came here first?' Cade asked, after waving for his friend's attention.

Quintus shrugged and pointed at the ground where their footsteps had tracked in sand and salt from the desert.

'No marks but our marks,' he said.

Cade sighed. He supposed it was for the best – retreading the same path the Roman army had taken could only lead to their defeat. After all, what could they achieve that three thousand trained soldiers could not?

'Codex, do we fight tomorrow?' Cade called.

Silence.

'Thanks, real helpful.'

Quintus shuffled his feet and kicked a small pebble down the cobbles.

'Come,' Quintus said. 'We must see if safe.'

The legionary staggered forwards, wincing at his aching muscles. Cade followed suit, but to his surprise, the entrance to the gatehouse and its tower was halfway up the stonework beside the gates, as if those who had once occupied it could fly. But of course, Cade realised, the entrance would have been at water level, which he now knew had been at least fifteen feet above them. The remnants of barnacles, calcified along the gatehouse's base, confirmed his theory.

They curved right, walking up the slope along the wall, until they found some stairs. There they walked back along the ramparts, peering into the village for a glimpse of their friends. But there must have been at least a hundred dwellings there blocking their view.

If Cade had been hoping for weaponry, or any other useful items on the walls, he was disappointed. The place had been picked clean, likely by the locals who had lived near the ruin over the years, as it lay empty in its harbour. Of course, that would have been before Abaddon had taken it.

They reached the gatehouse, and the tower at its top. This too was practically empty. A broken chair, simple and wooden, lay in the entrance. Dust, rags, the iron rim of an old barrel were within the main room, and an open room adjacent yielded only broken crockery and a splintered table. Nothing but firewood.

Still, there was a spiral staircase built into the inside, and after a brief pause to catch their breaths, the pair mounted the steps. It was like a small lighthouse, and when they reached the peak, Cade could see the remains of two giant braziers there, screwed so tightly into the walls that no one would have been able to scavenge them. These must have been used as signal fires.

But it was not these that fascinated him. 'Whoa,' Cade said, stumbling towards a catapult resting upon a stone platform. But the ancient piece of siege equipment was no longer workable. The ancient ropes that had once powered it had long since rotted away, and the timber that made up its frame had warped.

Beside it was a pile of perfectly round stones. At the very least, they could drop these on an invader's head as they rushed through the open harbour entrance.

It was a paltry find, but Cade was not willing to let their

39

good fortune go unnoticed. He held up his hand for a high five. Quintus stared at it blankly.

'Oh . . .' Cade said. 'Right, I forgot.'

High fives weren't a thing in Roman times.

Instead, he clapped his friend on the back.

'It's something,' he said, half to himself.

Quintus perched on the tower's edge and beckoned Cade to join him. They dangled their legs and stared out over the sunset. Tomorrow they may well die. But for now, he was with his best friend, watching the sun set.

They slept fitfully that night. The beds at the keep, paltry though they were, seemed like heaven compared to these simple mats of sackcloth laid out on the cold, uneven cobbles of Jomsborg's gatehouse.

To Cade's dismay, their search had turned up nothing. Only broken furniture that they used to fuel their hungry little fire, its low crackling echoing through the empty shell that was their new shelter.

It was a huge step down from their home at the keep. And as they had settled down for the night, Cade could think of nothing to say to lift their spirits.

So it was no surprise that as the dawn light filtered through the arrow slits of the gatehouse, he saw his friends were all awake as well.

The relief of the end of their desert trek had been replaced by trepidation. A battle was to come. And they might not all survive it.

Yet there was nothing to do but wait. The Codex remained

silent, no matter how often they cajoled it.

'So . . .' Scott said, stretching. 'Who's up for a bit of dinomeat?'

He reached into the sack he had been using as a pillow and tossed a shred of the stuff to Cade, before stuffing another into his mouth.

Cade looked at the wrinkled, black-singed morsel that was about as tough as leather. He lifted a tentative hand and placed it on his tongue.

To his surprise, it had a pleasant smoky taste, though he had to swig a gulp of water to help chew up the toughened flesh. At the very least, it was edible.

The crew huddled around Scott's bag, each taking a piece of their own and sighing with relief as their hunger abated. They had not tried the meat the day before, for it was packed deep among the sleds, and had preferred the sweet fruit from the orchards to keep them going.

Cade allowed himself a moment to relax, the sounds of concentrated chewing all that could be heard.

Or . . . was it?

There was a strange noise coming from outside. Halfway between a bird and an insect, a buzzy trill that was almost musical in its utterance.

In an instant, he was at the window, seeking out approaching enemies in the desert. He let out a strangled gasp, choking on the jerky as he pointed wildly.

The desert was no longer there. In its place . . . was another world.

EIGHT

Purple. Covering the rolling landscape like a cloak. There was not a single tree visible, only the waving fronds of violet fields, stretching on in an endless expanse.

Whatever creature had made the noise was nowhere to be seen, likely hidden among the tall grass. They were in another place. Lost, on a piece of another world.

'Holy shit,' Yoshi breathed beside Cade.

The others crowded around the single window, and then Cade heard footsteps running.

'Come on,' Amber called, and Cade turned to see her rushing up the stairs.

He followed, heart pounding, mounting the steps two at a time. At the top, he staggered to the parapet, careful of the crumbling rocks that dislodged as he leaned against it.

The rubble tumbled down, landing on a crust of sand and salt. Some of the desert remained, a perfect ring of it where the settlement had been teleported from one place to the next – and them with it.

But it was not this that fascinated him. Rather, it was the sheer expanse of the place. The ground, undulating gently as far as the eye could see. No mountains. No landmarks. Just the purple sea of grass.

Cade stared as the others caught up, a soft breeze that he had not felt in the desert cooling his sweat-damp skin. The raft of expletives from the others slowly petered out, as they surveyed the alien landscape for any sign of what would come next.

'Codex,' Cade said, his voice hardly above a whisper. 'What happens next?'

No answer.

'Can you even tell us if we're going to get help?' Cade asked. 'Is it just us, or are there other contenders here?'

Finally, the Codex swivelled in the air, fixing its robotic lens on him.

'You have your instructions. No more information regarding the game rules will be offered.'

Cade stared at it. The damned thing was as cryptic as it had been the very first day he had encountered it.

'Little git,' Amber growled, throwing a hand at it. The machine easily moved away, and almost mocked her as it hung out of reach in empty space.

'Tell us who the others are?' Trix asked.

But there was no response.

'Ask it something else,' Bea prompted. 'See what it *will* answer.'

'Codex . . . tell us about Jomsborg,' Grace said. 'Who lived here?'

The machine zoomed closer.

'*The Jomsvikings were a secretive order of elite pagan mercenaries from the tenth century AD, fighting for the highest bidder. The brotherhood swore never to flee, even in the face of overwhelming odds. No women or children were allowed in their fortress.*'

Cade was relieved it was still willing to answer general questions.

'Figures,' Amber grunted.

'Talk about a sausage fest,' Scott said, earning himself another prod from Grace. He grinned.

Cade took Amber's hand and stared out over the landscape. She squeezed it, and that simple gesture was enough to calm him. This was a game. It was time to start playing.

'Eight of us can't succeed where a legion of others failed,' Cade said. 'We can't take a stronghold on our own. We don't even know where it is. I say we find these "others" first. If Abaddon has added them to the game, he expects us to use them.'

'Right,' Yoshi said. 'So how do we do that?'

Cade scanned the horizon once more, walking slowly around the ring of the parapet. But there was nothing. Only the endless hillocks of purple grass.

'I don't know,' he said. 'We might just have to pick a direction and walk as far as we can but can still see Jomsborg. Don't want to get lost out there.'

Yoshi grunted in reluctant agreement.

'What kind of world is this?' Bea muttered. 'Purple grass? And hardly a tree or mountain in sight?'

'Purple doesn't surprise me,' Trix said. 'Didn't you pay attention in biology?'

'Go on, then,' Grace said. 'Tell us.'

'Chlorophyll is what makes plants green,' she said. 'It absorbs blue and red light. But there's another type . . . I forget its name . . . that absorbs green and yellow light. My teacher said all our plants might have been purple if evolution had gone a different way.'

'Right. So . . . why no trees?' Cade asked.

'The grass may have outcompeted everything else. Or maybe whatever dominant species we will face made them extinct. Impossible to say.'

'Thanks for the science lesson,' Bea laughed. 'Swot!'

'You just wish you had my brains,' Trix said, winking.

'So it's basically grass, for all intents and purposes,' Cade said. 'We can't eat it. But I heard something out there this morning. Maybe we can hunt them.'

'Can we even digest . . . like . . . aliens?' Scott asked.

'We'll find out, I guess,' Cade replied. 'But whoever these "others" are, they'll probably be able to tell us.'

'If they're human,' Yoshi said. 'And if they've been here longer than us. For all we know, Abaddon has dumped an army of Vikings out there this morning with no explanation.'

'You're probably right,' Amber groaned. 'It's not like this place was designed for eight people to defend. I think we're supposed to bring them here.'

Cade tightened his grip on the edge of the rampart, trying to focus. Abaddon did not do anything randomly. It was like a puzzle he wanted them to solve.

'If these guys *are* on foot,' Cade said slowly. 'We're the largest landmark for miles. The chances of us coming across them while wandering the landscape is tiny – we might not even be able to see further than a hundred yards with the grass. So we need to help them find us.'

'Yeah?' Scott said. 'And how are we going to do that?'

Cade closed his eyes, concentrating.

They couldn't use sound. He doubted any noise they could make would travel far.

How did people communicate before technology?

Carrier pigeons? Signal flags?

He opened his eyes. Only for them to settle on the exact answer to his problem.

Suddenly, the fort they were in made a lot more sense. It wasn't the walls themselves. It was the height of the tower . . . and what was at its top.

A plan slotted into his mind. It was risky, but they had no choice.

'Guys,' he said, 'I have a plan.'

It was the braziers that Cade had seen. Those giant metal cradles for fire, rusted into the stone itself but still serviceable at a pinch.

These would serve as a smoke signal in the dusk, and lighthouse through the night. But they had a problem. Fuel.

The day became a grueling affair, one where they roamed the ruined hulks of the old longhouses that made up most of the village, picking through the rubble and detritus for anything they might burn.

It was a near-fruitless affair, but charred remnants remained, half-buried in the dry earth. These scattered pieces were lugged to the tower's top and piled alongside four of their sleds, which they had decided to sacrifice for the cause.

But their search did make one useful discovery: there was a well at the centre of the village. Amber had said it was dry as a bone the day before, but in this new world, ground-water had seeped into it, giving them a source of water.

For now, they would stick to their own supply brought from the keep, for they had no idea what alien microbes might be lurking within. They would eventually need to find a new source of fuel to boil it.

The sun was beginning to set, and the team had filled one of the large embrasures with wood, stacked from smallest pieces to largest, and shredded sackcloth at its base for tinder.

Cade still had the lighter he had found in the jungles, which, though empty, was used to spark a light at the base of their pyre.

With a gentle blow of his breath, the pile slowly sputtered before crackling into life.

Now, they could only watch.

Slowly, a plume of black smoke began to form above. This air was strangely still, with hardly a breeze to speak of. It was strange to see the smoke go straight upwards, forming a thin, dark pillar in the sky.

The fire burned quickly, and for a while, Cade was worried that they might run out of wood before darkness fell. But luck was on their side, and they managed to keep the fire going for several hours in the darkness, huddled in silent worry as the fire blazed for the world to see.

NINE

'Cade.'

There was soft pressure on Cade's shoulder, pulling him from a dreamless sleep.

Quintus's face stared down at him. It pulled away as Cade squinted through the darkness.

'Your watch,' Quintus said, motioning at the spiral staircase above.

Cade groaned, looking enviously at the snoring crew sprawled around him. He nodded and struggled to his feet, still sore from the many trips they had made up and down the stairs to build the fire. To his surprise, Quintus led the way, returning to the tower's peak with him.

'Not going to sleep?' Cade asked.

Quintus shrugged.

'Only waiting now. I sleep when is warm.'

He motioned at the sun, peeking over the horizon. The young legionary hopped onto the parapet's edge, dangling his feet over the side. Cade joined him.

They stared out over the purple plains, tinged scarlet by the red-white of the twin moons above. For a while, they stared in silence, Cade's mind slowly awakening as the world grew brighter and brighter.

'Who do you think these others are?' Cade asked.

Quintus shrugged again.

'I think more humans. Many more. Hundreds.'

Cade nodded in agreement, scratching the beginnings of the beard on his chin.

It was new, and he wondered what he looked like these days – especially now he and Amber were . . . whatever they were. It had been some time since he had gazed at himself in a mirror, having only seen the warped reflection in a bucket of water.

He imagined he might look more man than boy now. He felt like it too. There was something about almost dying that shook the child out of you.

'Romans?' Cade asked.

Quintus inclined his head.

'But not contenders?' Cade asked. 'What does that mean?'

'Maybe they are not warriors,' Quintus said. 'Maybe they are like Amber. And you.'

Cade gasped in mock offence, and Quintus blushed as red as the grass beneath them.

'Not now,' Quintus said swiftly. 'Before. When you arrived.'

Cade laughed.

'I'm just messing with you,' he said. 'I have to hope you're wrong though. We'd have no weapons for them for a start.

There's just rocks, sand and grass out here.'

Quintus nodded. 'That is why I worry. When we defend, we can find things in the caldera. Here, we only have what we bring with us. We did not bring a lot.'

But Cade was not listening.

There was movement on the horizon.

He had not noticed it, but with the sunrise in full swing, he could see a furrow in the fields. One winding slowly towards them like a snake in the long grass.

'They're coming!' Cade yelled out.

Quintus scrambled down the stairs, and Cade stood on the parapet, as if it would somehow give him a better vantage.

They were moving fast. Marching in formation, or so it seemed. Heading in the direction of their gatehouse.

It was not long before the others came to join him, bleary eyes staring across the plains. By now, Cade could see the glint of weapons and armour in the sun. Bronze as the sun-swept sky.

'Warriors,' Cade breathed.

'Ours?' Yoshi asked.

'Who can say,' Cade said. 'But they're wearing armour. That's a good sign.'

He was in awe that his plan had worked. In truth, he had not expected it to.

'We need to get ready,' Amber said. 'That means putting on your own armour, Cade. If they're allies, at the very least we ought to look the part.'

'How long until they reach us?' Scott asked.

'One hour,' Quintus said. 'Possible it is less.'

51

'And if they aren't friendly?' Grace said. 'Do we just lie down and die?'

Cade scratched his head. They should have prepared for this earlier.

'The only way into the fort is through those gates,' he said, pointing at the ground. 'There's another gate on the other side of the fort, but that one is intact. So this is the entry point.'

'It's fifty feet across,' Grace groaned. 'Eight people can't hold that.'

'Not if we get the gates back up,' Amber said.

'And how would we keep them up?' Bea asked. 'There's nothing to attach them to.'

'We have half an hour to figure that out,' Cade said. 'Then we have to make other plans. Let's go take a look at them.'

The gates lay in the sand, so rusted and barnacled that Cade suspected they had steeped in the salt waters of the Baltic Sea for many years before Abaddon had taken the fort to Acies. The gateway still had the great hinges embedded in its walls, but the twin gates' connecting brackets on either side had broken, likely rusting through and then snapping under the gates' weight.

Cade stood at the edge of the grasslands, staring at the strange vegetation. Standing so close to it, he could see an iridescent blue to the grass's edges. They came as high as his waist, and he knew that beneath, like the placid surface of a lagoon . . . predators might lurk there.

He heard a grunt of anger, only to see Yoshi attempting

to lever up one of the gates' edges. The structure didn't move an inch.

'Ropes,' Quintus called.

The quick-thinking legionary had already brought their sackcloth ropes from their sleds, and now he tossed a rolled length of it to Cade and Amber, then proceeded to tie the end to the gate's tip.

'Leverage,' Cade breathed. 'Of course.'

The plan was swiftly explained, with the aid of a diagram drawn in the salt-crusted sand. Quintus had Bea and Trix holding the bottom of one of the gates in place beneath the arch, Grace, Scott and Yoshi levering up the top end, and he, Amber and Quintus hauling on the ropes as soon as the gate was lifted enough that their pulling would make a difference.

It was a brutal tug-of-war, and it was only with a monumental effort from Grace, standing on her tiptoes, that the gate lifted high enough for Cade's crew to find some momentum. Then it was a case of rushing forwards and holding the gate straight as it teetered back towards them.

Soon enough, Quintus had clambered up the rusting crosshatch of iron and tied knots between the great hinges and the gate itself. It was enough to keep the gate upright, without their holding it in place.

As the group cheered, Quintus climbed up again to untie the knots, struggling with them and then cutting them for ease. Time was fleeting.

'Right,' Cade announced as the group panted. 'Now for the next one.'

TEN

They had done what they could. With both gates up and tied together with threadbare ropes, it at least gave the impression of a secure gateway. As soon as the new arrivals came close, they would see it could be broken through with hardly more than a solid push.

In fact, the gates would not even entirely close, for in their haste, they were at angles to each other and could not be shifted in the sand. A man could walk between them if he turned sideways.

Still, it put Cade's mind at ease as they geared up for war, having dragged their sleds to the gatehouse interior. The others were ready before him, and they helped him put his armour on. It was dented and scratched from his battle with the alpha, and the helmet was in such a state that he left it aside. There would be time to try to bang it back into shape later, but for now he shuddered at the memory of the battle.

As they tugged straps and slotted armour into place, Cade was thinking ahead. There were a dozen ways to play

54

this. But a single idea had formed in his mind, a memory of a story his father had told him. He could not shake it. As the last piece of armour was tightened, Cade turned to survey his troops.

They were a sorry sight. Bea and Trix still wore their school uniforms, though patchily repaired with sackcloth and stitching where the cloth had been torn or worn away. Yoshi wore his old blue uniform too.

Grace and the others were clad in their linen clothing from their time in New Rome's arena, complete with the metal plates that came with it. Yet the cloth had become ingrained with dirt, blood, and grass stains in the months following the last round, which would not come out no matter how often they washed them.

'Now what?' the others panted, weapons ready.

'I'm going out there, alone.'

'Are you kidding me?' Amber snapped.

'I'm the one wearing the armour – if they shoot an arrow, I might just survive it. And if I'm the only one they see, they might think everyone in here is just as well armed and move off.'

Amber muttered under her breath, but said nothing further.

Cade peered through the arrow slit. Now, he could see the approaching figures clearly, though he still couldn't tell if they were human or alien.

'Bea, Trix, Yoshi. You go up the tower, and take our supplies with you. Stay hidden, but be ready to drop the stones if I call out.'

The trio nodded.

'The rest of you, I need you to dangle a rope from the gatehouse's window down to the ground outside. Hold on to it, and if you feel me tug, haul me up as fast as you can.'

'What then?' Amber said.

'If they're enemies, we retreat up the tower and hold them there – the narrow spiral staircase gives us the high ground, and they can only come one at a time. Plus they'll have to run up the beach and then back along the walls to reach us. If you pull me up quick enough, they might think I escaped out of the exit on the other side of the keep.'

'Might . . .' Amber said sullenly. 'I'm sick of you being the one in danger all the time.'

Cade didn't have time to argue. 'They're almost here. No time to change the plan now.'

He drew his blade and strode out, each step accompanied by the scrape of metal on metal. The armour was heavier than he remembered, and more constricting. But by the time he had made the long walk to the front gates, he had become used to wearing it again.

'Like riding a bike,' he whispered.

It was simple enough for him to ease between the gap in the gates and step beyond the gateway. He was taking a huge risk, for it was only a stone's throw away from the edge of the long grass, where the approaching figures would eventually emerge.

He had to appear relaxed, but be prepared to run. He only hoped he was fast enough.

Cade had brought the broken chair with him. It only had

three legs, and the seat was rotted, but it allowed him to balance semiprecariously on its edge and take the weight off his legs. If his plan worked, he was going to be there for quite some time.

And then, as the morning sun fully emerged from the horizon, they stepped out of the grasslands.

They came in twos and threes, diamond-shaped shields raised, forming a semicircle around the gatehouse, along the edge of the purple sea. Helmets obscured their features, and spears glinted in the light, raised over their shoulders at the ready.

Cade's heart fell as his gaze swept the arrayed soldiers, near fifty in all. These were no humans.

Their eyes stood out the most. Black orbs, large as fists, embedded in distended grey skulls. The noses were a pair of slits, and lipless mouths were drawn tight beneath.

Grey skin, mottled as a corpse's, stood out against the bronze armour, which was tarnished with edges of green. It might well have been torn from Greek myth, were it not for the strange creatures that wore it.

But now was not the time to show fear. As the enemy arrayed in their shield wall, Cade gave a great sigh and sat down on the chair, a lazy leg kicked out in front of him.

He stretched, then yawned, lifting his eyes to the sky as if he had not a care in the world. Yet all the while, his heart hammered and sweat dripped from his brow to pool in the hollow of his neck.

From his position, he could see the enemy's lips move, a mellifluous language that flowed like water. It was almost beautiful.

Still he sat, lowering his eyes to meet their gaze. More words, almost singing, as the grey folk discussed his presence.

Suddenly, a single grey soldier darted towards him, scurrying across the sand.

The movement made Cade's heart leap, but still he sat, forcing his smile steady as the soldier approached him.

As swiftly as it had advanced, the soldier retreated, its black eyes swivelling to gaze up at the silent battlements above. A feint.

Cade leaned back, hiding a grimace as the ancient chair groaned beneath his weight. He near-closed his eyes, feigning sleep.

He watched. And waited.

ELEVEN

They had moved back into the long grass, where they huddled in conversation. A pair of them kept watch, crouched at the edge of the grasslands. Though he could not see the direction of their gaze, only the strange swivelling of the black orbs in their sockets.

To them, he was behaving insane. And therein lay the rub.

What man would stand alone against an army? Moreover, why would a single soldier guard a fortress?

Yet, the very same had happened before. Not once but a half-dozen times, in ancient China. It was called the empty fort strategy, and though part history, part legend, the stories had fascinated him as a child.

Perhaps most famously, General Zhao Yung had defended his own fort, outnumbered a thousand to one. It had been a hopeless cause, yet he had opened the gates, hidden his men, and sat on its battlements plucking a tune on his musical instrument.

When the enemy had approached, they had feared a

trap, and retreated before the general's allies came to his aid.

An hour had passed. The longest hour of Cade's life, spent in a strange oscillation between absolute panic and nonchalance. It was a strange thing, to relax his body while ready to leap into action at any moment. He had to keep moving and flexing his limbs within his armour, in case they fell asleep. What an end that would be, if he had sat himself into being unable to run.

Even so, it was as if his body dictated his feelings. By acting relaxed, he was becoming so. At times, he almost tricked himself into sleep, so he distracted himself by examining his new enemy through half-lidded eyes.

These 'Greys' – as he had dubbed them – were only formidable in their armaments and numbers. They were scrawny things; no taller than five feet, and so skinny he could see their ribs beneath the armour. Whether this was a consequence of starvation or their natural state, he could not tell.

Their fingers, as far as he could make out, were like those of a pianist – long and delicate, though numbering only three fingers and a long, triple-jointed thumb.

Perhaps strangest of all though, were the tiny creatures that climbed upon them – scarab-like beetles that crawled in and out of the enemy armour.

At first, Cade had thought they were parasites, but the Greys made no move to remove them, even as the little insects scurried across the surface of their eyes. *It must be some sort of symbiotic relationship*, Cade figured.

Movement. The troop was advancing to their previous position. Their motions had purpose, and their speech was faster and louder.

Despite it all, Cade remained still. Every second he bought was another his friends were alive. Arrayed once more in their semicircle formation, as Cade watched, a pair of Greys shuffled forwards, their heads tilted up at the battlements above.

'Bea, Trix, now!'

Before he had even finished speaking, a stone ball thudded into the sand ahead of him. It was almost too close for comfort, and Cade was glad he had kept his seat within the shadow of the gatehouse arch. The pair startled at the sound, leaping back for the safety of the formation.

Yet even as Cade allowed himself a grin, a screech of annoyance from within the formation sent the pair forwards once more. Their leader, Cade saw, was a foot taller than the others, with a more ornate helmet, while the pair selected were the runts of the group, four feet tall. They advanced slowly, their dark eyes swivelling frantically in their sockets. Still Cade remained in place. If he ran now, they would catch up to him. He only wished he had kept up his training since his injury.

The two Greys stopped but six feet away from him, their spears extended. A jab spitted the air in front of Cade's face, but he had judged the distance and ignored it.

Then, with a screech, the two enemies closed, launching themselves forwards.

Cade stood and swept his blade up in a wide arc, knocking

61

the blows askew in a clatter of wood and metal. One stumbled, surprised by his speed, and a swift reverse of his blade took it in its throat beneath its helmet.

The Grey reeled away, even as its companion made a second thrust, aiming for Cade's belly. It scraped along his chest plate as Cade twisted aside, steel ringing as his own blow glanced across the bronze metal of the alien's helmet.

The alien made for another stab, but Cade riposted in kind, moving with explosive speed to skewer the Grey through its slitted mouth and deep within. Cade twisted and withdrew, kicking the alien back to sprawl on the ground beside the other.

For a moment, he stared at the pair, startled by blue blood pooling in the sand. He had moved almost by instinct, yet he was shocked at what he had done. Then he remembered himself, and glared up at the enemy, the arrayed faces unreadable as they stared.

With that, Cade righted his chair and sat down again, his blue-dripping blade laid out across his lap.

The Greys fluted and trilled in alarm. Had his display scared them into thinking again about attacking the grand fort . . . or agitated them into seeking revenge?

If it was the latter, they did not show it. Rather, they retreated back a few steps, with the leader huddling with what must have been a second in command. Cade could almost hear their trills in the still air.

Minutes crawled by as the Greys watched and waited. Cade was growing nervous, the sight of the two bodies before him driving the reality of the situation home.

And then, with a screech that set his teeth on edge . . . the formation charged.

'Bea! Trix!' Cade bellowed as he threw himself back, his sword sticking in the grate before being yanked free in his desperation to pass through the gates.

He seized the rope and yanked, feeling his feet lift from the ground almost instantly. Slowly, ever so slowly, he was hauled up.

The Greys piled into the gatehouse as stones tumbled from the battlements above. Cade caught a glimpse of a rock thudding into the masses, blue spray accompanied by squeals of pain.

The frontrunners pressed into the gates, the momentum of those behind pressing them into the grating, preventing them from squeezing through. Cade swung himself forwards, using an armoured foot to climb up the grate squares, as spears jabbed at him. The gates began to topple, the rope holding them in place fraying and snapping.

They slammed into the ground, and the Greys stampeded through. For one heart-pounding moment Cade dangled above the enemy, and felt the clatter of outstretched spearheads slicing at his feet. Then he was out of range, swinging as the army below trilled in anger.

He was safe . . . for now.

TWELVE

They were outnumbered five to one, if not more. And as they watched the Greys stumble into the sandy basin of the old harbour, this became ever more apparent.

A few were limping, injured by the falling rocks, and Cade knew at least one had died. But it did not make their odds any better.

They had faced greater numbers of vipers, it was true, but these creatures were more advanced. These were sentient beings, fighting in formation and armoured from head to toe. Defeating them seemed impossible. The best they could hope to do was make them pay so dearly that they gave up trying to kill them.

'What now?' Yoshi whispered.

They were peering out of the sea-gate entrance, which Cade had scrambled into moments before.

'It's a siege,' Cade muttered back. 'Just not of the fort. Of this gatehouse.'

Below, Cade saw the black eyes of the leader swivel in

their overlarge sockets, and moments later fluted orders split the Grey army in two.

'Shit,' Scott whispered. 'They figured that out fast.'

They were headed up the beach, where the wall met the ground and they could run along the battlements to the two doorways on either side of the large room they were in.

'Do we defend the doorways?' Amber asked.

'No,' Cade said. 'We stick to the plan. Up the stairs, now.'

They ran, stumbling in their panic up the steps, and it was twice as hard in Cade's armour. He collapsed at the top, the group gathering around the entrance with their blades drawn.

Cade took a moment to catch his breath. To think.

There was advantage in their retreat. The enemy did not know their numbers, even now. And if Cade held the stairs, the Greys would not know how many warriors were crowded at the top of the tower with him.

'They'll come up two at a time,' Cade said. 'Greys seem to be right-handed, like most of us. They'll struggle to stab their spears around the staircase's central column at us.'

'Greys?' Grace asked.

Cade shrugged. 'As good a name as any. Now, Grace has the longest reach and sword – she can take point. Their spears have better range than our swords, but with our longer arms it's about even. I'm the most protected in my armour, so I'll fight first.'

He lifted his blade and stood beside Grace, who drew her own enormous sword. Together, they listened to the sounds of tramping feet below. The enemy was moving quickly, giving them little time to prepare.

'The rest of you, gather the stones we have left and position them around the stairwell,' Cade whispered. 'Quietly.'

The others moved at his request as the first Grey shifted into view, its diamond-shaped shield raised, spear poised to strike.

But he was right about the angle. The Grey was forced to step into full view to get its spear into position, and Cade was quick to attack as it moved.

His sword struck like a snake, scraping over the shield's top and into the hissing face above. The blade jarred on the metal nasal crest, then passed through to send the beast reeling and tumbling into the next enemy, approaching behind.

In the confusion, Grace leaped down the steps, sweeping her enormous blade in a downward swing that cleaved through metal, bone and flesh.

She moved back as more Greys crowded into the stairway, trampling their fallen comrades in their haste to rush the defenders. The sounds of footsteps and fluting calls echoing from below were louder now – exactly what Cade had been waiting for.

'Now! Push 'em in,' Cade snarled.

Hands heaved on round balls, rolling them from the stairwell's edges down into the dingy steps. There was the clack of stone on stone, then, as the rocks began to tumble down the spiral, the crackle of broken bones. The balls rattled down the stairway, echoing in tandem with the screeches of agony as they pinballed through limbs.

'All of them!' Cade yelled.

More balls rolled down the steps, and the cries intensified. Soon, there were no rocks left, and Cade listened to the trilling groans of those below.

'Charge!' Cade yelled, leaping into the stairwell.

It was a grisly sight – the injured scattered across the steps like broken marionettes. One staggered to its feet, spear trembling in its hands, and Cade resisted hesitation as his blade took it through the neck.

Another stab finished another, and Grace's blade swung next, cleaving through a raised helmet before being wrenched free. But in those few seconds, the injured Greys were rallying, and Cade's next blow was met with a raised shield, and his chest plate clanged as a spear dented it.

'Back,' Cade snarled, kicking out to shove the shield back, gaining them the room to turn and retreat.

Panting, he turned at the top, where he found a shield wall two-deep blocking his view of the stairwell. The Greys were tenacious, even as the wails of the injured echoed from beneath.

'Get ready,' Cade gasped as Quintus nudged him aside and took his place.

Cade was thankful, exhausted by his efforts. He fell to his knees and gulped down some water from an amphora.

Just then, Grace cried out in warning.

The Greys were advancing. One step at a time, four shields held in a square edged up the stairs, spears poking through the gaps in a hedgehog of wood and metal.

It was all they could do but surround the stairs, waiting for the beasts to emerge and the real battle to begin.

'Here they come,' Cade snarled, leaning on his sword to struggle to his feet. The first spear tips came into view . . .

But the Greys were at a disadvantage. Their backs were exposed. From the stairwell behind them, Bea and Trix were slashing down. Spears weaved and stabbed in return, and the Greys behind lifted their shields in a makeshift shell to defend from the blows above.

Trix cried out in triumph as a Grey screeched and fell away. Yet within a second, another took its place. An endless queue of warriors choked the stairs, undaunted by the slashing blades above.

Cade stabbed forwards, his blade aimed at a gap between the shields, only to find his blade jar against the wood.

'It's no use,' Bea cried out, backing away and clutching a cut to her arm.

Their thin ring of warriors expanded as the Greys emerged from the staircase, limping, bleeding, but in formation.

'Drive them back,' Cade yelled, lifting his sword. 'Charge together . . . now!'

They moved in as one, the ferocity of their attack pushing the wall inward, pressing them into the Greys crowding behind. Swords rose and fell, splintering spear hafts and shields alike.

But no Greys fell beneath their onslaught. They bore the wave of violence like an impenetrable wall. Where blows did pass through, they were deflected by armour, and the spears stabbed back in riposte.

A flash of pain seared across Cade's wrist, and he felt the hot trickle of blood, his hilt slippery in his grip. This was not a battle they could win.

And then, almost lost among the calls of the trilling enemies, he heard it. A bellow from below. Then another, and another. Trills of alarm followed, Grey heads turning to listen.

'Again!' Cade roared.

They pressed forwards once more, and this time, the shield wall fell back, even as the clash of weapons echoed from below. Again and again Cade swung, the last vestiges of his energy spent in great, sweeping blows. The Greys, distracted, shuffled further and further back, the crush of those behind them seemingly gone as their reinforcements turned to face the new threat.

As suddenly as they had emerged, the Greys at the top retreated, their shields upheld, but only in defence as they scrambled to return to the stairs. Soon, they disappeared from view, turning and charging into the gloom beneath.

Breathing hoarsely, Cade fell to his knees, blocking the way as Quintus tried to follow down the stairs.

'Whatever's coming up,' Cade growled, 'it's more dangerous than those Greys.'

He stared into the darkness as the battle below intensified. Metal rang on metal, and the garbled screams of the dying set his teeth on edge.

Minutes ticked by. The black shadow of the staircase loomed.

Then, as the noise of battle petered out, a figure shuffled out of the gloom, shrouded in shadow. A man holding a shield stepped into the light.

His mouth opened, eyes flashing in recognition. He choked a single word.

'*Quintus?*'

THIRTEEN

A Roman.

Cade could hardly believe it, yet there he stood. A legionary in rusted armour, square shield and gladius clutched in bloodied hands.

Quintus's face was suddenly split by a broad grin, and he rushed forwards to hug the man.

'Marius!' a voice called from below, followed by a string of Latin too fast for Cade to follow. Marius called back in reply.

'Translate,' Cade hissed, and the Codex, suddenly invisible, whispered in his ear as it had done so many times before.

'. . . the last of them! But you won't believe who they were attacking.'

'Bring them to us,' the voice called back. 'We have wounded.'

Marius beckoned for them to follow, then stumbled down the stairs.

'Quintus?' Cade asked, but the young Roman was already

71

leaping down the stairs after Marius.

Cade followed, ignoring the clamour of questioning from the others behind.

The staircase was carnage, with massacred Greys splayed across the stairway like toys across a nursery floor. The walls were slick with blue and red blood, yet Cade could not help but lean against them as he navigated the butchered and broken bodies. Quintus didn't stop, no matter how loudly Cade called for him. Cade could only follow, until he emerged into the large central room of the gatehouse.

An unbelievable sight greeted him.

Legionaries, arrayed in formation, blue blood still dripping from their weapons. Nearby, a handful of injured soldiers lay on the ground, with a man in a red tunic rushing between them with needle and thread.

Cade counted as many as a hundred men standing to attention. The first man – Marius – was among them, while another in an elaborate helmet stood at their head.

It was strange to see the men in such neat rows, even as some clutched wounds or held others up. Stranger still for their leader to ignore their obvious pain.

Only when Quintus touched the second man's shoulder did he turn, and Cade was shocked to find a sneer of disdain across the leader's face. He had a cruel look about him, with an aquiline nose and pinched mouth beneath raven hair.

'So,' the man snorted. 'The gods have sent you to help us.'

He spat, then looked above Quintus's head, as if searching for something.

'Do you have the Codex?'

Quintus kept his lips pursed.

'Dumb donkey,' the man snarled, barging past Quintus and facing Cade. His face was beet red.

'You,' the man growled, stabbing a finger at Cade. 'Where is the Codex?'

Cade shrugged, earning himself a furious glare.

'Any of you?'

When no one replied, the man threw up his hands in anger. 'At least we have a new home,' he said.

He turned to Marius. 'Centurion,' he snapped. 'Return to our camp and instruct them that we are relocating our base of operations here.'

Marius blanched. 'Legatus, I ask dispensation for twenty men to accompany me.'

The commander – which was what the word *legatus* meant – snorted at the request.

'All the men are needed here in case of a counterattack. We do not know if the enemy patrol sent word back to their headquarters.'

Marius's face paled further. 'Legatus, if I am captured or killed, my message will not get through and our camp will be left vulnerable.'

The commander pursed his lips. 'Take the donkey's friends,' he said finally. 'They will be little use to me. In the meantime, I shall interrogate him.'

Cade moved to protest, but felt Quintus's grip tighten on his shoulder.

'Wait,' was all Quintus whispered.

Marius's face was drawn, but he nodded at the order.

73

'Go. Now,' the legatus ordered.

Marius nodded and marched away from the formation.

He stopped at the gatehouse's doorway, beckoning for Cade to follow. Quintus gave him a gentle shove, surprising him. Clearly his friend thought they would be safer out there than here. But as he turned to question Quintus, a glare of such feeling as Cade had never seen before greeted him.

'Come on,' Cade said, motioning at the others. 'We'll do as he says.'

Cade stopped at the doorway beside Marius and quickly unbuckled the armour he wore, leaving it in a pile beside the sledges. If this was to be a long march, the ill-fitting, heavy armour would be a bad idea.

'Get some water,' Cade said, picking up one of the smaller amphorae himself. 'We don't know how long we will be out there.'

With that done, Cade snatched up some bandages from a pile where the Roman medic had left them, and hurried after Marius, who was already walking outside.

'Cade,' Amber hissed as they emerged into the sunlight of the battlements. 'What are we doing?'

The others had likely understood little of the conversation, despite their now rudimentary understanding of Latin. But Cade was wondering the same himself. Everything was moving so quickly, he'd had hardly any time to think. But they were alive, and five minutes ago he hadn't thought that was possible.

Still, he somehow found little joy in the arrival of their new allies. The legatus had given them a cold welcome, and treated his men almost as badly. It did not bode well.

'We have to trust Quintus,' was all he could say. 'Right now, he knows more about these Romans than the rest of us. He wants us to go, so that's what we're doing.'

'We don't even know what's out there,' Scott chimed in. 'Marius looked terrified. He asked for twenty men, if I understood the Latin!'

'Well, good thing we're worth twice as many,' Cade said, forcing a smile.

His body ached, yet he did not want to lose Marius, so he broke into a stiff jog, cutting further conversation short. Luckily, once the Roman reached the shadow of the gatehouse, he had stopped to wait for them.

'Hurry, we must reach camp before nightfall,' the man said. 'But take a moment to bind your wounds.'

Cade sighed with relief. This Roman, at least, had some empathy.

He was a tall man, with a chiseled, shaven jaw, wide blue eyes, and mouse-brown hair. It was a face Cade instinctively trusted, and any friend of Quintus's was surely a friend of his.

'Your commander,' Cade said, his Latin broken and stilted, 'he did not seem . . . happy to see us.'

Marius lifted a finger to his lips.

'Not here,' he said. 'We will speak on the way.'

Cade's eyes widened. Marius had answered in English.

FOURTEEN

The grass was sticky-damp against their legs as they trudged through the grasslands, but Cade was grateful that their way had already been trampled by the Romans on their journey to the fort.

Their path was a clear swath through the purple sea, and Cade wondered how Marius would have navigated the landscape without it. They had walked for a good half hour by now, but Marius had not stopped for one minute, seemingly eager to get as far from the fort as possible before continuing their conversation.

They had hardly introduced themselves before Marius had outpaced them, his skinny legs belying a wiry strength and stamina that they could not match.

Trix and Yoshi, especially, were struggling to keep up, for both had superficial yet painful cuts to their legs. And Cade's own wrist was pulsing with every beat of his heart, where a spear had somehow slipped through the hinge of his armour.

'Marius,' Cade called, this time in English. 'We've got to slow down. Some of us are wounded.'

At those words, the Roman held up a hand, halting the procession.

'Come,' he said, sidling off their path and into the grasses. 'We rest here, away from any that follow.'

He lifted each foot with care as he walked, taking long steps and carefully threading it through the grass so as not to disturb it unduly. Cade mirrored his movements, and soon the group was seated amid the grass, close together and off the beaten path.

'I am sure you have many questions,' Marius said before Cade could open his mouth. 'But first, I must ask you to answer mine. Who are you, and how did you come to know Quintus?'

To Cade's surprise, he could almost detect a slight French accent among the more typical Latin one that he had first heard in New Rome.

Cade paused, struggling to encompass their past year in as few words as possible.

'We come from a time far beyond your own,' Cade said. 'Brought by the gods to replace you as contenders. I assume you were with Quintus's legion?'

Marius nodded.

'We have successfully won two rounds in defence,' Cade continued, 'but now we've been forced to attack. The eight of us were sent on our own.'

This time, Marius snorted. 'Of course. We suffer, and the new gods laugh.'

Cade wondered whether to tell Marius of the true identity of these so-called new gods, but thought better of it.

'How do you know English?' Cade asked.

'A man named Louis Le Prince,' Marius replied. 'He lived with us in this place for years, before he died from a sickness. From him, we learned the wonders of your future . . . and it was I who was tasked to learn it from him.'

So that explained the accent – Le Prince had been born in France.

'Not all of the wonders,' Cade said. 'We come from beyond Le Prince's time, by more than a century.'

Marius shrugged. 'The world does not change so quickly.'

Cade begged to differ, but now was not the time for a history lesson. 'What happened to you? How are you still alive?' he asked.

Now it was Marius's turn to pause.

'We came here with thousands of men,' he said. 'Even I did not know how many. In truth, I do not know the specifics of our mission here, for I am but a centurion, and our leader does not divulge his plans.'

'The . . . legatus?' Amber asked.

'Yes, Atticus Publius. A worse leader I have never known . . . but I stray from the path of your question. Our task was to attack the headquarters of our enemy, and leave none alive inside.'

'Those Greys we were fighting?' Scott interrupted.

'Yes . . . we call them the Tritons.'

Marius stood a little higher as he said their name, peering out across the grasslands. Satisfied, he resumed his seat.

'Our legion joined those who had been here on Acies before us. I did not know the leaders, for they led us but for a few days before their death. We had been given a year to defeat these . . . Greys . . . but it was our commanders' decision to attack as soon as we arrived, for we did not know the land – what to eat, what to drink.'

He spat to the side, as if disgusted by this decision, though Cade wondered if he would have done any different. Feeding several thousand men by living off an alien land seemed a daunting prospect.

'We sent scouts to discover their headquarters and attacked as soon as we found it. Apparently a surprise attack was to be better than a siege. But, as we charged . . . bright lights flashed . . . and our men who were struck by them turned to dust before my very eyes. It was as if Medusa herself stared out from their fortress. Yet our leaders refused to retreat, sending them on into the moving light. Halfway through the battle the lights stopped, but our men could only pound at their front gates as arrows rained from above. Only those in the baggage train at the back survived.'

He wiped at his eyes.

'Only the weakest, the sick and the injured were in the baggage train. And with it the most incompetent of their commanders . . . Atticus. It is he who has led us all this time since. Who let the timer expire, and thus let our Codex abandon us. Now, we only fight to survive. I had thought we would never see another human soul again. Yet here you are.'

'So . . . if we attack again, there will be another flash of light?' Amber asked. Cade could only guess it was a futuristic weapon of some sort.

Marius shook his head. 'We believe that they used all their . . . ammunition . . . in our first attack. Since then, we have never seen these lights again, even when we ambushed one of their patrols in front of their gates to try to draw them out. They appear to have been reduced to our level once more – it is the only reason we have been able to survive. They have attacked us many times, yet we prevailed. They are poor fighters.'

It was some relief to hear Marius say that.

'Do you think if you were to attack them now, with all your men, you could win?' Scott asked.

Marius shrugged.

'If they met us in open battle, perhaps. There are less than a thousand of them, as far as we can guess, and two hundred of us. But their fort is impenetrable. Our catapults could not pierce its shell when we attacked, though we have not tried since.'

With those words, he stood, and motioned for them to follow, even as Cade sat stunned. All that time . . . fighting for survival.

'Come,' Marius instructed. 'We have a long way to travel yet.'

FIFTEEN

They arrived at sunset. Early enough for Cade to see the sorry place that the Romans had come to call home.

It was a simple wooden fort. Most likely of earthly origin, for Cade had yet to see any trees on their long journey there. He doubted the half-rotten logs that made up the wall of the fort were from this world.

'Codex,' Cade whispered. 'What is this place?'

He did not see the Codex fly off, nor the blue flash as it scanned the fort, but he did hear the quiet reply in his ear.

'Remnant is Fort Caroline, built by several hundred French explorers attempting to colonise Florida in 1564. The settlers were massacred and the fort taken by Spanish conquistadors in 1565, only for the same to happen to them by avenging French soldiers in 1568. The Spanish retook the fort a final time, but later abandoned it. The fort, which was rebuilt three times in the various battles for control of Florida, has never been seen since.'

By the time the Codex finished its long explanation, Cade and his friends had followed Marius to a drawbridge that slowly creaked down over a narrow moat filled with stagnant water.

The fort was triangular in shape, with three bulwarks at each corner. These, in turn, had rusted cannons set in their walls, and sentries in Roman armour patrolled the battlements, their helmets shining bright against the setting sun.

'Marius!' bellowed a soldier in Latin. 'What news of the smoke?'

'Jupiter smiles upon us!' Marius replied. 'A new headquarters, a stone fort . . . and new friends!'

By now, more men had gathered on the battlements – their faces dirty, and almost as skinny as the Greys had been.

Still, their wide grins were welcoming enough, a stark contrast to Atticus's greeting. At least the rank and file were happy about their arrival.

As the drawbridge thudded to the ground, the men gathered behind it rushed out to greet them.

'Halt!' Marius yelled. 'All men but the sentries are to form up in the courtyard immediately.'

The crowd dispersed, much to Cade's relief.

'Come,' Marius said. 'We will bring you food and water. We shall have to work through the night if we are to be ready to leave by morning.'

Across the bridge, log cabins scattered across the grounds, with a larger and grander one sat at the camp's very centre. Marius motioned for them to enter.

'Make yourselves comfortable. I shall instruct the men.'

Despite Marius's orders to assemble, the men were staring at Amber, Grace, Bea and Trix. It was then that Cade noted that there was not a single woman present. From the uncomfortable looks of the girls, they had noticed this too.

'Come on,' Amber said.

The inside of the lodge was single storey, the walls painted orange by a crackling hearth built into one of the walls. Beams of daylight sliced through the gloom, where shooting slits and broken slats perforated the old shell of the building.

It was a relief to sit on the old logs by the fire, but somehow they had little to say as they stared into the flames. Their long walk had given Cade plenty of time to think, but he hadn't expected to find this.

Yes, there were soldiers. But the state of them and their camp had shocked him. These men were on their last legs. Two hundred of them against a thousand Greys? It was impossible.

As his mind drifted, Cade saw bundles of purple grass piled like straw beside the fire. Curious, he threw in a handful, and was surprised to see it smoulder and feed the flame slowly and steadily, rather than burn up in a flash as he had expected.

Some time later, Marius came back. He sighed and sat heavily beside them, before glancing up at their apparent fascination with the burning grass.

'A godsend,' he said. 'Or a curse, depending on how you look at it. The . . . Greys, you called them . . . they use this grass for everything. They pulp it and glue it to use as wood. They burn it for fuel, as we do. It is surprisingly versatile, though, sadly, we cannot eat it. We have ranged far and wide on this plain, and there is but grass, and the creatures that live here.'

'Before you go further, can you tell us how you know Quintus?' Cade asked. 'Will he be . . . OK? With Atticus?'

Marius sighed deeply and stared into the flames.

'I knew Quintus when he was a legionary. I looked out for him where I could. We didn't speak much, for I was his superior. But we were friends, of sorts. As for Atticus. Who can say? If the boy answers his questions, he will be safe. If not . . .'

He let his words trail off, and a man stumbled into the lodge, bowing to the new arrivals with reverence.

'Centurion, are your guests hungry?' the man asked in Latin.

Marius slapped his head and turned to Cade and his friends. 'Of course, I am so rude. Please, some food?'

The new arrival barked an order in Latin, and another man entered, carrying wooden bowls on a platter.

'I . . . thank you,' Cade mumbled as a bowl was handed to each of them.

His stomach turned as he saw what was within.

Insects. Or something very much like them. Stag beetles, if he had to make a close approximation, but with eight legs, and far more eyes – now sunken cavities after cooking – than even the most nightmarish of spiders.

They had been charred and roasted, such that he could not tell its original colour. The meal sat in a pool of its own juices, and Cade struggled to find a single thing appetising about it.

'I'm not sure if I can keep this down,' Bea said, her voice queasy.

She looked up at Marius, who smiled back.

'It's better if you think of it as a crab,' he said, cracking a leg free and slurping at the white meat within. 'It's almost all we have eaten since we arrived, beyond some parsnips we have managed to grow.'

Amber threw Cade a glance, motioning at the sack of jerky they had brought with them.

'Here,' she said. 'Try this.'

Marius took the bag and withdrew a morsel of the dried jerky. For a moment he stared at it as if it were a jewel.

He lay it on his tongue reverently and bit down, his eyes closed in apparent ecstasy. He chewed slowly, only gulping down when he had extracted the last bit of flavour from the food.

Marius proffered the sack back to Amber, but she held up her hands.

'It's all yours,' she said, glaring at Scott as he groaned softly.

Cade took hold of an insectile leg and pulled it free with a soft crack. He held it up, then sucked the meat into his mouth.

To his surprise, it was bland and rubbery – like unseasoned tofu.

'Thank you,' he said as the starving Marius stuffed a handful of jerky into his mouth. 'For everything. We won't forget this.'

SIXTEEN

Cade woke to the sound of deep voices calling to one another outside. It was strange to be in the presence of so many. He had become used to the soft voices of his companions, and the lazy mornings that had made up the last few months.

They had slept around the fire, exhausted by the battle and their walk, though not before a medic had bandaged their wounds. Now, the others preferred to rest inside, but as Marius's voice barked orders at the men, Cade's curiosity outweighed his tiredness. Quintus had been a Roman, true, and Cade had spent many an hour learning the reality of Roman history from him. But now he could actually *see* a legionary camp in action.

Disappointingly, when Cade emerged from the cabin, he found no camp at all. Rather, a dismantled shell, with the very palisade and surrounding cabins reduced to a few scattered logs.

The sun had hardly risen, and the sky was a wan dark-blue that put Cade on edge. The area remained a hive of activity, men running to and fro, loading tools and supplies onto rickety wagons, alongside the piles of logs that had once made up the small fort. There were no animals in the traces, and instead the soldiers themselves were harnessed to the front.

'Good, you're awake.'

It was Marius, his eyes shadowed after what must have been a sleepless night.

'You work fast,' Cade said.

Marius grinned. 'The men were eager to leave. And once the walls come down we are open to attack. Fear is the greatest enemy of idle hands.'

He waved away the look of worry on Cade's face. 'I have scouts keeping watch. That is one benefit of this flat, cursed land. No surprises.'

Cade relaxed, if only slightly. There was no telling what technology the Greys had at their disposal. They may have put up with the Romans in their land thus far, perhaps reserving their soldiers and resources for whatever challenge their equivalent of Abaddon had in store for them.

But this was now part of the game. And with the slaughter of their patrol – one tenth of their entire army no less, if Marius's guess at their numbers was accurate – they would be making moves soon.

'Should I tell the others to come out, so you can take their wood too?' Cade asked.

'We cannot take everything here,' Marius said, scratching the shadow of stubble on his chin. 'There are only six wagons – all we could salvage after we lost our first battle. A waste to leave all this wood. Perhaps we will return.'

Cade saw that it was not just the cabin that remained. The cannons set in the walls had also been abandoned, left in the dirt where the gun platforms had once been.

'You aren't seriously leaving the cannons too?' Cade asked, pointing at the rusted hulks and the iron balls scattered beside them.

Marius chuckled. 'Our friend Louis told us what they were,' he said. 'But we have never been able to use them. No . . . powder, I think he called it.'

Cade sighed. Of course. Gunpowder had existed in the time of the Romans, but had only been used in east Asia. They would have little idea of how to make it. Then again, even if they had known, they would have had little chance of gathering the ingredients in this alien world.

'What will you do when we move to the new fort?' Cade asked. 'Now that my friends and I are here, things must be different.'

Marius laughed. 'Ask Atticus,' he said. 'The man tells us nothing of his plans. Long we have asked to attack once more, to end this eternal waiting. But instead he still tries to draw them out. Over the years, we have ambushed their patrols, whittled down their numbers. But look at us.'

He gestured to his own, skinny body.

'We waste away, living off a barren land of grass and vermin. Our men sicken and die, our weapons rust. It cannot continue.'

'It won't,' Cade said, his words more confident than he felt. 'We only have five days to defeat the Greys.'

'And what happens if you fail?' Marius asked.

Cade hesitated. 'Our world will be destroyed. Earth. I know everyone you left behind is long dead, but . . . would you still fight for it?'

Marius bit his lip. 'I had not thought of it. We came here because the gods told us to, and our commanders ordered us the same. Now, our men want this to end. But five days . . . there is little time to prepare.'

Then he shrugged. 'What we want is not the question. It is Atticus you must convince.'

Cade shuddered. The man he had met at Jomsborg had not seemed like a man who could be easily swayed, nor one who had particularly welcomed their arrival. Even now, he would be interrogating Quintus.

'Now that we speak of Atticus . . . tell me,' Marius began, his voice lowered all of a sudden. 'Atticus asked if you have the . . . Codex. Is there such a thing?'

Cade hesitated, and Marius moved closed still.

'Our commanders kept it hidden from us. Even Atticus has never seen it. It is said to be an Oracle. One that could answer any question, and allowed them to commune with the new gods. Was it a lie, to convince us to follow?'

Cade stepped back, his heart suddenly pumping. The Codex was their only advantage over the Romans. The only thing that set them apart as contenders. In truth, it was the only bargaining chip they had against Atticus.

Yet, as Marius stared at him with desperate eyes, Cade found it hard to lie to him. The man had shown them nothing but kindness.

'We'll talk about it later,' Cade said, unable to come to a

decision either way. 'We should get going.'

Marius sighed, then nodded curtly.

'Gather your friends,' he said. 'It is time to leave.'

SEVENTEEN

The silhouette of Jomsborg was a welcome sight. The march had been even more arduous than their last – for they took their turn in helping the Romans pulling the old carts full of wood and equipment.

Every minute felt fraught with danger, despite Marius's assurances that there were scouts in the vicinity. So when they trundled through the gates, Cade fell to his knees with relief.

Still, he scanned the surroundings, hoping to catch a glimpse of Quintus. He could only hope his friend had managed to fend off any questions from Atticus. For once, their fate was in someone else's hands, yet that made Cade no less uneasy.

But there was no sign of Quintus. The camp had been lit up in anticipation of the coming night, rusted embrasures and sconces filled with bundles of the hardy purple grass.

Men patrolled the walls, dangling slings from their arms, and beyond the fortified town, pyres of grass were lit to illuminate any approach from the enemy.

The century of Roman soldiers they had left behind had been busy too. Men knelt in the sand, tying together bundles of purple grass, while others thatched the roofs of crumbling longhouses, the spear hafts of the dead Greys forming the structure the grass was tied to.

The newly arrived Romans cheered at the sight of their new camp, but their voices fell silent when Atticus strode out from the shadows. His face was grim, mouth drawn tight.

'Bring them to me,' he barked, pointing at Cade and the others.

There was a moment of silence. For a brief second, Cade caught Marius's gaze, before the man lowered his eyes and rough hands took hold of his arms.

He did not resist – he knew he could never overpower these men. And beyond these walls . . . was only death. No, this was all part of the game. He and his fellow contenders were the players, and these Romans were the pieces. He had to learn how to play them.

The longhouse they were shoved into was smoky, lit by flickering torchlight.

But Cade was more concerned with the sight of Quintus, tied to a frame made of spears, his body naked but for a loincloth. His flesh was a mess of red welts, and Cade forced himself to choke back a cry.

They had not kept Quintus for interrogation. They had kept him back for torture.

Cade was pushed to his knees in front of Quintus, the others falling to the floor beside him. Atticus strode in front of them, a knotted rope in his hand.

'Your boy here refuses to speak,' the legatus said in Latin. 'But I know he can. What secret are you hiding?'

The Codex whispered the translation in Cade's ear.

'Marius!' Atticus bellowed.

Marius's footsteps thudded closer to Cade. 'Yes, Legatus.'

'Ask this boy where the Codex is. Ask him where the flying ball that speaks is.'

Marius crouched beside Cade. 'The Codex,' he whispered. 'Now is the time to speak.'

His words were urgent, but Cade hardly registered them. Instead, he looked to Quintus.

The boy's face was taut with pain, his body drenched in sweat. Yet, despite his obvious discomfort and exhaustion, Quintus's eyes were bright – he knew exactly what was going on.

A soft shake of his head was all the answer Cade needed.

'We have no Codex. No ball,' Cade replied in halting Latin.

Atticus raised a brow, surprised. 'At least one of them speaks,' he snarled. 'How are you here? Have you not communed with the gods?'

Cade breathed deeply, biting his lip and lifting his eyes as if thinking of the Latin words. In the walk back, he'd had time to consider what he would say to Marius. Now, he would say it to Atticus instead.

Without the Codex, they were expendable. They needed Atticus to need them as much as they needed him.

'Our commander stays in the keep – our home. He controls the Codex,' Cade said, stuttering awkwardly with the Latin.

He spoke as loudly and clearly as he could. This was for the soldiers who held the contenders down to hear, and the men who would be eavesdropping outside. If this was to be his opportunity to speak, then he would have to make it count.

'We are from the future. Even further than Louis Le Prince. We are here to help you.'

He could hear the soft murmuring of the men inside, and the rustle of men pressing their ears to the walls of the log house.

'We brought you this castle. We brought you a victory. We brought out the . . . Tritons . . . for you to kill. Why do you act as if we are your enemy?'

The murmuring grew louder, such that Atticus was forced to raise his hand for silence. 'Your commander sent only eight fighters to help us,' he said. 'Some help you are.'

Cade brought one foot forwards, moving from kneeling into taking a single knee. There was no move to push him down again.

'We are few, yes,' Cade said. 'But we could not leave the keep with nobody to defend it. If we fail . . . the world ends.'

Atticus scoffed. 'The same lie our own commanders told us. Leading us to our deaths on a foolhardy assault. I keep my men alive. I care not for this game.'

'But if you win here, you go back to the keep. Win again, and you go back to . . .'

He struggled with the Latin word for planet, but Marius finished it for him.

'Home,' Marius said simply.

'Yes,' Cade said.

Atticus laughed. 'We have been fighting the Tritons for years. How do eight pathetic fighters make any difference at all? This fort is only good for defence. The catapults on the roof are broken, and the ones we used during that first battle did no more than dent their doors.'

Cade had no answer for that. Or at least, not one he believed. 'We have knowledge. Knowledge from the future.'

Atticus brought his face close to Cade's. 'If you can break open their fort, or bring the Tritons into open battle, come talk to me. Otherwise, stay out of sight.'

'But we only have five days!' Cade shouted. 'Five days, or we are here forever. All of us.'

Atticus froze. 'What did you say?'

'If we don't kill the Tritons in five days, the gods will abandon us here. This is your only chance to escape.'

His words rang out, leaving the longhouse deathly quiet. Any murmuring in the background had stopped.

Atticus stared at him, a look of shock stamped across his face. Then, it turned into a rictus of anger.

'Lies!' he snarled, gripping Cade's chin in his hand and shoving him back in disgust. 'The same lies our dead leaders told us, to rush us into a battle we could not win.'

He turned to the men, and Cade managed a quick glance over his shoulder. At least fifty legionaries had filed into the longhouse. Enough to spread the word throughout the entire camp.

'This boy is here for his own reasons, and he will say anything to get what he wants,' Atticus barked. 'He has no

Codex. No proof of what he and his friends are doing here. Any soldier who speaks to any of them will be whipped.'

Atticus nodded to the guards, and they began to cut Quintus down from the frame.

'Get them out of my sight,' he snarled. 'We're done here.'

EIGHTEEN

They sat in the ruined shell of a longhouse on the periphery of the camp. Quintus lay on a makeshift bed made from their sleds – these, at least, the Romans had not touched.

The young legionary seemed almost annoyed at their attentions, refusing to lie still despite the red welts peppering his body. He wanted the situation resolved, and quickly.

'The legion must know the truth,' he croaked. 'They must know the timer is running out.'

'Why didn't we tell them about the Codex?' Grace asked. 'Surely that is proof enough?'

Cade shook his head. 'If we revealed the Codex, we wouldn't be here right now. Atticus wants it for himself.'

'Can he even do that?' Yoshi asked. 'Force us to transfer the Codex to him?'

'If he couldn't, he could force us to ask it questions,' Cade said. 'Or declare himself a contender again, or kill us all so it attaches to him.'

'So why not just give it to him?' Amber asked. 'Would that be so bad?'

'Yes,' Quintus groaned. 'The man is a . . . fool.'

'I think the soldiers are convinced already,' Cade said. 'We have no reason to lie. But it changes nothing.'

'Why?' Grace asked.

'Because attacking the Greys' fortress is suicide,' Cade said. 'Even if the Romans agreed to fight with us, we would never break through. We need to present a solution *and* the Codex to the Romans at the same time. Proof, and a way forwards. One doesn't work without the other.'

Scott sighed and rubbed his eyes. 'So . . . we have two options. Bring the Greys out into open battle . . . or find a way into their stronghold.'

'Well, we won't get them to come out of there,' Bea said. 'They will have a timer, just like we do. I bet that patrol only attacked Jomsborg because they weren't aware a new round had begun. The Greys at their HQ will have withdrawn all their patrols by now. They just have to wait us out.'

Cade closed his eyes, letting the conversation wash over him. Bea was right. Even if the Greys could be tempted out into the open, whatever skeleton crew was left to guard their home would still be able to hold off the Romans in the impregnable fort. They had to kill each and every Grey inside, not just defeat the army that was sent out.

'There is a solution,' Cade said, speaking his thoughts out loud.

There was silence for a few moments.

'Err . . . are you going to enlighten us?' Grace asked.

Cade shrugged.

'I didn't say I knew what it was. I just know for a fact that there is one.'

Scott put an arm around his shoulders. 'I think you've finally cracked, buddy. Quintus, shift over. I think Cade needs to lie down.'

Cade laughed, though with a hint of bitterness. 'That's not what I mean. Abaddon sent these Romans here to attack an impregnable fortress. He would have known their catapults would do nothing to the gates. He would have known the Greys had a weapon capable of destroying an entire army. But he sent the Romans here anyway. And not with just a week, but months.'

'So?' Trix asked.

'So, he wouldn't have done that if they didn't have a way to win. Every round, he agrees the rules of the game with the other Pantheon member that rules the game. How long the timer is, what resources he can send here, all of that.'

'And?' Yoshi said.

'He wouldn't send *us* here if there was no solution. Every time we've gone into battle, there've been resources available to us. Weapons, armour . . . if we're smart enough to find them.'

'Unless he doesn't want us to win,' Scott said. 'Maybe he wants us to lose, so he can wipe Earth out and start again. Just like he did with Mars before it.'

Cade scratched his fledgling beard. 'He could do that anytime he wanted. Leave us with nothing. Instead, he left us with this fort, and the Romans. Those two things on their own are not enough though. So there *must* be something else.'

'Well, what did he give the Romans?' Amber asked. 'There's Fort Caroline. Maybe *that* had the tools they needed.'

Cade nodded slowly. 'Fort Caroline may just have been a base for them. But . . . why such a small fort? Why not Jomsborg? There were thousands of Romans at the beginning. Maybe Abaddon knew that most of the army would be blown away, but he couldn't be sure they would attack immediately.'

It was like his mind was scratching around the edges of a grand realisation, but it just wouldn't come.

'They had cannons,' Cade said slowly. 'But they were rusty, with no gunpowder. There was a moat . . . but that doesn't seem important. Wood, yes, but that's not exactly a game changer.'

He buried his head in his hands. 'Think, Cade,' he whispered to himself.

'What if there is more?' Quintus asked.

The boy had been his usual silent self, his eyes darting from one speaker to the next, reading their lips, listening keenly to their words. As usual, they were speaking louder when in his presence.

'More?' Cade asked.

'Yes. We received Jomsborg, and the Romans, and Fort Caroline. What if I know about one other thing?'

Cade's eyes widened. 'They told you about somewhere else?'

Quintus shook his head, then flashed him a smile. 'There is . . . good . . . in my silent ears,' he said slowly. 'I can see a man's lips move and know what they speak.'

Cade's eyes widened. 'What did they say?'

Quintus bit his lip thoughtfully. 'They spoke of another place. One where they took shelter when the rains came. A place that was not Fort Caroline. They said Jomsborg is much better than the other home the gods offered them.'

Cade leaned closer. 'Did they say where it was? Or anything else?'

Quintus shook his head. 'They spoke of the smell there. It smelled of death, so they said. A cruel joke from the gods.'

Scott threw up his hands. 'Oh great. Let's go wandering around an alien land, seeking out the place that smells like death, so we can see if it's a clue to how to break into a place thousands of trained soldiers couldn't.'

Cade allowed himself a thin smile. 'You got a better idea?'

They packed their sleds immediately – sleep could wait. Their water jars were refilled surreptitiously from the Roman wagons, which were still waiting to be unpacked as the soldiers celebrated their new home.

They could not leave just yet though. It was all well and good to seek out the second Roman base. But without at least a direction to head in, they had no hope of finding it in time.

Now, it was up to Quintus, who had told them more about Marius. His friendship with the centurion was one that had spanned years. It was Marius who had championed the young legionary's right to fight in the Ninth Legion, despite his hearing impediment. He who had shielded the boy from the worst of the bullying, and ensured Quintus was fed when his food was taken from him.

So they could do nothing but wait by the gate entrance as

Quintus slunk between the campfires scattered across the harbour's dry basin, seeking out his old friend.

He was gone for quite some time, and they had to endure the curious glances from passing Romans. In a way, Atticus's proclamation protected them from further investigation – none wanted to incur the despotic leader's wrath.

Quintus returned breathless, his eyes ringed with dark circles. But though his face was haggard, a smile was stamped across it.

'Marius could not speak to me. He ignored me when I asked him to show me the other place. But I walked away and watched. He drew this, and threw it behind him.'

He passed a rag to Cade, who held it up to the red light of the rising moon.

It was rough, scratched into the fabric with charcoal. Jomsborg, at its centre, marked by a square with crenellations at its top.

There was Fort Caroline, a spike-topped circle to indicate the palisade around it. And a third object, a strange, jagged triangle, directly above the conquistador's fort.

By luck or Abaddon's twisted logic, their journey was a straight line, one that would return them to Fort Caroline. They would have a place to rest up, and would be able to investigate both locations further.

But there were disadvantages too. The Greys might well be holed up in their fort, but it was possible they would have sent scouts out to investigate what the Romans were up to. No doubt they would have discovered the location of Fort Caroline.

If there *were* scouts out there, they would be watching it. Perhaps even patrolling the route between the fort and Jomsborg.

Their only advantage was speed . . . and the cover of night.

NINETEEN

Quintus was hardly able to walk by the time they reached Fort Caroline, with the chirrups and calls of the local fauna announcing the arrival of the sun.

They had trekked through the night, watching the horizon for approaching Greys. But none had come. Still, the Greys could arrive at any moment, and as they staggered into the log cabin, the last structure remaining there, they left Quintus to sleep in a makeshift cot on one of their sleds. He only took the time to gulp down some water and jerky before he was out like a light.

'We can't stay here,' Cade said as Quintus snored softly. 'We're better off stopping at the—'

'—place that smells of death?' Scott interjected.

'Can you give me a break?' Cade snapped.

Scott froze, surprised by Cade's reaction.

'Hey,' Grace said, giving Scott a gentle nudge. 'Give the plan a chance. Has Cade ever let us down? He's a player.'

'You can say that again,' Amber said, flashing Cade a

smile. She swatted him away playfully.

It was enough to lift some of the tension, and Cade sighed. It felt good to be so close to her. He'd been so engrossed in their survival, he'd hardly had a chance to talk to her.

'You know what I mean,' Grace said, grinning. 'Cade knows this game. Knows how Abaddon thinks. If this smelly place was part of Abaddon's plan for the Romans, at the very least we can find out what was there.'

Cade felt his head nodding, his chin bouncing on his chest. It would be so easy to sleep here. The cabin was already warming to the sun's rays above.

But he could not allow them to rest. They had to move on, make camp in the spot where they had the best chance of discovering what new tools Abaddon had given the Romans.

'You know, this might all be a waste of time,' Yoshi said. 'The Romans definitely checked out this death place, right? So what could we possibly find there that they overlooked?'

Cade shrugged. 'Our advantage has to be the Codex. It sounds like the Romans attacked so soon after their arrival, they didn't have time to find out what everything was. Marius said he only learned what the cannons were because Louis Le Prince told him.'

He thought a moment longer. 'In fact, that's a second thing. Even without the Codex, we are *modern* humans. More so than even Louis – if they could understand him properly then. Maybe there's something there that he wouldn't have recognised.'

'A rocket launcher?' Scott joked.

'Maybe,' Cade said, dead serious. 'It could be a tank for all we know.' He sighed. 'We won't know for sure until we go there. But I know there's *something* we can use. There has to be.'

'Well, all right then,' Scott announced, leaping to his feet, then wincing and clutching his head. 'Oh man, I think I need some water.'

Cade smiled and handed him his amphora.

'Thanks. And hey, I didn't mean to put you down earlier. Just making a bad joke.'

Cade shook his head. 'We're all exhausted, man. Don't worry about it.'

'You are right though,' Amber said, standing too. 'We need to get going. I say we pull Quintus along; he's had even less sleep than we have. I don't know how accurate that map is, but it looks close. Maybe we can get there before nightfall, investigate in the daylight, and finally sleep when the sun sets.'

'Now you're speaking my language,' Yoshi said. 'I don't *care* how bad it smells. I'd crawl up an elephant's ass if I could get some sleep.'

There were groans all round, and then they were off again, Quintus snoring in one of the sleds.

As they trundled over the drawbridge, circling to the other side of the fort, Cade kept his eyes peeled for any Grey scouts. To his relief, he could see nothing but endless fields of purple grass, swaying against a soft breeze. It might have been beautiful . . . were it not for the timer, ticking away.

'Codex,' Cade said as they rounded the opposite side of the fort. 'How long do we have?'

00:96:01:54
00:96:01:53
00:96:01:52

It was an ominous number, but there was nothing he could do. Only trudge on, ignoring the pain from his aching, blistered feet and the exhaustion that weighed his body like a suit of lead.

'What's that smell?' Grace groaned, wrinkling her nose.

'It can't be what we're looking for,' Cade said. 'We've hardly left the fort.'

But as he stepped further into the grass, he noticed a well-worn path had carved a furrow, leaving black soil exposed. People had walked here, many times.

They followed the path, more for ease of travel than anything else, and the stench grew stronger. It was not the smell of death. Cade had smelled enough of that in the previous rounds of the Pantheon's game to know.

Soon enough, they discovered the source of the scent. An enormous, round pit, rimmed on one side with a bench of wood, holes cut into its top.

He almost choked at the smell. It was a cesspit – where the Romans defecated and urinated.

'My god,' Amber said, her voice nasal from her fingers pinching her nose. 'That is *disgusting.*'

'I bet they missed the toilets back at the keep,' Scott

said. 'I know I do.'

Cade shuffled closer, the fetid air almost muggy as he peered over the bench's edge. The pit was deep and wide, so much so that you could drop double-decker bus in and it would hardly touch the sides.

'Come on,' Cade said. 'We should keep moving.'

They saw it as a smudge on the horizon, hardly an hour after they left the fort. But it still seemed too far off. The going was tougher, for they had to wade through the tall grass with every step, and the struts of the sled kept tangling in the grass.

The smudge was a good sign, but the contenders were flagging. There was only so much they could ask of their bodies. Fuelled on strips of hard jerky and a few mouthfuls of water, with hardly any sleep for two days, each step was a torment, and their progress imperceptible.

Cade almost wanted to give up – to return to the Romans and plead his case again. Perhaps they were wasting precious time, precious *energy* on this endeavour. Worse still, as doubts plagued his mind, Cade began to wonder if it was his own curiosity driving him more than logic.

If curiosity drove him to walk on, perhaps it would the others.

'So, any guesses what it is?' Cade called out, his voice hoarse from heavy breathing.

For a moment there was no reply, only the panting of the others as they staggered on like zombies.

Then Scott's voice piped up.

'All I've got is a triangle shape that smells like death,' he said. 'Maybe . . . Yoshi's underwear?'

It was a poor joke, but it elicited a laugh from the others.

'Joke's on you,' Yoshi called out. 'I haven't worn any for months.'

Another laugh, this time more heartfelt.

'Seriously though,' Cade said. 'Let's guess.'

Silence. Then:

'Another fort?' Amber said. 'Maybe one full of bodies after a battle. I mean, we've got Fort Caroline and Jomsborg. Why not another?'

Cade considered it.

'Would have to be a pretty crappy fort for them to want to go to Fort Caroline instead,' he said. 'But I hear you on the bodies part.'

'It has to be a place with a roof, right?' Trix asked. 'If the Romans considered making it their base? Like a church, with the triangle shape? Like, the Vikings raided English churches all the time, killed all the monks. Maybe Abaddon stuck with the Viking theme.'

'Right,' Cade said. 'Could be.'

He thought for a moment. 'I'd love it if it was a modern building,' he said. 'From our time. Or even post-First World War. Imagine how much better things would be if we had actual guns?'

Bea gave a bitter laugh. 'I think Abaddon likes to watch us bleed.'

Cade didn't doubt that. But he could dream.

The black smudge grew larger and clearer with each mile they travelled. It was grey-brown in colour and shaped like a leaning shard poking from the ground.

It was only when they were a hundred feet away that Cade recognised it for what it was.

A ship.

TWENTY

The ship was a rusted hulk, broken down the middle with its back half-flat along the ground. Its front end pointed upwards, as if it had fallen from the sky and bent from the impact before tipping back and resting.

So this was their triangle. A five-hundred-foot metal ship. Modern, perhaps. It was hard to say; the thing was so rusted that no lettering or detail remained.

And the smell. It hit them like a physical wall, leaving their eyes watering and nostrils stinging.

'That's not dead bodies,' Cade choked.

'I think this is worse,' Scott groaned.

It was no wonder the Romans had abandoned this place. There was no getting used to that.

The odour was strangely similar to that of the cesspit, but more chemical in nature, like rotten eggs. But it gave Cade hope in some strange way. The smell was unusual. And unusual meant this thing had been abandoned here for a reason.

'How do we get in?' Scott asked, dropping the handholds

of the sled and rubbing his cracked, blistered hands.

Cade jogged closer, curiosity fuelling his aching body. There was a huge rent down the ship's middle, a crack yawning like a jagged mouth. As he approached, the miasma in the air seemed to thicken, and he held a sleeve up to his nose.

There was something different about the ground outside the crack. No grass grew there, and the ground was not the black soil of this alien region. Rather, it seemed to be coated in a fine yellow powder.

'Codex,' Cade coughed. 'What is this place?'

The drone flashed blue light and spoke.

'*Remnant is the SS* Marine Sulphur Queen, *which disappeared when travelling through the Bermuda Triangle in 1963. It had a crew of thirty-nine and carried a tank of 15,260 tons of molten sulphur in its hold.*'

Cade staggered away, giving himself a break from the smell. He allowed himself to collapse on the ground, and the others followed. Here, the stench was just about bearable.

'The . . . *Sulphur Queen?*' Scott said first. 'What kind of name is that? Sounds like Grace after a bean stew, if you know what I mean.'

He winked, only to wheeze a moment later as Grace's elbow found his belly.

'Not funny, Scott.'

Cade wondered how thoroughly the Romans had investigated the ship. It didn't look like there was anything of use left there. Scrap metal perhaps. But whatever was inside had likely rusted away already.

Nor was the ship a wartime vessel. There would be no rocket launcher here. No guns, nor any other weapons. He would explore the ship, but he had little hope of finding anything that would solve their siege weapon problem.

'So, sulphur,' Amber said matter-of-factly.

Cade rubbed his eyes and forced a smile. 'Yeah?'

'Well . . . that's it, isn't it? That's what Abaddon gave to the Romans. And I guess, that's what he gave us.'

He rubbed his eyes some more. This was going to be more complicated than he had thought. 'I mean, I don't—'

'Acid!' Yoshi announced triumphantly.

Cade stared at him.

'We make sulphuric acid,' he explained. 'I remember it from chemistry class. Remember, Bunsen burners and all that?'

Cade rubbed his chin. It was not a bad guess. Though he doubted they would ever be able to make anything potent enough to eat through a door of what he imagined was solid metal or stone.

'Codex, what is the simplest way to make sulphuric acid from raw sulphur?' Cade asked.

'Burn sulphur to create a gas, and direct the gas into a reactor bed with vanadium pentoxide catalyst and oxygen gas to make sulphur trioxide—'

Cade held up his hand.

'That's enough, thank you, Codex.'

Yoshi sighed under his breath before collapsing back and closing his eyes. 'Well, that's all I've got. Anyone else?'

'Unless we can build a reactor and find some vanadium whatever, I don't think we can make acid,' Amber said.

113

'Let alone something powerful enough to be of any use.'

'All right, all right,' Yoshi groaned. 'I get it, bad idea.'

'Yoshi is right, sort of,' Cade said, trying to settle the tension that had crept in. 'It's chemistry, right? Sulphur doesn't do anything but smell on its own. I think if you burn it, the gas is quite toxic, but I don't think we can smoke the Greys out – normal smoke would work just as well.'

'And they'd be chucking javelins at us the whole time we were setting the fire,' Trix muttered.

'Think,' Cade said, putting his head in his hands. For a moment he stayed like that, resting his eyes as thoughts rattled around his head. Chemistry was clearly the answer. In fact, he had solved a problem just like this one in the first round. That time he had made quicklime.

'It's an ingredient to a substance that we need to create. I think we need to look at the ancient uses for sulphur, not the modern ones. They wouldn't have had chemicals and reactors and whatnot. Just clay pots, water, soil, that sort of thing.'

As he spoke, a memory swam to the surface. It was there on the edge. Something he had considered, all those months ago, when contemplating the exact same problem. But he had discounted it due to the ingredients.

'Codex,' Cade asked, crossing his fingers, 'what are the basic ingredients for gunpowder?'

'*Sulphur, charcoal and potassium nitrate.*'

Cade narrowed his eyes. Two out of three. Damn.

'See?' Yoshi said, still lying on his back. 'Potassium nitrate. Where are we gonna get that?'

114

Cade turned to the Codex.

'Codex, how did humans make potassium nitrate back when it was invented?'

The answer came lightning-fast.

'They would mix manure, wood ash, straw and urine. After approximately eight months, they would boil and filter the remaining liquid with charcoal and cloth, then cool the liquid to form potassium nitrate crystals.'

For a moment, they sat in stunned, disappointed silence.

'Eight months!' Bea choked. 'We don't even have that many days!'

Cade pinched the bridge of his nose. The Romans had been given a whole year. If they had been patient, they might have been able to figure this out and could have begun making gunpowder with all the time to spare.

Now it was too late.

'This is an old answer to an old game,' Yoshi said. 'It's a dead end.'

The words rang hollow in Cade's ears. He had misread the game. Misread everything. Perhaps Abaddon truly had abandoned them to death.

Whatever member of the Pantheon who ruled this part of Acies might have become sick of these Romans living here. And as a favour, Abaddon had sent Cade's crew to convince the Romans into suicidal attack. To rid himself of Earth forever, and start anew – as he said he had done with Mars billions of years before.

Despair had become a familiar feeling since he had first arrived on Acies, and this moment was no different. But a kernel of stubbornness remained.

Abaddon had spent a long time creating the caldera. Populating it with remnants, cherry-picking people and artifacts from Earth. Most had never been used.

And while an immortal being like Abaddon would have immeasurable patience, Cade imagined that a so-called god would be loath to leave so much wasted potential behind.

'No,' Cade growled. 'There's something to this, I *know* it.'

'Cade . . .' Amber said, touching him gently on the arm. 'No one blames you. We'll find another way.'

Cade shook his head. 'We're taking some of this back with us,' he said. 'As much as we can carry. Metal too. The going will be easier now that we've beaten a path.'

'Seriously?' Yoshi moaned.

Cade pursed his lips and lifted his chin. 'I know you don't all agree with me,' he said, trying to lace his words with confidence. 'But I'm asking you to trust me. If we grab it all now, we can be back to Fort Caroline this evening, and we'll sleep then.'

Cade stood and walked over to the ship, heading for the immense crack where the sulphur spilled out.

'I'm going inside,' he said. 'See if there's anything useful.'

As Cade eased himself into the fume-filled ship, he held his sleeve up to his nose and realised he would not be able to stay long. The acrid air burned his eyes and nose, and each breath felt hoarse and tight in his chest. The rotten-egg scent coated his mouth and tongue, making him want to gag.

It was immediately obvious that hardly anything here was

116

salvageable. In fact, it seemed the ship had spent many years underwater before being brought here, and it was only because the sulphur had been kept in an airtight tank that it had not all dissolved away. He could see the tank on his right, a section of it twisted aside in its crash onto Acies, letting the sulphur spill across the floor in yellow piles.

The rusted walls were caked with calcified limpets and coral, and many of the surfaces had been completely eaten through. Access to the living areas above was possible via a rusted ladder, but when Cade went to put his foot on the first rung, it dislodged, clanging to the ground.

He managed to struggle up the remaining rungs and poke his head out to see what was above, but it was all much the same. Cade hauled himself up, panting as he lay on the floor. He was dead tired, and the effort had been surprisingly difficult.

He did not want to venture too far, for the rust had eaten through the metal beneath, leaving jagged holes. If his feet burst through the floor, he might slice his flesh open to the bone. Tetanus would be the least of his concerns then.

With some disappointment, he lowered himself back to the level below and returned to the crack, almost holding his breath in desperation to get out into the fresh air.

The others were waiting for him, and to Cade's relief, they held up an outstretched amphora, perhaps the largest one they had – now empty after their long journey. They also each held a roll of sackcloth to use as a makeshift bag. They were ready to collect the sulphur.

'Thank you, guys,' Cade said, tears pricking the corners of

his eyes. 'I know I'll figure it out.'

Scott walked past him and clapped Cade on the shoulder with a grin.

'You take first watch tonight,' he said.

TWENTY-ONE

It was dark when they approached the fort. Every amphora that did not contain water was filled to the brim with sulphur, as were the sackcloths they had intended to use as tents. Shards of rusted metal were also brought, if only because Cade knew that metal was hard to come by. Perhaps they could use it to forge arrowheads, or to repair Jomsborg's gates.

Now, he sat alone, listening to the soft snores of the others inside. They had earned their rest, and then some.

Despite the nodding of his head onto his chest, Cade knew he had to stay awake and watch for approaching Greys. If he spotted them before they spotted him, the contenders could slip out of the log cabin and hide in the grass, leaving the enemy to think the place had been abandoned.

A sad consequence of this was they had not set a fire, leaving him bitterly cold as he sat upon an old cannon, staring out over the swaying purple grass.

The moons were clouded that evening, the red and white spheres casting a wan glow over the purple fields. It was difficult to see much at all, and he worried that he had no idea which direction the Greys might come from.

As the minutes ticked by, Cade found himself walking the perimeter; any time sitting down risked falling asleep. Quintus, who had managed to sleep for much of the day in the sled, would take next watch, but it was not for a few hours yet.

It was on one of his circuits of the fort that Cade caught a whiff of the cesspit. Realising he needed to go, he wandered closer, wrinkling his nose at the stench.

Cade stood at the edge of the giant pit, careful not to get too close as he relieved himself off its edge, careful not to fall in. What an ugly end that would be.

And the smell didn't bother him so much any more – they all stank of sulphur.

It was an odd thing to do, going to the pit, when he could have easily gone in the grass. But curiosity had taken his feet there. If anything, it broke up the monotony of the night.

The cesspit was more than a hand-dug hole; Cade saw that the Romans had tiled the insides of the pit with clay bricks. This was a useful piece of information – somewhere near here was soil that could be turned into clay. With that, they could make pots, perhaps even mortar and more bricks to repair the broken walls of the fort.

Not that they had time for that. Still, it was an idea.

But there was something strange about the pit's walls. They shone strangely pale in the moonlight, almost reflected by a white sheen that coated patches of the tiles.

'What is that?' Cade wondered aloud.

There was a flash of blue behind him.

'*This substance is potassium nitrate, also known as saltpeter, or salt of the rock.*'

Cade gaped, leaning precariously to get a closer look. He swept a fingernail across the clay brick of the rim, only to find a crystalline substance beneath his fingernail.

'Codex, what other way was potassium nitrate harvested, historically?'

'*Saltpeter men were known throughout Britain and France in the eighteenth century. By royal decree, these men could enter any premises to harvest saltpeter that had formed on the walls and soil – such was the demand for gunpowder at the time. Saltpeter efflorescence typically formed on the walls of sewers and stables, where the combination of urine and excrement allowed the crystals to form on the surrounding surfaces over time.*'

Cade felt the hairs on the back of his neck stand up. This was their solution. Abaddon had given the Romans a year because that was how long they would have taken to make the saltpeter. But over the years they had been abandoned here, they had been producing it in a more . . . organic way.

That was why the new contenders had only been given a week.

They had the sulphur. They had the wood to turn into charcoal. Now . . . they had the saltpeter. The only question was, would it be enough?

'Codex, what are the basic ratios of charcoal, sulphur, and potassium nitrate to make gunpowder?'

'*Seventy-five percent potassium nitrate, fifteen percent charcoal, ten percent sulphur,*' came the reply.

Cade grunted in frustration. The primary ingredient was also the substance they lacked the most.

But now another idea came to him. This was not the only place to have sewers. If they were lucky, Jomsborg would have its own sewage system, long dried and empty, but potentially loaded with crystals too.

The only thing was, they could not rely on that. They would have to harvest what they could here.

'Cade,' a voice called.

Quintus stumbled down the path from the fort, rubbing his bleary eyes.

'Quintus, come see,' Cade called.

The young legionary hurried over, and Cade wrapped him in a hug.

'It's the solution to all our problems!' Cade said.

Quintus extricated himself and peered into the hole, before wrinkling his nose and turning away.

'Very . . . nice,' he said politely, then paused. 'I am confused.'

Cade laughed, realising that Quintus had been fast asleep when they had seen the cesspit on their way to the *Sulphur Queen*, and they had detoured around it on their way back.

'Do we still have some of that rope on the sleds?' Cade asked.

Now Quintus seemed utterly baffled, but he followed his friend as Cade hurried back to where they had left the sleds and began to knot a rope around himself, tucking the loop beneath his armpit.

'Think you can hold my weight?' Cade asked.

'Are you OK, Cade?' Quintus asked. 'Maybe you need to sleep.'

'No time,' Cade said breathlessly, hurrying back to the pit. 'I want to prove this can work by morning.'

He approached the rim of the cesspit, staring down at the horrible, gloopy mass at the bottom. Cade really, really hoped the rope wouldn't break.

TWENTY-TWO

'What are you still doing awake?'

Cade looked up from his work, and Amber almost recoiled from him as she caught his bloodshot eyes and haggard face.

'You look like hell,' she said.

Cade laughed. 'I feel great though.'

It was a half truth. He was swaying on his feet, and it took concentrated effort to keep his eyes open. If Quintus hadn't been there to help him, he'd have collapsed long ago.

But he'd done it. It had taken all night, and hours of scraping away at the crusted, disgusting walls of the cesspit, dangling on a threadbare rope above a pool of vile waste.

By the time the sun had risen, he had gathered almost all of it, leaving him with an entire sackful of brown-white crystal.

At the same time, Quintus had made charcoal, setting a fire and baking wood within a sealed ceramic pot, leaving it blackened. They were lucky the Romans had been forced to abandon so much.

In the early hours of the morning, the pair had toiled with a blunt stub of palisade each, pounding sulphur, saltpeter, and charcoal into a fine powder.

Now, the finishing touch. There were no scales here, but Cade used the end of an old clay pipe to measure out seven and a half dashes of saltpeter, one and a half of charcoal dust, and another of sulphur crystal. This used up a good tenth of their saltpeter supplies, but it was a necessary sample to see if it had worked.

The black powder mixture that remained was now being poured gently into a scrap of Roman parchment, taken from the dusty interior of the log cabin. He made the final twist, grinning as the others emerged from the cabin.

'What is that?' Grace asked, staring at Cade's sooty hands and Quintus's worried expression.

'This . . .' Cade said, seeing double as he held up the package to the light, 'is going to get us into the Greys' fort.'

Cade woke to the sound of Latin shouts, and the scrape of the sled moving onto pebbled sand. He jerked upright, only to find himself in the shadow of the gates, Scott and Yoshi grunting as they hauled him over the rough surface.

He had resisted riding the sled for the first half of the journey, near delirious as he shambled behind the others, but Amber forced him to lie down on the sled and rest when he began to slow them down.

'I'm up, I'm up,' Cade groaned, rolling off the moving sled and sprawling on the ground. They were in the harbour basin of Jomsborg, where the campfires of the Romans were

125

already lit, and curious glances were tossed in their direction.

He saw Marius at the head of a half-dozen men and checked surreptitiously to see if the Codex was still visible. Lucky for him, it had a knack for knowing when to hide itself from others. How thoughtful of Abaddon to programme it that way.

'The liars have returned,' Atticus's voice called from behind, in Latin. Cade turned to see Atticus standing on the thin lip of the gatehouse doors, the same one he had hauled himself into when the Greys had attacked.

'We come bearing gifts,' Cade called back in Latin, his voice surprisingly hoarse.

The sun was beginning to set, for the poor contenders had trekked all day to return to Jomsborg. But they had no time to dally.

'Gifts, you say?' Atticus laughed. 'Perhaps the Codex, in exchange for our protection?'

Cade shook his head. 'A weapon,' he called back. 'The key to the Triton fortress.'

His answer seemed to catch Atticus by surprise, and Cade thought he saw the man's face pale. Emboldened, he drew the package from where he had placed it in the sled and held it up to the Romans.

'Quintus,' Cade said. 'Tell them.'

Quintus bit his lip, but took a few steps away from them and cupped his hands around his mouth.

'Romans,' he yelled. 'Hear me!'

Atticus disappeared from the doorway, and Cade heard the slap of his footsteps.

126

'Quickly,' Cade said urgently. 'He's coming.'

'We have with us a substance from the future. Greek fire, but more potent. Lightning straight from Zeus's fingertips.'

'Seize them,' Atticus screamed, now on the ramparts. 'I will tolerate their corruption no longer!'

Quintus ignored him, even as Romans stood from their campfires, peering at them with curiosity. Only Marius moved, passing unheard orders to his men, who jogged in tandem down the beach.

Cade stumbled forwards as Quintus spoke, finding a small fire where a pair of men warmed their hands beside it.

'Leave,' Cade hissed in Latin, jabbing the package at them as if it were a poisonous snake.

The men scrambled away, and Cade held the package aloft for all to see once more. By now Marius's men were closing on him, but Cade had circled the fire, putting it between the approaching soldiers and himself.

'Look!' Cade bellowed.

He hurled the package into the fire, then threw his hands up to protect his face.

There was a fizzle. Silence, but for the chatter of men.

Laughter. Then . . .

Crack.

Cade felt the heat hit him like a wave, accompanied by a sudden flare of light. Coals scattered from the fire, pelting him across the hands and torso.

He fell on his back, half-blinded by the light, and smoke billowed in a mini-mushroom cloud into the sky.

'Whoa,' he breathed.

It had not been as spectacular as he had thought it would be, but it was enough to get his point across. He lay there, waiting for his world to stop spinning. Whether it was exhaustion, hunger, dehydration or the explosion, he did not know, but for the life of him he could not find the energy to bring himself to his feet.

So he lay there, staring as the breeze pulled the ash cloud away, until hardly a trace remained.

A shadow fell across his face. Marius stared down at him, his face twisted in a strange mix of consternation and anger. Rough hands pulled him up, and Atticus's visage swam into view.

'Filth,' the man hissed, taking Cade's throat in his hands. 'Filth and lies.'

Cade's world darkened, the grip of the soldiers pinning his hands to his sides. The edges of his vision blurred, and he could only focus on choking down a last breath before the vice-like fingers tightened.

As Atticus's face swam, Cade kicked his feet, and Atticus's laughter at his feeble efforts rang out. Beyond, he could hear Amber's screams, seeming to come from far away.

The pressure eased. Pain flared in his neck as a ragged fingernail dug down, prising Atticus's fingers away, one by one.

He collapsed to his knees and caught the blurry sight of Marius standing in front of him.

'We will hear him speak,' Marius said.

Cade fell onto his side and saw the rage in Atticus's face.

'You dare touch me?' Atticus spat. 'I will see your men decimated. Step aside.'

But Marius stood firm.

'You would entertain this charlatan's tricks?' Atticus said, spinning and addressing the men. 'You would allow him to con you into throwing yourselves against the Triton walls?'

His words seemed to rouse the Romans, though through the haze of pain and suffocation, Cade could hardly discern what they were saying – the Codex did not whisper a translation of everyone in his ears, only those of Atticus and Marius.

'Continue with this nonsense and I shall declare a decimation!' Atticus yelled, his voice taking on a high-pitched whine.

The murmuring of the soldiers grew louder. And from the recesses of Cade's memory, the meaning of Atticus's repeated threat came to him.

The origin of the word *decimation* came from a different meaning, back in the days of the Romans. Where soldiers who were to be punished were separated into tens and drew straws. One man in each group would eventually draw the short straw, and then his comrades would be forced to execute him together, often through stoning or clubs.

It was a brutal form of discipline, and one that had only been used in the direst of circumstances. Atticus's threat was a foolish one, though, and showed to Cade just what a poor tactician the legatus was.

To lose one tenth of his men was foolish enough, let alone forcing comrades to harm one another in such a random fashion. These men who had lived through so much together would never submit to such an order.

'No, Atticus,' Marius said. 'I think not.'

His words were almost gentle as he pulled the legatus aside. He spoke softly, and it was only the dagger in his hand, pressed into Atticus's spine, that told Cade of the veiled threat.

'You will step down as legatus,' Marius murmured. 'You will do so without complaint, nor violence. We can afford your cowardice no longer.'

This was mutiny. There was no denying it.

Cade knew not of the politics in this Roman camp. If there were men loyal to Atticus, or Marius, or both. But what was clear was that Atticus had overplayed his hand.

'We thank you for your leadership,' Marius said, this time loudly for the benefit of the others. 'But if there is a chance to leave this place, we will listen.'

His words met with approval from the legionaries, who clapped and nodded their heads.

Marius turned to Cade and motioned for him to rise.

'Speak, Cade,' Marius said. 'Tell us how we will end this.'

TWENTY-THREE

The legion crowded close as Cade stood beside the crater that had once been the fire, while Atticus stared silently.

Men watched him with hungry, hope-filled eyes. And despite the truth he knew he would speak now, he felt a surge of guilt. He had lied to these men about the Codex. About the imaginary leader of theirs waiting back at the keep.

Now, he would ask them to risk their lives on a half-baked plan.

'The substance that I threw into the fire is called "gunpowder",' Cade called out, sweeping his hand at the blackened sand. 'It is an . . . invention . . . from my time.'

He struggled to form the words, his fuddled mind forgetting his rudimentary Latin.

'At your . . . old home . . . there were metal weapons called "cannons",' Cade said, and the murmuring and nodding of the men told him Marius had shared what Louis Le Prince had spoken of before he died.

'Gunpowder is what makes them work,' Cade went on,

each word seeming to scrape his battered throat as it came out. 'We know how to make it.'

A man stepped forwards, his eyes flicking to Marius as if asking permission to speak. Marius inclined his head.

'Will it destroy the doors to their fortress?' he asked.

Cade nodded. His response elicited a cheer, and he felt the back of his neck burn with shame.

But these men needed confidence in him. He could not sow seeds of doubt – not when they were mutinying for his cause.

'If we are to make this work,' Cade said, his words silencing the crowd as they listened eagerly for more, 'I will need your help. Some will need to bring the cannons here. Others must help make . . .'

He struggled for the word for charcoal, then plowed on.

'. . . the powder. But have no doubt. Tomorrow, we march to war.'

His final words were said breathlessly, trailing off as he lost his confidence, yet another cheer rocked the dry harbour and hands clapped him on the back. He grinned, and felt Marius's arm about his shoulders.

But when Cade turned to him, Marius did not look at him with joy, or friendship in his eyes. There was a warning there, and the first green shoots of hope in Cade's chest shriveled at the sight.

Marius steered Cade towards the other contenders, beckoning them to follow as they walked beside the sleds. Marius paused, then bent down.

'Tonight, we have meat!' Marius bellowed, lifting a sack

of sauropod jerky from the sleds.

More cheers followed, and Marius tossed the sack to one of his men. Famished hands reached in, and Marius took one sack, then another, throwing them to the grasping fingers of the legionaries crowding forwards.

Cade did not begrudge them it, but Marius's requisition of their supplies made him uneasy – not to mention the firm grip about his shoulders as they walked through the thronging legionaries, Marius's entourage following.

It was not long before they were walking through the doorway of the longhouse, and Marius grunted for the accompanying guards to wait outside.

He led Cade into the furthest recesses of the room, the others following. Cade could see the alarm on their faces, but Marius did not seem to mind being alone with them – at the very least, violence appeared not to be his aim.

'Sit,' Marius instructed in English, pushing Cade down onto the hunks of stone that served as seats, beside a crumbling fireplace. A small smouldering pile of grass burned there, casting a low light through the room.

Marius groaned as he sat opposite Cade, and the others sat too, waiting for Marius to speak. Cade had no idea what he could have done wrong. Had he not caused Marius's rise to power?

'You lied to me,' Marius said.

Cade opened his mouth, but Marius held up a hand, shaking his head.

'Do not deny it,' he said.

Then he pointed his finger over Cade's shoulder.

Cade turned his head, and his heart fell. Even in the dim light of the longhouse, he could see what Marius had.

The explosion had sent debris flying everywhere, ash and sand included. And though it was hard to spot if you were not looking for it, a strange half-moon shadow hung in the air, where the dust had settled on the invisible sphere that was the Codex.

'Speak,' Marius said. 'Now.'

Cade wrung his hands, his mind racing. 'We did not trust Atticus,' he said, stumbling over his words.

It was hard to focus with the world spinning the way it was. His throat felt like it was closing up, and it hurt to swallow. Cade could not remember when he had last had a drink of water, and the half-snatched sleep of the bumpy sled ride had done little to alleviate his exhaustion.

'What you mean is, you did not trust me,' Marius chided him, though there was an edge to his voice. 'And now . . . I cannot trust you.'

Cade rubbed his temples, trying to think. 'If we had told Atticus about the Codex, he might have taken it from us. Even killed us for it.'

Marius shrugged. 'It matters not. If you tell both lies and truths, I cannot tell which you speak on other matters. Who is to say the cannons can destroy the doors of the fortress? Even Louis Le Prince said the cannons were a weapon they no longer used in his time.'

Cade hung his head. 'If you want the truth, I'll give it to you now. It's up to you whether you trust me.'

Marius leaned back and crossed his arms, then motioned

134

with his chin for Cade to go on.

'The cannons are old and rusted,' Cade confessed, the doubts and fears of his mind manifesting on his tongue. 'I think they'll fire, but I do not know if they will work and fire accurately, or if they do, whether they will crack or explode before a second shot.'

Marius rubbed his chin. 'The powder will not work alone?' he asked.

Cade shook his head slowly. 'It might, but we would need a lot of it, and we would need to pile it against the door itself rather than shoot from far away.'

His words hung in the air, but Marius only stared at him in response. 'Where did this powder come from?'

'The place that smelled of death,' Scott interjected. 'It was full of—'

Marius stabbed a finger in the boy's direction. 'I did not ask you to speak. I am asking Cade,' he said in a low voice.

Scott held up his hands and fell silent.

'Cade?' Marius asked.

Cade bit his lip. 'Scott's right. The yellow powder there is an ingredient. The other is charcoal, and the third . . . well, I scraped it from the walls of your cesspit.'

'Nitrum,' Marius murmured. 'It is used for . . .' He searched for the right word, then shook his head. 'It helps our plants grow.'

Cade was surprised that the Romans had known of the substance, but he plowed on regardless. 'When crushed and combined in the right amounts, together they make a powder that explodes. When you place it inside a cannon behind a cannonball, the explosion shoots the cannonball out like a sling stone.'

Marius nodded slowly, though Cade could tell some of the words he had used were not ones that the new legatus was used to.

'You have enough of this gunpowder?' Marius asked.

'We can make more by morning. But your men have to scrape more of this . . . nitrum . . . from the sewers here, if there is any. We've already gathered all we could from Fort Caroline.'

Marius furrowed his brows. 'Caroline?'

Cade forced a smile. 'That's what the Codex told us your old encampment was called.'

If he had expected a smile from Marius, he was disappointed.

'You hide such power from us,' Marius said, his voice low and angry. 'You are here three days, and you already know more than we have discovered in years.'

He lifted his chin. 'Tomorrow, we will march to war. We will camp outside their walls. You contenders shall be tasked with opening their gates. You alone. Should you fail, you will transfer the power of the Codex to me. The attack will be called off. And you will begin a new life here, with us.'

TWENTY-FOUR

The men slept through the morning and into the afternoon, and now Cade could feel the urgency as the timer ticked away. But Marius had insisted that tired men could not fight, and would not be swayed on the matter, especially after they wasted several hours digging, only to find that Jomsborg's sewers contained no saltpeter at all.

Still, Cade had time to sharpen his blade and grease his armour with sauropod fat, rendered over a campfire. More time still to sleep, and hold Amber close in his arms.

They hardly spoke when they did so, only kissing and talking as they lazed in the warmth of day. Somehow, the impending battle was pushed aside in the face of their desire to touch and be touched.

So the sun was high in the sky and well on its way towards the horizon when they marched from Jomsborg towards the enemy base.

Cade watched as they marched through the gates, newly repaired by the men. And to Marius's credit, he left no men behind to guard it. This was real. If Cade could open the doors – they were going in, full force.

But what *was* full force? The men wore rusted armour, hanging from threadbare straps. Their footwear had been repaired so often they were more patch than sandal. And their spears, though sharp and bright, hung from rusted nails in their hafts, while the hafts of their gladiuses dangled unraveling strips of leather.

As for the legionaries, they were in no better condition. Every man showed signs of starvation – hollow cheeked and skinny as rakes, no better than Quintus had been when Cade had first met him.

Two hundred men who looked like they belonged in a hospital ward. Men who limped from long hours of marching, from wounds sustained in their recent battle.

But still they marched. Their eyes were sunken, but shone bright with life. Their scrawny chests still puffed with pride as their new leader surveyed them.

There was fight in them yet. Cade could only hope it was enough to defeat ten times their number, and away from home turf.

Soon enough, Cade joined the head of the column, walking alongside Marius and the carriage that carried the cannons, twenty men hauling on traces at its head. It had taken the same number to lift the largest, and the cannon's hollow faces pointed ominously at their backs, preloaded with their charges and ready to fire at the touch of a flame.

'We will reach the enemy fort at nightfall,' Marius said, guessing Cade's unspoken question as the sun neared the horizon.

Cade nodded slowly. He was bone tired, mentally and physically. His preparations and planning for their attempted breach had taken much of the afternoon, and the brief hours he had snatched had not made a dent in the bank of sleep he owed his body when all of this was over.

The march had been a silent one, and any attempts at conversation were silenced by Marius. Sound travelled far on the flat steppe of the Greys' world.

It was only when the sun had nearly set that Marius ordered the men to halt and make camp, though no campfires were allowed. And beyond, in the darkening sky, Cade saw a smudge that was the enemy fort.

'Come,' Marius said, motioning at Cade. 'We go alone. Less chance of being seen.'

Then he turned to his centurions – two in all. Atticus was nowhere to be seen, but Cade had seen him walking with the legionaries at the back, seemingly under guard, and his fine armour now adorned Marius's body.

'In one hour, follow me,' Marius instructed his subordinates.

Amber flashed Cade a worried look, but he motioned that it was OK. He had to do the same to Quintus, waving him back down as the young legionary stood. The others seemed grateful for the rest, and Cade did not begrudge them for it.

Marius seemed to squat in the long grass, then motioned Cade to follow, shuffling slowly in a bow-legged stance. It was going to be a long night.

* * *

The fort stretched into the dark sky, ominous in its scale. It was a veritable mountain, as if a giant spar of red rock had buried itself vertically in the earth, all cracks, gullies and ridges. It reminded him of the Devil's Tower in Wyoming, a naturally formed 'butte' he had once visited on a metal-detecting trip with his father.

The Greys must have carved their fort from the bones of a natural rock formation, but Cade could only see apertures at the very front, above where the door was set in the stone.

And what a door it was. Even from a distance, Cade could see its stature, tall as ten men by his estimate, and just as wide. A dark line down the middle told him it was an entrance that could be opened, for the rust that had formed on its exterior blended closely with the red of the stone surrounding it.

'They must not care for the light, then,' Cade whispered as he stared at the forbidding sight.

'Oh?' Marius breathed back.

'No windows from what I can see. One entrance, and only slits at the front, probably to throw spears or fire arrows. They don't need natural light like we do.'

Marius shrugged. 'It makes attack harder.'

Cade wasn't so sure. 'Let's say we charge the door from here,' he said. 'They will send projectiles at us as we attack, right?'

Marius nodded, his brows furrowed.

'But what if we go in from the sides?' Cade said, motioning in a pincer movement with his hands. 'They can't hurt us until we're directly underneath. Or at least, if there are some holes for them to attack us from, there aren't as many as the front.'

Marius stared, then groaned and shook his head.

'That is a good plan,' he said, scratching his beard. 'We haven't considered a direct attack for quite some time, but I had not thought of that.'

Cade grinned. 'Fresh pair of eyes,' he whispered. 'Now, here's the other problem. We get those doors open, they're going to rush to close them again. Remember, it's only the bar that we can break. We don't follow up, they'll close them and shove their spears where the bar was.'

Marius rubbed his eyes and sighed. 'So even if the cannons work, it might all be for nothing?'

'If we're lucky, the doors will come off their hinges, but there's no guarantee that will happen. All I need from you is for your men to be ready to charge as soon as I give the signal.'

Marius closed his eyes. 'The only way my men reach those doors before the Tritons do is if we stand close – even if we do come in from the sides.'

'That's what the testudo formation is for,' Cade said, not unkindly.

'You know about the testudo?' Marius asked.

Cade nodded. 'We studied the Romans in school.'

This time, it was Marius's turn to grin. 'When this is over, I must hear more about your world.'

Cade smiled back. 'You can count on it.'

TWENTY-FIVE

Cade stood in silence, waiting for the legionaries to catch their breath as they came to a stop ahead of him. There was no hiding their approach – the carriage carrying the cannons saw to that. By now, the men had disguised the cannon muzzles with bundles of grass, so the Greys would be none the wiser.

At least, not until Cade enacted his plan.

Marius had already given instructions to his centurions, and now, two groups of ninety men were crawling through the grass, circling the fortress to wait on either side. At the firing of the cannon, they would charge in from the sides, before running along the fortress's curved edges to meet at the front doors.

Meanwhile, the remaining twenty men would walk between the campfires they were setting up, making it appear that the rest of the army was sitting down, below the tops of the grass.

This had been Marius's idea, and Cade was all for it. And those twenty men would be needed soon enough.

Cade had originally intended to follow a similar route to

the pincers with his carriage, but as he and Marius had crawled closer, they had seen that the ground on either side of the doors and beyond was strewn with rubble and uneven patches – too dangerous for the carriage's rickety wheels. He and his group would need to attack head-on, down the clear, well-trodden path that the Greys took when they moved in and out of the fort.

'Cade.'

Scott's voice jarred Cade from going over his plan, and he found the other contenders waiting for him, worry upon their faces.

'Hey . . .' Cade said, a flash of guilt pushing through his belly.

He had hardly spoken to them since Marius's interrogation. There had just been so much to do, so much to plan with Marius. Between sleep, work and planning, they had hardly exchanged glances, let alone words.

'What's the plan?' Grace asked. 'Even those guys know more than us, 'cause the centurions told them in Latin.'

Quintus crossed his arms, giving Cade a worried glance.

'I'm sorry,' Cade said, wiping a hand across his forehead. 'I just . . . I knew what we had to do. I should have asked you for help.'

'Our help?' Yoshi said. 'What about our opinion? We trust you, man, but you didn't even let us decide if this attack is a good idea.'

Amber stepped forwards to stand next to Cade, if a little apart.

'We understand that we're running out of time,' Amber

said. 'But we're about to charge an enemy fort with some rusted old cannons, right? Couldn't you have let us in on it a little?'

Cade felt a wave of exhaustion come over him. He sat down and clutched his knees.

'I really am sorry,' he whispered. 'I'm trying. I really am. I don't want us to die here. That's all I want. If we had more time—'

'Hey,' Scott said, stepping forwards with his hands in the air. 'We're not attacking you, dude. We know the pressure you're under. We know time's running out. Just keep us in the loop, OK? How about you tell us what the plan is and we take it from there.'

Cade felt the edges of his lips curl a little. 'We're gonna form a testudo, behind the cannon cart, and shove it down that path,' he said, motioning in the fortress's direction. 'Then when we get close, we light the fuse.'

'But what if that . . . laser thing shoots again?' Bea asked, her voice barely above a whisper.

'We can't worry about that,' Cade said. 'As far as we know, they had one shot with that thing.'

'Why would you think that?' Scott asked. 'Just because they didn't shoot the Romans when they lay siege here last time doesn't mean they didn't have it up their sleeve.'

Cade shook his head. 'We've only got one shot with that big cannon,' he said. 'These guys are just like us – fighting using remnants of their past. I mean, the Greys in that fortress might be from a time before technology even developed on their planet, just like our Romans. Maybe they found some super weapon, with a single round in it. We just don't know.'

'Wish we found a super weapon,' Scott said, kicking at the ground. 'Not some rusted old relics.'

Cade inclined his head. 'We'll see just how super this stuff is in a few minutes,' he said.

There was no movement from the fortress. Not even when the carriage was surreptitiously moved onto the trodden path at the front, or when the score of men who would push it gathered behind.

Cade and his contenders pressed together, crouched behind the canvas-top carriage, where bales of purple hay had been piled within. The canvas top had been removed – it was Cade's hope that the Greys would confuse their attack as an attempt to burn down the doors, which of course would not work on metal and leave the Greys complacent.

The back of the carriage had been affixed with two long pieces of wood, ones that the contenders and accompanying legionaries would use to propel the cart down the track and right up against the doors themselves. There was also a flaming torch slotted in a holder at the very back, ready for Cade to ignite the cannons.

These torches would be held by each contender in one hand, while the other would hold a shield above in a makeshift testudo formation, to protect his friends' heads from javelins and arrows.

Now, they stood waiting, and Cade wished that Marius was with him. But the commander had chosen to lead one of the pincers, preferring to stay with the majority of his men.

Which meant it fell to him to give the order. He could almost feel the hot breath of the waiting men on his neck, and with it the weight of the lives of a further two hundred soldiers. But far greater was the weight of billions on a planet far, far away.

It was hard to imagine, how the fate of so many could rely on the actions of so few. On a plan so haphazard, in a time so short.

Yet his voice did not tremble when he yelled the order.

'*Impetus!*'

Attack.

They heaved forwards, the rickety wheels and rusted axles of the cart complaining as they trundled over the uneven ground. They edged ahead, picking up speed, Cade's world in shadow as shields clattered above their heads.

There were no war cries, no whistle of arrows. Only the heavy breathing of his compatriots, amplified beneath their fragile shell of wood and iron.

Still they went, feet pounding the path, the cart juddering beneath the weight of the cannons. Cade stared through the ever-shifting crack of the shields above, their thin protection shifting as they shoved the cart forwards. The fortress loomed large, its rust-tinged peaks dark against the black sky.

Then it came. A whine, buzzing over his head like an angry bee before a woody *thunk* sounded behind him. More projectiles hissed by, rattling and banging as they ripped into their formation.

A scream tore at his ears, and moonlight washed through

as a man behind him dropped away, only for darkness to return as another stepped into his place.

There was no time for mercy, no time to think of anything but getting to those doors.

'Go!' Cade yelled. 'Go, go, go!'

The world turned dark as they entered the fortress's shadow, and now the scattered projectiles turned into a torrent. His arm numbed as the shield above splintered and shuddered, a spear tip erupting through to glint before his eyes, slicing his wrist to the bone.

He felt no pain, only the frantic beating of his heart.

'Faster,' he yelled. 'Come on!'

The cart's wheels crackled as they entered the rocky foreground of the doors, and now Cade shoved with all his might, Quintus heaving beside him.

And then the thud of the doors. Men pressed into his back, momentum crushing him against the cart's rear, his shield pushing up into the straw to leave him exposed.

He could hear the fluting calls of the enemy above and around him, and a rock thudded down behind him. Blood sprayed his hair.

His hand grasped the torch, and touched it to the trailing twine coated in gunpowder that ran into the main cannon's touch hole.

Light flared, casting the gateway in flickering light, as men sobbed and yelled at the torrent of spears, rocks, and arrows that tore at them.

The light sputtered out, the flame disappearing into the cannon's top, leaving its charred remains behind.

One second.

Two.

Boom.

TWENTY-SIX

The explosion sent the cart barrelling back, the world flipping as Cade fell into a mass of fallen men. Smoke billowed, filling the cave-like doorway with acrid fog.

Cade staggered upright, his arm aching as he stared through the grey mist, where the metal doors had bent back to the walls and revealed a tunnel beyond.

Miraculously, the onslaught of projectiles paused, the shock of the sound and smoke stunning the defenders.

'With me,' Cade yelled in Latin, half-choking from the smoke. 'We stand here!'

He snatched up the torch from where it had fallen and stumbled past the cart, using it to hold himself up. The doors, though warped by the cannonball, were still intact and on their hinges. The splintered, broken bar was on the floor, but a spear haft could easily replace it if the Greys closed the doors again.

They had not secured the entrance yet.

Soldiers pressed forwards, raising shields peppered with

broken javelins and arrows. They stood shoulder to shoulder beside him, Quintus to his right, Amber to his left. The other contenders, miraculously, seemed to be alive and well, mixed in among the Romans. In the lee of the entrance, the javelins could not reach them, but Cade saw that hardly ten soldiers had survived their charge. Their shield wall was awfully thin, and most, if not all, of his small squad were injured.

He was only grateful that his own team had been protected by the grass bales and the bulk of the cannons beneath, having been positioned just behind the cart. Those further back had not been so lucky, and a glance back revealed the broken trail of bodies they had left behind them.

By now, near two hundred legionaries would be charging towards the fortress, then running along its sides to reinforce them. Two hundred soldiers against a thousand were thin odds. But right now, it was less than a score, holding the doors. And the Greys would be coming.

Already he could see shapes moving in the darkness beyond, and Cade's fear was confirmed. The Greys worked in darkness. There were no artificial lights here. Only a strange blue glow emitting from the walls, which were covered in luminescent lichen. Cade might have been fascinated were he not trying to keep his heart from beating out of his chest.

The screeches of the enemy were intensifying, and the shapes were taking form. A shield wall.

'Hold,' Cade growled, lifting the blazing torch.

The sounds of trilling voices echoed down the tunnel. It was melodic, rising and falling in tandem with the crash of spear against shield.

They were singing. A battle song to strike fear into the hearts of their enemies, but all Cade felt was pity. These were not enemies of his choosing. In another world, another time, they might have spoken. Learned from one another.

He was the aggressor here, and they were only defending their home. Their species. Their planet.

But he had a job to do. He was going to kill them.

'We can't hold against that lot,' Scott called. 'What do we do?'

'We won't have to,' Cade yelled back. 'Stand firm.'

The Romans were snarling in Latin, calling for the enemy to come closer. This was their last stand. Their revenge. There was anger here, borne from years of misery and conflict.

The Greys advanced in response, stepping forwards with each crash of spear on shield. Slowly at first, but as Cade's pitiful numbers became apparent, their tempo increased.

Now, Cade could see the dark globes of their eyes, and see their slitted mouths open as they screeched their fury. Twenty steps away. Ten.

'Get down!' Cade bellowed.

He dropped to his knees, even as he ignited the second and third cannons, each trailing fuses that hung from the cart's front. The powder-encrusted twine flared and sparked. Cade stared as the flame travelled up and into the cart, his back turned to the enemy. Around him, the Romans fell to the floor, calling prayers to their gods.

He cursed the slow travel of the fire, expecting a blade to stab home at any second. Instead, he heard the Greys' song stop, and the clatter of weapons being dropped. He turned to see the Greys nearest pushing back, screeching at those from behind who could not see what was about to happen.

But it was too late for them. Too late for all of them.

He put his fingers in his ears.

Cade's world erupted in smoke, the force of the explosion rippling above him and throwing him forwards. For the second time in as many minutes, Cade stumbled through smoke and sputtering flames.

The haze cleared faster than the others, for the cannons were smaller. But the devastation they had wreaked was far greater than he could ever have imagined.

The smaller cannons had been packed with scraps of metal taken from the *Sulphur Queen*, sharpened upon the coarse stone of Jomsborg's walls and packed inside the black cylinders from base to tip.

In the explosion, the metal had come flying out, an oversized shotgun blast that had funnelled through the tunnel, ricocheting off the walls and into the crowd of enemies beyond.

He hurled his torch down the tunnel, and choked in horror at the devastation he had wrought.

It was a charnel house. Blood, blue and caustic, coated the walls. Greys lay dead and dying, packing the tunnel in a gory mess. It was a wall of bodies, and those that had survived the mincer were dragging themselves back to the safety of the tunnel depths.

'Attack!' Cade roared, drawing his sword and staggering forwards.

There were living among the dead. Wounded beyond

belief, such that Cade felt little guilt as he stabbed and stabbed again, aiming through the gaps in their helmets, gritting his teeth as the blade scraped through bone and teeth.

It was a mercy, he told himself. That, and the fact that every Grey needed to die. There was no room for pity here. Only the butchery of all-out war.

Around him, the Romans followed suit, finishing the bloody business alongside his contenders. They shouted with joy. With pride. He did not begrudge them their feelings, even as he choked back his own sobs of horror and relief. It was a heady mixture, one he hardly understood.

Soon, they were virtually crawling over the mass of bodies, stabbing their blades like ski poles as they hurried to progress the slaughter.

Behind, he heard the roar of their reinforcements, the trample of feet. Men overtook him, and it was only when a rough hand dragged him back did he allow himself to falter, right at the edge of the sprawling mass of the dead.

'Cade,' Marius said, snapping his fingers in front of Cade's face. 'Are you all right?'

Cade nodded dumbly, swaying with exhaustion, dizziness and shock. There was a wild excitement in Marius's eyes, and Cade could only stare back as the world shook and spun around him.

'Thank you, Cade,' Marius breathed, pressing him into the wall as men thundered past him.

'We haven't won yet,' Cade croaked. 'There are hundreds more.'

Marius shook his head before calling on his bodyguards to

move on as they paused at his side and stemmed the flow of soldiers. He turned back and planted a kiss on Cade's bloodied, sooty cheek.

'That was the flower of their army you just killed. Their greatest warriors. The workers, the children, that is all that is left. We will kill them all.'

Cade's mind reeled. He hadn't imagined there would be innocents here. Civilians.

'You stay here,' Marius said, pushing Cade down to his knees and crouching beside him. 'My men will finish what you started.'

Then he was gone, his figure disappearing into the crowd of charging bodies flowing through the tunnel. He could hear the crash of battle, and screams of pain and fury ahead.

Cade's squad pressed against the walls, alongside him, their identities obvious from their wounds and soot-streaked faces. They cringed as their comrades thundered past, shell-shocked by the horror they had witnessed, too exhausted to match the pace as more and more Romans poured into the fortress.

It felt like hours before the Roman army had finally passed by, though Cade knew it was only a few seconds. Only then did he allow himself to bury his head in his hands. Only then did he allow himself to cry.

TWENTY-SEVEN

'Cade.'

Amber's voice seemed distant, yet he felt her arm wrap around his shoulders as he rocked back and forth among the dead.

It was as if a dam had broken in him. And all that was left was a flood of . . . nothing. Not despair. Not relief. Not even something in between. Just an emptiness. A dark pit at his centre, devoid of hope or happiness.

He only knew he wanted to get away.

'We won, Cade. Did you hear? The Codex just announced it.'

Cade shuddered at Amber's words. He never wanted to see that thing again.

He stood, swaying as the world came into focus. Outside, the first rays of sun were rising. Had he slept? It was impossible to say.

The Romans had gone, including those in his squad. Only the contenders remained, watching him from where they sat, concern in their eyes.

'You've been out for ages, man,' he heard Yoshi say. 'We were worried. It was like you couldn't hear us.'

Cade felt numb. Maybe once he would have felt proud, but now it all felt so pointless. No matter what he did, no matter who he killed. It was all for the entertainment of some sick master.

He was a pit bull in a dogfight. Even if he won, he didn't win. It was back in the cage, back to being kicked and beaten. Only his master won. Only Abaddon won.

Worst of all, he knew it was just a passing amusement. One fraction of focus. Abaddon had said so himself. The alien's mind was so advanced, he had a thousand, thousand thoughts at once.

'Cade, talk. Please,' Quintus said, struggling to his feet. The legionary's arm hung limp by his side, where some spear or javelin had sliced deep.

But it was Cade's arm that took Amber's interest.

'You're hurt!' Amber cried, grasping at him.

Cade looked down to see red dripping between the joints of his armour. He had a flash of memory from their headlong charge, where a javelin had broken through his shield.

The others crowded in, pawing at his arm to see the extent of the damage. Pain. Pain that had always been there, like a dull drumming at the back of his mind. Blood dripped from his armour, and Cade could see where the javelin had skewered between the plates. A lucky shot, though one he had hardly noticed in the battle as adrenaline drove him on.

'We should wrap it . . .'

'. . . stitches . . .'

'Don't touch it.'

'. . . had some water . . .'

The voices swirled and merged, a crescendo in Cade's ears. He pulled away, staggering a few feet to the side.

'Please,' Cade said. 'I just . . . I need to be alone.'

'Cade . . .' Amber pleaded.

But already his feet were moving, taking him deeper into the tunnel.

It was a strange home, this place. Walls that glowed blue, blue as the blood that seemed to drip from the very ceilings, so brutal had the butchery of the Romans been.

The bodies were nowhere to be seen, and he spun to make sure he was not mistaken, looking back at where the falconets had fired. Understanding dawned as he spotted the flames at the end of the tunnel, where the purple of the grass had been replaced by orange flames. The Romans were burning the bodies outside.

And then he saw it. The Codex, following him. No timer this time. No new challenge just yet. Even so, he knew Abaddon – at least in some fraction of his focus – was watching.

With the Romans burning the bodies, Cade had a chance to see the place the Greys had called home. He staggered on, ignoring the calls of his friends, taking one branch, then another, passing by splintered doors. He caught glimpses of bunks carved into walls, but his curiosity was tempered by the hints at the massacres that the Romans had enacted within.

His feet took him deeper into the depths of the warren, passing by the occasional Roman carrying weapons and armour. The tunnels opened up, even as they moved higher and twisted in angular slopes. There was beauty in the design, alien though it was. Brutalist and empty, yet sculpted with precision and care.

He walked through great chambers, strewn with the wreckage of the assault. Tables and chairs, carved from that strange grass-glue wood. The legs widened and narrowed in geometric shapes he could not name, only admire the artistry that had gone into their design. Tables, flat-topped though they were, followed similar patterns in the light and dark-purple patterns, kaleidoscopic and ever-shifting as his eyes drifted across their surfaces.

But there was more than furniture. Musical instruments lay in splinters along the ground, smashed by Roman boots and blades. Stringed ones, not unlike violins, but coupled with holes along their sides and spouts where mouths would have blown.

There was artistry here. Beauty, even. He could see those who had lived here, eating and singing in their fluting voices. Delicate fingers plucking strings and dancing along the sides, while eerie notes drifted from the eaves.

He had enabled a genocide. That was the word for what had happened here. An entire species wiped off a world. An entire planet brought one step closer to annihilation.

Perhaps their red line on the leaderboard had been higher than Earth's. He might be responsible for the deaths of billions.

On he walked, his eyes taking in the spatters of blood. He imagined the legionaries rampaging through the place, putting innocents to the sword with wild abandon.

This was different from before.

These were not savage beasts. This had not been an act of self-defence. The choice he had been given by Abaddon had been an impossible one, but that did little to ease his guilt.

There was life here. Sentient life. Life that loved. Life that created.

And he had ended it all.

Cade walked on, letting the horror sink in. He dared not enter the chambers scattered throughout the fortress, the rooms of those he'd had murdered. Where he would see more of their possessions, those little hints of culture that spoke to the horror of what he had done.

In another time, another place, he would have been fascinated to see an alien civilisation up close. And not just in its present form, but one he knew would be an amalgamation of the species' entire history.

Instead, he let his eyes skip across the detail of the place, wanting to see and yet not wanting to at the same time. Some legionaries still remained, wandering the halls as he was. He ignored these men, sickened by what they had done. Then again, was he any better?

His feet wandered, even as blood dripped from his arm, and the Codex watched with a silent stare. Was Abaddon watching too? Reveling in the misery he had caused?

He did not even know what Abaddon *could* see. Was his vision limited to what could be seen through Codexes? A billion eyes, scattered across the vast universe, watching as species evolved, rose and fell?

And then . . . he smelled it. It was fleeting. Yet so pleasant that he could not help but stop and turn his head, seeking the scent's source.

He followed his nose, turning his head left and right, taking him back the way he had come. Deeper into the spiralling tunnels.

Soon, the sloping tunnels were narrowing, and the chambers on either side becoming fewer and fewer, until there were none left at all. With each twist and turn, the smell grew stronger.

It was a strange fragrance. Almost floral, but at the same time making him salivate. His empty stomach twisted with hunger.

He was almost suspicious of it, but curiosity outweighed his fear. That, and the fact that there was no blood here. In fact, from the dust that gathered on the walls, it seemed nobody had been here for many years. His own feet left prints where he walked, showing no one before had passed this way, and the luminescence of the walls dimmed with every step he took.

Finally, the tunnel stopped. Its ending was rough, as if this tunnel had been left incomplete, abandoned halfway through its boring.

The smell was now overpowering, yet there was no source of the heady aroma that had drawn him here. He stood there, silent in the darkness, wondering if the ceiling would collapse upon him, a trap he had fallen into of his own volition.

'Well, this was a waste of time,' he said aloud.

The Codex, his only companion, remained silent, staring

at him through its unreadable lens. He stared back at it, waiting for a response. Wondering if Abaddon had drawn him here for a private audience.

Still, nothing.

And then . . . a throb.

There was no other way to describe it. As if the very world had shuddered without moving, pulsing along some unseen plane. He felt it deep in his guts, though the world around him remained unchanged.

The Codex fell. Plummeting to the ground with an audible crack, then rolling like a marble down the incline of the slope.

Cade watched it roll, eyes widening, only to gasp as the sphere disappeared into the very rock itself.

A voice spoke.

'We do not have much time,' it said. 'Follow, quickly.'

TWENTY-EIGHT

Cade stared.

Breathed. Waited.

His mind teetered on the edge of a full-blown panic attack. Yet the voice spoke again.

'Cade, please.'

It was the Codex's voice. Artificial. Flat-toned.

'Abaddon?' he hissed.

There was a pause. Then:

'Walk towards this voice. Hurry.'

Cade put his hand to the wall, letting his fingers graze along its surface. Only, they touched nothing but air, passing through the wall as if it were not there at all.

He took a step forwards, leaning his face towards the wall. Something grasped his breastplate and pulled him through.

Cade staggered, the unexpected emptiness of what he passed through making him lose his balance. Light, so bright it blinded him, glared from where he fell.

The tunnel continued. But only for a few yards. It

morphed into a cave bereft of lichen, with walls smooth and white as porcelain. Turning, he saw the fake wall remained. A hologram.

He blinked in the new light, raising his eyes to protect them. A figure stood before him.

A Grey.

One dressed in a simple white robe, and no weapons to speak of.

It watched him from its black protruding eyes, the slitted mouth pursed in inscrutable expression. Its hand, outstretched from where it had grabbed him, fell to its side.

'What . . .' was all Cade could manage.

But there was too much to take in for him to formulate a question. The cave was vast. So large it could fit the entire keep within its confines. Size, though, was not the greatest shock here.

Technology was. There was no other word for it.

Terminals lined the walls, complete with wires and flashing lights. And above, screens. Hundreds of them, empty of image or movement, yet startling in their number. They stretched up into the very recesses of the ceiling's space, where artificial light shone dazzlingly bright.

This was no part of the medieval, alien fortress. A spear and shield would be as strange here as a caveman in an arcade.

'Forgive my use of scent to bring you here. It is the only sense the Pantheon's Codexes cannot detect.'

Cade blinked, lifting his hand to shield his eyes.

'Too bright?' the voice asked as the lights dimmed to half their level.

The Grey's lipless mouth moved as the voice spoke. But the source of the voice was not the Grey, but rather an object on a plinth at the very centre of the room.

A Codex. But not as he knew it.

The drone had been taken apart, its parts splayed like a deconstructed watch, with wiring plugged to a half-dozen elements. These wires, in turn, split and split again, running along the floors to the terminals on the walls.

'You will have questions,' the Grey said. 'But we have little time to answer them. I will answer some to gain your trust, but then you must follow my instruction. If you do not . . . it will not be just my world that ends, but yours. Yours and countless others, from now until the end of time. Know this. And ask.'

Cade moved into a crouch, his hand straying to his sword.

Startled, the Grey moved back, its hands held up in supplication.

'If I had wished you harm, you would not be here. I beg you, do not waste time. Ask.'

Cade let his hand fall to his side, his mind racing. This was not supposed to be here. If Abaddon discovered it, they would fail the round.

His thoughts strayed to a dark place. One where he cut this unarmed creature down. Where he returned to the tunnel and spoke not a word of what he had seen.

But he turned away from those imaginings. He was sick of the killing. Of the death.

'If you will not ask, I shall tell,' the Grey said.

The creature folded its spindly legs, sitting in a meditative pose on the ground. Its eyes, seen so close, stirred within their sockets.

'You may call me Song. That is the meaning of my name in your language. I have been here for almost a hundred of your Earth years. And I have been watching you since you arrived on this planet.'

Cade fell back, sitting opposite the creature. A sense of unreality moved through him. He felt detached. As if it were all happening to someone else.

'When I first came here, we did not fight as you have seen us. We fought with guns. Airships. Technology more advanced than you humans have dreamed of.'

'Why am I here?' Cade blurted.

In the background, Cade heard his words parroted back in the fluting language of the Greys.

Song's lips pursed closed, his nostrils flaring.

'You will understand soon enough,' Song replied, this time so forcefully that Cade could hear its fluting voice beneath the dull intonation of the dissected Codex beyond.

'It was in a battle against a race not dissimilar to our own that it happened. A weapon of immense power was used by our enemy. An electromagnetic pulse so powerful that it disabled every piece of technology on the planet. And in its use, the powers of the Pantheon were disabled. Abaddon included.'

Cade could only stare, incredulous. To hurt the Pantheon had seemed an impossibility.

'They let them use it?' Cade asked.

Song seemed to smile at the question, though it was hard

to tell. His facial expressions were very different from a human's.

'Call it hubris. We believe the Pantheon have long forgotten how their technology works. It was built by their predecessors. They have no respect for the weapons of mere mortals such as us. An opinion they held at their peril.'

'What happened?' Cade asked, perhaps stupidly. But what else could he ask? Abaddon was still here, after all.

'We ended our battle in the face of the Pantheon's silence. Made peace with the enemy – for after all, we fought only to preserve ourselves. But while they focused on building a means of returning home, we knew the Pantheon were not finished yet. We planned for their resurgence.'

Cade could not believe what he was hearing.

'For seven blessed days, we were free from their influence. It was during that time that this place was built. A place invisible to them and protected from any future electromagnetic pulses. This place is currently surrounded by what you humans would call a Faraday cage, one I deployed just before I fired our EMP.'

'Why?' Cade asked. 'Why not destroy the Pantheon?'

The Grey sighed, though there was no equivalent sound from the deconstructed Codex.

'Because in disabling their technology, our own was destroyed too. We had no time to build something powerful enough to destroy them, nor did we have the resources. But we could build this.'

Song motioned at the monitors behind him. 'In repairing and backward engineering this disabled Codex, I can see what the Pantheon can see. Or at least, a fraction of it at a time. There are thousands of Codexes on this planet alone, and millions more across the universe. It is through these many eyes that they observe us.'

Cade was stunned. 'So there are Codexes floating around Earth?' he asked.

The Grey nodded this time. 'All around this planet too,' he said. 'Invisible, and fast enough to avoid anything that might touch them. Shielded from anything that might see them – heat, movement, magnetism – nothing works when they do not want to be seen. It is an incredible technology. One we have learned much from, here in this place. It is how we have stayed hidden for so long.'

'We?' Cade asked.

Song was silent for a moment. 'I am the last of the research team. The others aged into death many years ago. We have waited so long for an opportunity to end this. To strike back at the Pantheon – to destroy them for good.'

Cade felt pity for the creature. 'You've been alone for that long?' he asked. 'I'm so sorry.'

To Cade's surprise, a blue tear rolled from the corner of Song's eye.

'Our species has fallen too low on the leaderboard, and has been destroyed,' the Grey said. 'I watched it happen. Saw the fires rain from the sky. I am the last of my kind.'

If there was bitterness in the Grey's voice, Cade could not tell. He only heard the dull intonation of the Codex. Song closed his eyes as he spoke again.

'Now, I must ask you – the one who brought about our

destruction – to do what I could not.'

'I can't stay here,' Cade whispered. 'I can't take your place.'

Song shook his head.

'No, little one,' the Grey said, his fluting voice soft. 'I ask much more of you.'

He opened his eyes.

'You must destroy the Pantheon.'

TWENTY-NINE

Cade was speechless. It seemed impossible. More so than anything Abaddon had asked him to do.

'You're joking, right?' Cade said. 'What could I possibly do that you couldn't, with all that you have here?'

'We could not communicate with our brethren in the fortress, nor did we have the materials to build a weapon, here in this place. In truth, they have forgotten us, for new generations have been brought here, and those who were here before have died. And of course, any who remembered us could not discuss our presence with the newcomers. The Pantheon is always watching. Come.'

Song stood and motioned for him to follow. Cade pushed himself to his feet and padded after him, struggling to keep up. Song was surprisingly fast on his feet, and he turned down into an antechamber just before Cade lost sight of him.

A strange machine filled the space as large as an aircraft hangar. Copper coils twisted around a giant pillar of metal, with a terminal at its base.

'This is how I disabled their ship, so we could have this conversation,' Song said, running his hands along the rings of bronzed wiring. 'It is the same weapon as the one that gave us those seven days of freedom all those years ago.'

Here, the Codex's translation crackled through speakers, hidden somewhere above.

Cade was amazed. Finally, a way to strike back at Abaddon.

'An EMP?' Cade asked.

'That is the closest translation to what your species is aware of, though it is more sophisticated than that.'

Cade strode closer, craning his neck to take in the full scale of it.

'Why not keep using it?' Cade asked.

Song shook his head. 'This took almost a decade to charge up for the single pulse I used today. The Pantheon will have recovered long before I can produce a second. Worse still, they will know where the attack came from. When they come back online, this place will be destroyed. As will I.'

'And how long will that be?' Cade asked.

Song's mouth pursed. 'The first time the Pantheon were unprepared, and unfamiliar with this type of attack. We have watched their preparations for another attack of a similar kind, though it does not seem they were too concerned about a repeat. You see, when they returned, they made sure to teleport away any weapons that might be capable of such a thing again. But they did not know we had been busy down here, preparing for an opportune moment.'

Cade grinned. 'Hubris seems to be a theme here.'

Song nodded. 'They have been unable to protect

themselves fully, for in blocking an EMP, so too do they block their ability to interact with the outside world. Were they to build a similar Faraday cage to the one that surrounds us now, they would be unable to manipulate anything beyond. It blocks all signals, inside and out.'

'Surely they're advanced enough to figure out a solution?' Cade asked.

Song let out a trill, one that Cade assumed was laughter.

'The Pantheon are not who you think they are,' he said. 'I have watched them for many years. The members we suffer under today have no understanding of the machines they use now. The Codexes, their teleportation technology – even the ship they reside on – was built by their ancestors. They simply inherited it. The Pantheon are but spoiled children.'

He held up a finger before Cade could speak, though he had a thousand questions to ask.

'Do not misunderstand me. They are creatures of vast intellect. Capable of multitasking to a degree that I once thought was impossible. Able to simultaneously monitor and process billions of viewpoints at once. But their technology is beyond their understanding. The vast machines that built the tools they use have long been lost. They repair and maintain, and teleport from elsewhere. They do not create.'

'So we have a week?' Cade asked.

He was excited by that prospect . . . though he had no idea how they would be able to do anything beyond what Song had prepared.

But his joy was immediately dashed as Song shook his head.

'They have become much more accomplished at repairing

the damage that these attacks do, even if they are unable to prevent them. My analysis of what they have prepared gives us no more than an hour before they recover. But I cannot be sure – we must hurry.'

Cade's heart fell. 'So what do we do now?' he asked.

'We have one more of these, hidden elsewhere on the planet. Just one,' Song said. 'The next time it is used, we *must* have a weapon capable of destroying them for good.'

'And?' Cade demanded. 'Do you have one?'

'No,' Song said. 'But you do.'

Cade scoffed. 'Yeah, right.'

Song stared at him. 'So you know, then?'

Cade paused, confused, then realised that the Grey had not understood his sarcasm.

'No, sorry. Tell me.'

Song pointed at one of the screens, one of the larger ones that lined the walls of the antechamber.

It depicted something that Cade instantly recognised: a satellite image of the caldera, seen from far, far above. Earth's region.

'Your race is one of violence. The tragedies you have inflicted upon your own people are as cruel as any species I have encountered. And I have seen many through the Pantheon's Codexes. In that, you have an advantage.'

He moved his hands, and the image zoomed closer.

'Here. You are already aware of this remnant. An A-4E Skyhawk attack aircraft loaded with a B43 nuclear weapon. It is this that you will use to destroy the Pantheon.'

Cade looked on, amazed. He was looking at a clearing in

the midst of the jungles. There was a plane at its centre, surrounded by long grass.

'You want me to fly a . . . crashed fighter jet? I can't even drive a car!'

The Grey seemed to laugh again, the trill setting Cade's teeth on edge.

'I do not need you to fly such a thing. I want you to fly *this*.'

The picture blurred as the satellite image swept across the jungles before settling above a pool of water.

Cade squinted. 'Hey . . . that's the waterfall outside our keep.'

Song laughed some more, and then gestured with his hands again.

The screen flickered, and the image changed to black and white. It almost looked like an X-ray. Now, he could see something beneath the water. An oblong shape, all in white.

'Fifty years ago, a battle took place between one of our ships and six of your planes. I believe the planes were called Flight 19, taken from your planet in Earth's year of 1945.'

Cade raised his brows.

'During the battle, our pilot was killed by a bullet through his windshield. The autopilot brought the ship down to the nearest safe landing zone – the plunge pool of the waterfall. It has remained there ever since, hidden beneath the boulders that the Pantheon placed above it.'

'Why would they keep it there?' Cade asked.

Song waggled his head, which Cade guessed was the Grey equivalent of a shrug.

'We believed it was for a future game of theirs. Something for you humans to discover. Lucky for you, the layer of water protects it from the EMP. The cockpit will be flooded, and there will be a space suit for you to wear to help you breathe while flying it out of the atmosphere, but it should remain fully functional.'

'Wait, wait, wait,' Cade said, holding up his hands. 'You want me to fly it into *space*?!'

The Grey trilled again. 'I have prepared a disguised tool for you to use.' Song withdrew something from his simple white robe. It looked for all the world like a carved Grey, made from the same purple wood. A child's toy. 'If Abaddon questions your possession of it, you must claim it is a memento of your victory here.'

He lifted the toy and pressed a delicate digit into its eye, which clicked down after some gentle pressure.

'Press the left eye once to set off the EMP. Twice to command the ship to lift from the pool and land beside it. The right eye three times to command it to land on the Pantheon's ship. Both eyes four times for it to detonate, which you must do when pressing it to the tip of the atomic bomb.'

Cade swayed on his feet, though whether from shock or exhaustion he could not tell. He tried to commit the instructions to memory, but he was also trying to process what Song was saying.

'I land on their ship?' Cade whispered.

'Yes,' Song replied, gesturing with his hands once again. The screen changed.

Now it depicted a giant structure. It could not be called a

ship so much as an enormous mass. Clearly aesthetics had not been a concern of the Pantheon's ancestors when they built it. The structure was an uneven mass of metal, a jumble of pylons, panels, dishes and girders.

It was floating above the planet Acies.

And what a planet it was. This was no random mess of continents and oceans. Rather, it was a world divided into thousands of near-perfect squares, parcelled out like a patchwork quilt. Territories for the various species the Pantheon had played with in their cruel game.

'We have found an ideal point of entry, as close to the centre as possible. The route inside will take you direct to the heart of the ship. It is there where you must detonate your bomb. Only there will it do enough damage to destroy them for good.'

'Inside . . .' Cade muttered, his mind spinning.

He'd had his share of risky plans. But this one was something else. Another thought dawned on him as he processed the information.

'Did you say detonate? Not set a timer?' Cade asked.

Song shifted on his feet. 'It is the only way. If the Pantheon come online before the timer runs out, all will be lost.'

Cade gritted his teeth. 'So the best-case scenario ends with me *dying*?' he demanded.

The Grey took a step back and held his hands up in peace. 'And for me?' he asked. 'What is my best-case scenario?'

Cade felt his anger seep from him, soon replaced by pity.

'I am the last of my kind,' Song said. 'And as soon as the Pantheon return, my life will be extinguished. Perhaps they will torture me first. Tear me apart, atom by atom. But I do it. I do it so you can have this chance. To save your species. Save the universe, because I could not.'

Cade swallowed. 'Can you give me a chance to escape the detonation?' he asked. 'Five minutes?'

Song shook his head. 'I could lie to you and say I have. But I will not. I have watched you ever since you were brought to this planet. It is you, not any other human, who I chose to bring here and task with this mission. When the time comes, I know you will do the right thing.'

He pressed the toy into Cade's hand and strode out of the antechamber.

'It is time,' the voice echoed as Song walked away. 'Do your duty.'

THIRTY

Cade stumbled through the hologram wall, back into the darkness of the tunnel. The Codex, now clutched in his arms, seemed to stare at him with its blank lens.

He hurried up the slope, his heart full of mixed emotion. Hope and despair. Bittersweet in his mouth. A chance to win, and a chance to die.

But there was no time to think on it now. He had to find the others. Tell them what he had seen, before the Pantheon reawakened.

His legs, weighed down by armour and exhaustion, burned and shook as he staggered uphill. He called to the others. Screamed their names.

None came. He could only stagger on.

Worst of all, he was lost. The tunnels branched in myriad ways, left, right, up and down. He could only guess, turning back at dead ends, cursing through snatched, ragged breaths.

It felt like an hour before he made it back to the large, central chamber of the fortress. A legionary was there, slumped at a table, his eyes gazing ahead in a thousand-yard stare.

He mumbled something in Latin, but Cade ignored him. He knew where to go, as more legionaries moved in from a tunnel to his right, arms full of spears, armour and shields. The looting had begun.

Cade shouldered past them, an outstretched hand balanced against the wall like a drunk's. He kept on. Even as his vision darkened at its edges, and the nausea of overexertion made his face twitch and his stomach roil.

'Quintus,' he wheezed. 'Amber.'

Light. He could see it at the end of the tunnel, and he forced himself to push on. Past the gouged walls, where the falconets had torn them. Past the blood that pooled through the cracks of his armoured feet.

He fell. Crawled, one-handed, the other clutching the Codex and the toy. His hands were sticky with blood.

Then, light. Fresh air, intoxicating as he gasped.

Only, his friends were not there. Just the smouldering embers of the Roman funeral pyre. Ash and bone, strewn among the long grass like an open wound.

'Cade,' Marius called.

The man appeared in Cade's blurring vision, strong arms lifting him to his feet. He vomited, then choked a question through his bile-burned throat.

'Where are my friends?'

Marius shook his head. 'Just a boy,' he muttered. 'I forget, he is just a boy.'

'Friends!' Cade demanded, falling to his knees as his

strength left him completely.

'They are in the fortress,' Marius said gently, wiping the vomit from Cade's chin. 'Looking for you.'

Cade grasped at Marius's skirt, his weight pulling the man closer.

'Find them,' he croaked. 'Find them! Now!'

Marius slowly prised Cade's fingers from him.

'Rest easy, my son,' Marius said. 'I will.'

Cade heard the orders shouted. Saw the feet of the legionaries passing by, as they hurried into the fortress.

Then, a crackle. A shift in his arms. The Codex rolled free, tumbling onto the ground before levitating into the air.

Cade stared into the empty eye of its lens, a silent hiss of frustration sputtering through gritted teeth. Behind him, Cade heard his friends call his name. And then . . . the world changed.

Like a blink that never happened. Faster even. No flicker, no blur. What had been before, no longer was.

He was on a mountaintop. No. A spire.

His feet were splayed upon a rough-stone platform, one so narrow he could topple from it with a single step. Beneath him, the rock sloped out and out again, a curving pyramid of crags and bluffs, as if some giant had pinched a tablecloth plateau between its fingers and pulled it high and taut.

It was devastating in its height. And the surrounding air was clear as day, such that he could see for miles. And all was desert. Not a single living thing.

Cade could have been anywhere. Another planet. Another galaxy. A hard reminder to the awful power of the Pantheon. They could pluck him from existence with hardly a thought.

He still wore his armour, and it hung heavy on his body. The toy Grey remained in his hand, and he wondered if throwing it from the cliff would save him from Abaddon's wrath. He was so tired.

'Cade.'

The voice crackled, as if the Codex had been damaged in the EMP attack. And it was indeed the Codex. Hanging before him in the air, its empty gaze focused upon him.

Then, she appeared. Skipping through the air like a ghost, yet so real he could reach out and touch her. Abaddon's avatar. The girl.

'Did you enjoy it?' Abaddon asked. The girl's voice did not belay the veiled fury beneath it.

'Enjoy what?' Cade asked.

The girl flickered, though whether it was emotive or glitching, Cade could not tell. 'Your brief interlude of freedom.'

Cade felt himself gulp involuntarily, even as the little girl's eyes bore into his. Though he knew they were but a projection, and Abaddon observed him through other means, it made him no less nervous.

'Just because the Codex ran out of battery doesn't mean I was free,' Cade said, furrowing his brows in an attempted look of confusion.

The little girl giggled and twirled, the image crackling briefly. 'That's right, Cade. Don't you forget it.'

Cade said nothing. He wanted to go back to his friends.

'What's that?' the girl asked suddenly. She pointed a dainty finger at the Grey toy in Cade's hand.

He looked down at it. Inside, his heart pounded, but

he turned the fear into rage. 'To remember,' Cade said in a low voice.

'Remember what?'

'What you made me do,' Cade said.

He held up the toy, jabbing it in Abaddon's face. 'There were children in there!' he said. 'Civilians. Innocents.'

Abaddon's avatar shrugged. 'So?' she asked mildly.

'You made me a murderer!' Cade bellowed through his raw, bile-bitten throat. 'They didn't have to die!'

The girl giggled. 'Well, of course they didn't *have* to. Nothing *has* to happen. But wasn't it fun? This is real war, Cade. Don't you like the taste?'

Cade spat, phlegm passing through the avatar and plummeting below.

'Now now,' Abaddon said, wagging her dainty finger. 'I'll forgive you this once. Do it again and I will transport you into the sun.'

Cade opened his arms wide. 'Why shouldn't I?' he asked. 'What's the point? There's nothing for me here. No joy. I might as well give up now.'

He lied easily enough; it was how he had felt in his despair but a few hours earlier.

'Then why don't you jump?' the little girl asked in a chocolate-sweet voice.

'Maybe I will,' Cade bit back.

There was no response this time. Only the movement of the Codex, shooting into the sky.

And then, he was alone. No girl. No Codex.

Just him, alone on the spire.

181

THIRTY-ONE

It was cool on the rock, despite the sun in the cloudless sky. Cade sat upon the spire's edge, letting his feet dangle.

Cade was on another planet. He knew this by the enormous white moon in the sky, just visible upon the line of the horizon.

He was alone as any man had ever been, he imagined. Even Neil Armstrong had company.

Thoughts consumed him. Imaginings of his journey into the jungles. Collecting the bomb, and returning to the keep. Flying into the sky.

Dying.

Joy and triumph. Then oblivion.

Tears dribbled down his face, left to dry as he stared across the empty plains.

It was bittersweet, dreaming of a victory that only ended in death. Yet it was not for himself that he cried. First his family. His father, who had taught him so much. And his mother, whose love had been unconditional.

But most of all, Amber. Or rather, her absence from his life.

That he would never know her. Truly know her, the way only time spent in comfortable companionship allowed.

Not moments snatched in a battle for survival. But walks along the beach. Kissing in the rain. Netflix and chill. All the clichés, and then some.

But if he did succeed, she would live on. Humanity would. People across time immemorial would love where he could not. He was willing to make that sacrifice.

Because what was the alternative? To live one more year? Two? Then die anyway, for the entertainment of a psychopathic god.

Given the choice between a long, happy life and what Song had proposed, he might have found temptation eat away at his resolve. It was not the choice in front of him.

And there was selfishness in it too. Better to die quickly, in a flash of light, than be torn to pieces by slavering beasts. That was the fate that awaited him. The fate that awaited Amber and his friends, if he did not do what he had to.

He stared out for a while longer. It was peaceful here, in the empty sky. No dangers. No timer, counting down. Not even the Codex, watching over his shoulder.

Here, he would make peace with himself. With his choice. Alone on a nameless planet.

Cade did not know how long he waited. Time ran into itself, with only his thirst and hunger to measure it. He did not need anything else. Just a break. A break from the relentlessness of it all.

It was only when his head began to nod, exhaustion endangering a fall from his perch, that he stood and screamed at the sky.

'I'll fight,' he yelled. 'Is that what you want to hear? I'll fight!'

The Codex materialised in front of him.

'Good boy,' Abaddon's voice said.

Desert. White as a lamb's back, stretching to the horizon. Cade turned slowly, then breathed a sigh of relief as he saw the bone fields, and the walls of the keep at its end.

Abaddon had taken him home. He had almost thought Abaddon had another punishment for him – a trek through the desert to reach home. Small mercy, but mercy nonetheless.

He walked forwards, his armour clanking, legs burning. He still clutched the Grey's toy, so tightly he had to relax his grip. It was his lifeline. His path to vengeance.

The keep neared as his feet scattered bones and squelched through the mire. He reveled in the cool mud, sopping his aching feet.

He pictured the cold, clear water of the keep's baths. Imagined the sweat, grime and blood of an entire week sloughing from him like a second skin. Heaven was but minutes away.

And then, a yell. Faces appeared over the wall, alongside javelins and drawn bows. For a moment, Cade was startled. He was so used to the keep being near empty.

But he recognised the helmets of the legionaries, even

some of the faces above the parapet – men he had fought alongside in the battle.

He frowned. Their weapons were still drawn.

His frown deepened as his eyes scanned the walls. There was plenty he did not recognise. The walls, once crumbling, had been repaired and refaced. There were stakes in the ground too, and a deep trench in front of them. Only a narrow path allowed entry to the keep, and he navigated it with care, even as he saw smaller stakes, tips just above the mud, waiting for an unwary foot to step onto them.

Had he really waited that long?

A cry came from above.

'Cade!'

It was a frantic cry, one drawn deep from the lungs. He caught a flash of dark hair and pale skin, but it was gone before he could look. He trudged to the doorway.

His hands reached for the wood, only to have the door open, and a figure come barrelling out, near knocking him off his feet in an embrace.

'Cade,' Amber sobbed. 'Cade, you're alive.'

He laughed, relief flooding through him. She was here. She was alive.

At the back of his mind, he had imagined Abaddon abandoning his friends in the Grey territory, a final twist of the knife to complete Cade's misery.

'Of course I am,' Cade said as Quintus emerged from the doorway, a broad grin on the young legionary's face. 'You think Abaddon was gonna let me wriggle out of the next round?'

He extricated himself from her grip and took her hand, pulling her behind him as he passed through the doors, and on through a crowd of confused-looking soldiers.

Quintus followed, and Cade took note of the young man's new clothing. He was dressed in red cloth, with Roman armour in far better condition than that of the other men.

'Where . . . what . . .' Amber stuttered.

'Let's talk in the baths,' Cade croaked. 'I'm desperate to get out of this armour.'

He hurried on through the keep, stopping briefly in amazement. This too had changed. Long tables and benches had returned to the atrium. New shutters, complete with wooden bars to block them, covered the windows, and torches crackled merrily in their sconces.

'These guys work fast,' Cade murmured, limping on through to the stairs, and down into the depths of the baths.

Here, thankfully, it was empty. Cade tore at his armour, aided by Amber's and Quintus's fingers.

'Cade, where have you *been*?' Amber asked.

'In a minute,' Cade said, groaning with relief as the armour fell away, piece by piece.

Soon, he was in just his underwear, and he had the forethought to jump into the cold pool before Amber had a chance to see the ragged state of them. He only took care to place the Grey toy safely beside the stairs before he did so – who knew if the thing was waterproof?

It was a blessed relief to sit in the cool water, and he buried his head beneath the surface. He remained there for as long as his breath would allow, letting the liquid slough away the grime and sweat, rubbing himself with his hands.

He erupted to the surface with a gasp, pulling his long hair back from his eyes.

'Cade, you're hurt!' Amber pointed at his arm, where water had dissolved the coagulated blood, and red-stained rivulets travelled down his wrist to stain the pool red.

'Yeah, I should get that looked at,' Cade said. 'But it's not too bad. Already starting to scab.'

With the armour removed, he was finally able to look at the wound. Up on the spire, he'd hardly noticed the pain.

It was deep, but hardly wider than a bottlecap. He wiggled his fingers and was glad to see the tendons were unharmed. It would leave a nasty scar, but he'd live.

'How did it happen?' Amber asked.

Cade shrugged. 'A javelin, I think.'

Amber leaned forwards, taking a closer look. 'Was it another species on the leaderboard? Did Abaddon have you fighting another round while you were away?'

Cade stared at her. 'No . . .' he said slowly. 'You know about this. I got it in the battle. Quintus got hurt too.'

He pointed at Quintus's arm as he did so, only to slowly drop his finger. Quintus's arm had a puckered scar. No wound.

'But it's bleeding,' Amber said. 'You'd ha . . .'

She trailed off.

'How long have I been missing?' Cade whispered, realisation hitting him like a sledgehammer.

Amber took his hand and brought it to her lips.

'Six months,' she said.

THIRTY-TWO

Cade was numb. He said little as they led him, wrapped in sackcloth, to bed. Ignored their questions, their hugs and touches.

And now he lay on a cot within the storeroom, among renewed piles of broken weaponry, wood planks, and other detritus – and not the commander's bed where he had slept all those months before.

The contenders had been given the room for their quarters, as the barracks were full of Roman soldiers. It had a door they could lock behind them, which gave them some comfort from the unknown dangers of time-lost soldiers.

It was a long, dreamless sleep. Cade woke twice, only to chew down jerky, use the toilets, and have his wound cleaned and stitched by the Roman physician. But each time he returned to bed, a black, numbing exhaustion robbed him of the ability to talk, listen or respond.

He was in a fugue state. Almost out-of-body, his consciousness floating beyond as his friends coaxed him with questions or spooned food into his mouth.

It was hard to return. To let himself wake up. Acknowledge the great task ahead of him, and learn of what had transpired while he had been away, frozen in time by Abaddon in some cruel trick.

Six months had been stolen from him. Months he could have spent with Amber and his friends, with no timer hanging over them, no struggling for food and survival. The Romans seemed to have no trouble cultivating food in the orchards, or catching fish and small game in the jungles.

Abaddon had given him no respite. Those glorious, empty hours alone on the spire had been traded for a goodbye. He knew, one way or another, he would have time to make peace with his friends. To say what needed to be said, even if he could not tell them why.

With his arrival had come the Codex. There was no timer yet. No terrible danger hanging over them yet. Even so, he knew as soon as he woke, the game would start again.

The Romans might rule here. But Cade was the player.

Only now, Abaddon was in the game. A greater game, one only he and Cade would play. Abaddon just didn't know it yet.

'Come on, lad,' the voice said, drifting through his consciousness. 'We've waited long enough.'

Cade opened his eyes, and Marius's face swam into view.

'That's it,' Marius said, squeezing Cade's shoulders. 'Up you get.'

A hand pressed his back, and Cade sat up, taking in the

room properly for what felt like the first time.

Marius sat on a stool beside him, with the contenders crowding around. It was some relief to Cade to see the others there. He had seen them, briefly, in his strange, wakeful walks to the baths.

'You've been through a lot, I can see that,' Marius said, not unkindly. 'But you're back now. And we need the Codex.'

He waved behind him, where the Codex hung motionless in the air.

'Jesus, give him a min—' Scott began, but a look from Marius clapped his mouth shut.

'It won't respond to your friends, let alone me,' Marius said, his voice firm. 'So I think it's time you swore us in as contenders and passed control to me.'

Cade rubbed his eyes and let out a sigh. He had not even considered this situation.

He was just so *tired*. Even despite his long sleep.

So he laughed. It was a bitter laugh, but one that lasted until his breath ran out. He wheezed, then faced Marius.

'The Codex is mine. Kill me if you want to. But Abaddon was quite clear.' He looked Marius dead in the eye. 'You're a good man, Marius. But you're not an idiot. So tell me, why do you think *we* won against the Greys, when you had failed for years?'

Marius's face was grim, but he leaned back and considered Cade's question. 'You breached their stronghold,' he allowed grudgingly.

'How?' Cade asked.

Marius furrowed his brow. 'We all know what happened,'

he growled. 'Don't ask me stupid questions.'

Cade held up his hands in peace. 'Just tell me, how many rounds did you win before we came along?' he asked.

'I've won more battles than you've hairs on your balls, whelp,' Marius snarled. 'You had better get to your point quickly, before I present my own point to you.'

He gripped the hilt of his sword tellingly, but Cade was unfazed. Marius needed him, and there was something of a performance in his voice. As if the man regretted his words even before he said them.

'I'm not talking about battles, I'm talking about *rounds*,' Cade said. 'We've won two. Three if you count the battle with the vipers. I'm sure the others have told you about that by now.'

Marius relaxed his grip and nodded for Cade to continue.

'I don't care who leads here. I have no desire to be commander. But you cannot forget, this is a *game*, not a war. We're nothing more than pawns.'

'Pawns?' Marius asked.

Cade shook his head. Obviously Marius's vocabulary did not extend to chess. It probably hadn't even existed in the Roman's era.

'All I'm saying is, I'm good at this game. I've won, and I keep winning. We are one round from freedom. One round from returning to Earth. Let me keep doing what I'm good at. You keep doing what you're good at. It worked against the Gre— Tritons, didn't it?'

Marius sighed and rubbed his eyes. It seemed Cade wasn't the only one who was exhausted.

'What do you want to know?' Cade asked. 'You want to see the remnants? A map of the area? That's about all it's good for.'

Marius nodded slowly, clearly considering Cade's words. 'You'll let me ask it any question?'

Cade smiled. 'Why wouldn't I?' he said. 'We're all on the same team. Codex, show me the map.'

The drone turned towards Cade, and the map appeared, semi-translucent in the air. Marius hissed a breath between his teeth.

'Such . . . power,' he said.

The commander reached out, rubbing his fingers together as they passed through the holographic screen.

'This is . . . from above?' he asked.

Cade nodded.

'Almost half of our men died in the attack,' Marius said. 'Only a few of the Romans who once lived here, before my legion was summoned, are alive.'

He gestured at the walls. 'They are all common legionaries, so they knew little of the area, or the game. I have been fighting blind ever since I arrived on this planet. But I know I cannot win alone. It is your knowledge of the future that has won the rounds.'

'*Your* future.' Cade inclined his head in mild disagreement. 'My past. If we had the weapons of my time, or even my recent history . . . those Tritons wouldn't have stood a chance.'

Marius smiled for the first time. 'If you will allow me access to the Codex whenever I need it, there is no need for further disagreement. We work together, yes?'

192

Cade grinned in return, and extended a hand.

'Together.'

THIRTY-THREE

Cade sat in silent contemplation, watching the jungle's trees sway in the wind. Amber sat beside him, just as silent. Only the soft squeezing of her hand gave him comfort, even as she allowed him his time. She seemed to know Cade needed to think. And time to heal, both inside and out.

The afternoon had passed in a blur, though he had hardly left the storeroom. His friends had talked his ear off, and then some. So much seemed to have happened while he had been away, yet at the same time, nothing of true consequence.

They were alive, healthy and content, at least for the moment. That was all Cade truly cared about.

Quintus had been made tesserarius, a sort of squad leader or sergeant in the legion. It came with a small squad of ten soldiers, who followed his every command. They seemed in awe of their young leader, and Quintus had come into his own, leading hunts in the jungles for prey and keeping a careful watch over the jungles in case of slaver attacks.

As for the others, they were just glad there was food on the table and soldiers to keep them safe. The hard scrabble for survival among the ruins was behind them; life now was more restful, for Marius did not order them to do anything beyond their fair share of the chores and fishing.

Now, Cade had emerged for some fresh air, and to see what the legionaries had done to the keep. The orchards were tilled, stripped and planted, and the harvest boiled in clay jars and stoppered with corkwood to preserve them.

He wished *they* had thought of that. All the knowledge in the world was only useful if you thought to ask the right questions.

The keep had been repaired, clay used as mortar and rocks from the waterfall used as filling. Cade was glad that the Grey ship had not been discovered – that would have thrown quite a wrench into Song's plan.

'Codex,' Cade said softly. 'Show me the caldera.'

The machine flickered into life, slower and more glitchy since the EMP. Clearly, the Pantheon had yet to recover from the attack fully, and Cade was glad of it.

But now was the time to plan. The contenders had hardly managed to scrape through alive in the past, focusing on keeping themselves from starving.

They had to take the initiative. To mount an expedition of their own, before the timer began again and they were forced to rush into danger without thought or preparation.

'What are you thinking, Cade?' Amber asked gently, laying her head on his shoulder.

Cade turned his head and gave her a soft kiss on the forehead. He wished he could take a day off. Walk alone with her beneath the waterfall and pass the evening watching the twin moons.

Instead, he breathed deep and pointed at the hologram, where the blue dots glowed amid the sea of jungles.

'I want to go out again,' Cade said.

Amber stiffened and lifted her head.

'So soon?' she asked.

Cade closed his eyes and nodded. Every second he delayed was another that his plan could be found out. Another in which the second EMP device could be found. Perhaps Song was being tortured at this very moment, to tell the Pantheon of the Grey's plans. No, there was no time to rest.

'It's my . . . duty. Our duty,' he said.

Amber bit her lip, then nodded and returned her head to his shoulder.

'You're right,' she whispered. 'I wish you weren't, but you're right.'

Cade squeezed her hand tight, then released it and pointed at the map.

'We don't know what the rules of the next game will be. What weapons we can use, what obstacles we will have to overcome. But if Abaddon is going to force us to attack the top of the leaderboard, well . . . the least we can do is be prepared. No desperate battles where we've barely had a second to prepare. If we bring back the best of what's out there, in our own time . . .'

He left his sentence unfinished. It was hard to live in a world of hypotheticals. Would he be advocating for the same had he never met Song?

'I trust your judgment,' Amber said, snuggling closer into the crook of his shoulder.

Cade sighed, his eyes flicking up to the unwavering gaze of the Codex. Always there. Always following.

For a moment, he wondered if he *should* give the Codex to Marius. With the drone elsewhere, he could fill in his friends on the plan. But he knew it was too great a risk. Who knew what other drones hung above him, silent and invisible? Perhaps Abaddon liked to watch him suffer through multiple angles. He wouldn't put it past the sadistic voyeur.

No, he would have to do this himself. Convince his friends of two reasonings at once. For now, they intersected – both plans involved heading into the jungle. But when it came to bringing nuclear weapons back – how would they react?

But now was the time to 'realise' that the bomb was what they needed.

'Show me the remnants within fifteen miles from here that the current contenders have not seen before with their own eyes.'

The screen flashed, and blue dots scattered across the map winked out. He cursed silently. The crashed plane was just out of range – the clearing where it sat must have been a mile further.

'Make that thirty,' he said.

The screen flickered again, and this time the blue dot he was looking for appeared. He tried not to look at it directly.

'Oh?' Amber asked. 'Were those not enough for you? There's at least ten we could go for.'

Cade cleared his throat. 'Yes, well. It would be silly to go so far if there was something *really* good a little bit further. We'll only go for them if they're worth it.'

Amber hummed. 'I guess that makes sense. Remember, we've never spent the night in the jungles. Not without shelter anyway. Maybe there's somewhere we can use as base camp on the way?'

Cade moved his fingers over the screen. 'Remove this one, and this one, this, this, this . . .'

He swiftly ran through the remnants they had encountered in the past or he already knew of that would be useless for their endeavours. What remained were only a few dozen remnants. More than Cade had expected really.

The Romans had been lucky, considering their two expeditions had effectively been random wandering through the jungles. There *were* advantages to following the Roman routes, made obvious by the string of blue dots that followed a winding but semi-direct route along the map.

For one thing they knew it was safe. Well, forgetting the area where the slavers tended to hunt. If there were places rife with predators, the Romans had survived them.

At the same time, if they followed the same route, they had no chance of stumbling upon new remnants of their own. But ultimately, it did not matter. Because at the very end of one of the Roman expeditions, deep in the heart of the jungles . . . was the nuclear bomb he needed.

He swiftly skimmed through the remnants that lay within the range. Several he recognised from when they had sought Władysław's armour all those months ago.

Spearhafoc the monk, with stolen treasure. Many

explorers. Benjamin Church, the British spy, along with the prison ship he was on at the time. And of course, the nuclear bomb, along with the plane it sat upon.

There was a train called Dolly, some semi-modern civilian ships that would contain no guns; nothing that would be a game changer.

But it was the other items he had not considered before that drew his interest. If a nuclear bomb was not enough to tempt his friends into another expedition into the jungles, he would have to find something else.

'Let's get the others,' Cade said. 'We've got some planning to do.'

THIRTY-FOUR

'Codex, run us through the remaining remnants within the twenty-mile radius.'

As the group sat on the old tree stumps outside the tunnel, Cade only hoped there was something they had overlooked close by. That, at least, would get the conversation on leaving on an expedition moving.

A dot flashed.

'Charles Redheffer, con man who claimed to have invented a perpetual motion machine, disappeared in 1820.'

Cade shrugged. 'Anyone want a fake perpetual motion machine?'

'Next,' the group chorused.

'John Jeffrey, Scottish botanist, disappeared while researching plants in the Colorado desert in 1854.'

'Another desert one,' Cade said. 'It's like Abaddon just watches over deserts, waiting for someone to wander through it.'

'Next,' Amber said. 'Unless someone wants to learn about plants.'

'*Bela Kiss, insane serial killer, disappeared in 1916 after murdering twenty-three women.*'

'Moving swiftly on,' Amber growled. 'I'd only stop there to spit on his corpse.'

'*That is all,*' the Codex replied.

Cade sighed. This was not going to be so easy.

'Show us the remnants within thirty miles,' Cade said, trying not to let the desperation show through to his voice. The nuclear bomb would be a hard sell. Without some way of setting it off remotely, it was basically a very large suicide bomb – and an unwieldy one at that.

'*Imperial German Army Zeppelin LZ 90 disappeared without a trace after it broke loose in a storm and was blown out to sea in 1916.*'

'Now, that's more like it,' Cade said, pounding his fist into his palm. 'They could have guns on there, right?'

'*No,*' the Codex replied flatly. '*It was unmanned.*'

Cade cursed. 'Next, then.'

'*Panfilo de Narvaez, a Spanish conquistador, and a raft he built following a shipwreck,*' the Codex intoned.

'Useless,' Cade muttered.

He peered at the screen, where a cluster of blue dots stood out, deep in the jungles.

'*The tombs of: Imhotep, 2950 BC; Alexander the Great, 205 BC; Cleopatra and Mark Anthony, 30 BC; Boudicca, 61 AD; Attila the Hun, 453 AD; Genghis Khan, 1227 AD; Atahuallpa, 1533 AD.*'

Cade gaped at the blue dots flashing on the screen.

'What, all together?' Cade asked.

'*Yes*,' the Codex intoned.

'That's . . . messed up,' Scott said.

'What use is that?' Cade asked, half to himself. 'There might be weapons in there, but we need guns, explosives . . .'

'*You can trade*,' the Codex said. '*Treasure for favours.*'

'Favours?' Scott asked.

'*Information, teleportation to locations. Most anything within Abaddon's power. Primarily remnants, undiscovered or otherwise*,' the Codex replied. '*It is how the Ninth Legion was summoned by the previous contenders.*'

'Could we use it to trade for guns?' Cade asked.

'*If Abaddon deems the trade worthy*,' the Codex replied.

'Well, what did the Ninth Legion cost?' Cade asked.

'*The Ninth Legion cost the entire contents of the* Las Cinque Chagas, *a Spanish treasure ship that disappeared in 1594. It contained two thousand tonnes of precious metals and jewels.*'

Another dot flashed blue on the map, the furthest point on the long string of dots that marked the Roman expedition's progress. Clearly, that was what the Romans had been looking for.

'Can we trade it then and there?' Cade asked. 'As soon as we find it?'

'*Yes*,' the Codex replied.

Cade cursed quietly.

'Wait, why is that a problem?' Scott asked. 'If we find treasure out there, we won't have to lug it back to the keep.'

'Correct,' Cade said, his fists balled with frustration. 'But that means the Romans didn't have to either. Any remnant on the map there that had treasure in it was probably traded – gold's heavy, remember. And if they didn't know what to do with it, they would have paid some of it to have the rest teleported back. We won't find any left out there.'

'Oh . . . right,' Scott replied dejectedly.

A grim silence descended on the group.

'Was there treasure found in the tombs, then?' Cade asked, dejected.

'*Unknown,*' the Codex replied. '*The tombs were only scanned from the exterior.*'

Cade looked up, his eyes widening.

'Why?' he asked.

'*I cannot answer that question,*' the Codex replied.

Cade leaned back, a flutter of hope within his chest. The tombs had been found on the second expedition's way back to the keep, before they had been chased from their course by the slavers. Perhaps they were in a hurry to return, having found treasure enough already.

'Well, that's one avenue,' he said after a moment's pondering. 'Tombs mean treasure. Lara Croft taught me that.'

'I'm a Nathan Drake guy myself,' Yoshi said. 'But you're right.'

'Whatever that means,' Grace said, rolling her eyes.

'Weirdos,' Trix said, prodding Yoshi good-naturedly.

Cade scratched at his scruffy beard, staring at the map. There were far fewer remnants in the depths of the jungles, for only the second expedition had explored that far.

'What's left?' he asked the Codex.

'*An A-4E Skyhawk attack aircraft loaded with a B43 nuclear weapon fell from the deck of the USS* Ticonderoga *in 1965.*

Pilot, plane and weapon were never found.'

Cade held his breath, but nobody proffered an opinion.

'Anything else?' Amber asked.

'*That is all*,' the Codex replied.

Cade sighed and rested his chin on his hands. He had to play this right.

'It's a risk,' he announced after a moment's thought.

'Duh,' Scott said. 'Dino-infested jungles aren't exactly a walk in the park.'

Amber glared at him, then turned to Cade with a reassuring smile. 'What are you thinking?'

Cade's heart twisted. If only he *could* tell them what he was thinking. He didn't care about the treasure. If it was up to him, they'd make a beeline for the nuclear bomb, drag it back, and be done with it.

'Our end goal is the tombs. Abaddon placed all these tombs together for a reason. He wants us to explore them, and I bet there's treasure inside.'

'That's like . . . the second furthest thing,' Scott moaned.

'Well, I doubt that monk's treasure is still around, and I don't see any guns either. The only thing that's useful is that nuclear bomb.'

Amber scoffed.

'You don't think so?' Cade asked.

'Have you *seen* a nuclear bomb?' she asked. 'They're huge.'

'Yeah, and who knows how long it's been there – at least a few years, right?' Grace said. 'I bet it's rusted as hell. Might even be radioactive.'

'Codex, how much does the bomb weigh?' Amber asked.

'*Nine hundred and thirty-five kilograms.*'

Cade's stomach twisted. He felt like throwing up.

'Well, that's out, then,' Scott said. 'That's like moving a car, only without wheels, through a jungle, surrounded by predators. Oh, and the car has a rusted nuclear bomb inside it.'

Cade closed his eyes, letting the nausea fade. He had mentioned it offhandedly, but he should have put more thought into his argument. Worst of all, they were right. How the hell was he going to get it back here?

'And how do we set it off?' Yoshi asked. 'Smack it on the nose until it blows up? And say that works: won't we blow ourselves to kingdom come?'

Cade held up his hands, a fake smile pasted across his face.

'All right, all right. But say we *do* manage to set it off, remotely. Maybe we trade some treasure for a remote timer, right? And pay Abaddon to teleport it where it needs to be? It's game over for whatever we face then. They send an army? We blow them to kingdom come.'

Amber bit her lip. 'Either way, we need treasure,' she said, though Cade saw his logic was not holding water. 'So the tombs are the plan, no matter what. When we see how much treasure is there, *then* we decide what we do with it.'

Cade held his tongue, knowing there would be no winning them over right now. He needed to convince them to do the expedition first. The bomb could come later.

'If we're going to travel into the jungles, we need to plan a route. We can't camp in the open, so we need to use the remnants the Romans found as places to camp,' he said.

The others nodded along.

205

'We could take the river – it would be faster and safer from predators. But we know the slavers hunt on that route. I vote we walk instead.'

'Agreed,' Amber said.

The others blanched, fear stamped across their features. Yoshi, Bea and Trix in particular.

'Are you sure?' Bea asked. 'A dinosaur would . . . you know. Eat us. The slavers are trying to take us alive.'

'You guys haven't seen predators yet,' Cade said to the group. 'And some of you haven't seen the slavers. I'm the only one who has experienced both. Trust me, the slavers aren't better.'

Quintus held up a hand. 'I was in the jungles for a long time,' he said haltingly. 'Slavers are . . . worse.'

Yoshi nodded slowly. 'OK, so where do we camp?' he asked.

Cade rubbed his eyes, looking at the map. 'First place we stop is Benjamin Church's prison ship,' he said. 'We can get there by nightfall if we walk there directly. The Romans took longer because they did not do that.'

'They didn't?' Bea asked.

'No, they were searching for remnants. Based on the time stamps of each remnant discovery, I'm guessing they would explore one area after another thoroughly, setting up camp in appropriate locations and ranging out during the day. I doubt they would have come across so many remnants if they'd travelled in a straight line.'

He traced the route with his finger. 'Next, we hit the Leifsbudir. That's the first ever settlement in North America, made by the Vikings.'

'Wasn't that Columbus?' Amber asked.

'Nope,' Cade said, somewhat pleased he could share one of his favourite pieces of trivia. 'I mean, he was an idiot who just got lost on his way to India. The Vikings settled in Newfoundland, or Vinland as they called it, in the year 1000 AD.'

'Nerd,' Scott muttered.

'Not to mention the Roman ships they found wrecked in Brazil,' Cade said, then held up his hands as the others began to speak all at once. 'Anyway, hopefully there's a hut of some kind there we can shelter in.'

He grinned, looking at the map again. 'OK, so then we head for the tombs from there. We'd have to shelter in them overnight, explore them and all that. Better take some torches with us to be safe.'

'Wait,' Amber said. 'Didn't you say we would walk five miles a day last time?' She pointed at the tombs. 'This is almost thirty miles. That's six days there, six days back.'

Cade nodded. 'I was thinking about that earlier. I massively underestimated how fast we could travel before. The jungles aren't so overgrown. We walked between Hueitapalan and the *Sea Dragon* in around an hour. That's about a mile, right? If we walk ten hours a day, we'd make it there in three days. That's two sleeps there, two sleeps back, plus one sleep at the tombs. It works.'

Amber grimaced. 'Those jungles had been burned. And who's to say we won't run into a swamp or heavy bush?'

Cade hugged her close and felt her relax in his arms. 'We won't know until we do it,' he said. 'I just know we have to try.'

THIRTY-FIVE

Cade realised his problem only when they returned to the storeroom. In the heat of the moment, alone with his contenders, he had been thinking in the old way. Where all decisions were their own.

But that was not what he had agreed with Marius.

He was supposed to stay here. He was their access to the Codex. Instead, he was about to abandon the Romans, taking the Codex with him.

Leaving it here was not an option – the contenders needed it to scan discoveries, and to make any deals for the treasure they found. Nor was Cade staying and letting the others go an option either, even if they could somehow summon the Codex when they needed it. He now knew they hated his bomb idea. Left to their own devices and having to make a decision on what to trade with Abaddon then and there . . . they couldn't be trusted to teleport the bomb to the keep.

He'd have enough trouble convincing them to do it

if he *was* there. But that was a bridge to cross for another time.

The good thing was, they didn't need to build a raft this time. And thanks to the Romans, the food, water and equipment needed for a trip into the jungles were in plentiful supply. The legionaries even had backpacks, and there were hundreds to choose from, piled high in the storeroom while they were not in use.

Still, Cade knew that abandoning the Romans without telling them their plans would be seen as an act of betrayal. Returning with treasure, or the results thereof, would do little to calm Marius down. Their leaving would undermine his leadership and leave him simmering with anger the entire time they were away.

He needed to speak to Marius.

'Coming to bed, Cade?' Amber asked, poking her head out from behind a shelf.

Cade turned, only to see her settled in the cot beside his. It had been pulled surreptitiously behind some shelves where they could have some privacy. Cade's heart beat a little faster, and Amber blushed as his eyes flicked between her and the cot's new location.

'Uh . . .' Cade felt his stomach twist with a sudden rush of anxiety.

Amber usually slept with the other girls. Something had changed while he'd been gone.

'I need to speak to Marius,' Cade said. 'I'll be right back.'

He hurried out of the room, strangely relieved for the excuse. He'd have to think about why that was later.

Still, now he was standing in the atrium, the eyes of a score of legionaries having a late-night meal upon him. He smiled awkwardly and walked up the stairs, his mind spinning. It was not a conversation he was prepared to have, yet he needed to gauge what Marius's views were on expeditions and remnants. What would he even say?

'What do you want?' His way was blocked by a legionary. The man raised his eyebrows.

'Marius,' Cade replied simply, too tired to drag the Latin words from his memory.

The legionary stood aside, and to Cade's dismay, the commander was in the hall between the two rooms of the top floor, poring over something upon the table. No time to gather his thoughts.

Marius turned to see Cade and gave him a smile, beckoning him closer.

'Cade!' he said. 'We were just talking about you. Come look at this.'

Cade stepped forwards and saw a large map laid out on the round table at the hall's centre. Other men, officers, stood around it, deep discussions interrupted as Cade walked closer. Their eyes followed with a strange mix of fear and annoyance.

What was he to these men? An aberration from the future. A stranger of even stranger origin, who had somehow given them victory. They owed him, yet they did not want to.

The map was of the caldera. It was a crude thing, though the scale was off, and it did not, of course, show remnants.

Instead, wood-carved figurines had been placed to delineate the locations the Romans knew of so far.

'Codex,' Cade said, trying to hide the hesitation in his voice. 'Show me the map.'

Instantly, the map appeared at the table's centre, floating horizontally above the one the Romans had been so carefully poring over.

This was followed by a collective intake of breath and a flurry of Latin, too fast and intermixed for Cade to follow.

'It is a . . . this Codex is . . .'

Cade tried to hide his wince. But if he was to convince Marius of the value of the remnants in the jungles, he had to show them its powers. Now was the time to balance the benefits of keeping it here against the discovery of remnants.

'Do you see the blue . . . things?' Cade asked. He spoke in Latin for the benefit of the officers, even as he struggled to find the right word for *dot*.

Marius understood though and nodded.

'These are more objects. Like the cannons. Some from my time, or close to it.'

'More cannons?' one of the Roman officers asked, overpronouncing the new word.

Cade nodded. 'Maybe. But those are not . . .'

He paused, then turned to the Codex. 'Translate for me, would you?'

'*Yes.*'

'Any cannons we bring here would be useless,' Cade continued. 'They need powder, and we don't have deposits of potassium nitrate – that white powder we used – here.'

The man scoffed and chuckled. 'So what use are they?'

Cade jabbed his finger at the map. 'Imagine if I could wipe away an entire city with a click of my fingers.'

This time, the officer fell silent.

'Codex, please tell them how many people died in the bombing of Hiroshima.'

'*The death toll of the 1945 Hiroshima nuclear bombing resulted in an estimated two hundred thousand deaths.*'

Cade brought his finger closer to the blue dot. 'You thought the cannon was powerful? The remnant here is a million times more powerful.'

The men around him stared, their faces horrified.

'Such . . . power,' Marius whispered, horrorstruck.

'There are enough of these weapons on Earth now to destroy it ten times over,' Cade said. 'They are used as a deterrent for war.'

Marius brought a hand to his mouth, his eyes wide with shock.

'It doesn't just set the world on fire,' Cade pressed on. 'It poisons the air, as far as the wind will take it. The ground is infected, so much so that people can't walk on it for a hundred years. It causes an invisible disease, so that even those who survive the initial blast will die a slow death of cancer and blood sickness.'

Silence now.

'I would never use such a weapon,' Marius finally said. 'Would you have us caught in its web, for the sake of the destruction of our enemies? I would not turn such a weapon on those forced into battle the way that we are.'

'Were the Tritons any different?' Cade retorted.

Marius glared at him, anger and shame apparent on his face.

'We had no choice,' he said in a low growl. 'And they had already used a similar weapon against us.'

Cade shook his head. 'Don't you get it? If we have the bomb, then Abaddon's rivals in the Pantheon will know we do. How could they ever attack us again, knowing we could destroy their contenders easily?'

Marius took a step back, and Cade hammered him with his words.

'Imagine if we'd had this weapon against the Tritons,' Cade said. 'Not a single one of your men would have had to die. We wouldn't have even had to place it that close to their gates. We could've just hidden it in the long grass, retreated to a safe distance, and then . . .'

He clicked his fingers.

With each word, he felt more ashamed of himself. He had forced himself to turn to the darkest of his thoughts, that cruel, selfish side of his human soul he had not known he possessed, in order to appeal to that same nature in the man before him.

Marius held up a hand. 'You say this . . . weapon . . . it is out there?'

Cade nodded. 'And more. We think we know where to find treasure we can use to barter with Abaddon. We could get more troops. Even more advanced weapons.'

Marius shook his head, disbelief stamped across his features.

'Give me an hour, just me, you and the Codex,' Cade said. 'Let me show you the future.'

THIRTY-SIX

Cade jerked awake, then groaned as his back spasmed with pain. He was in a rickety chair, one that pressed into his spine as he levered himself upright. Sleep had overcome him, and Marius had suffered the same, collapsed on the bed's edge.

They had spoken long into the night, the Codex droning in its monotone voice, proving again and again in meticulous detail the horrors of the weapons of Cade's world.

There was no discussion of an expedition. Cade didn't think he even needed to bring it up. Marius grew more fascinated and horrified with every word, even as Cade's stomach grew sicker.

He felt like Lucifer in the Garden of Eden, tempting an innocent soul with knowledge of evil. Yet he had achieved his aim. Marius was now interested in expeditions into the jungles. Now he had to convert it into permission.

Cade descended the stairs with heavy steps and even heavier eyelids. All he wanted was to go to sleep. To just not . . . be, for a while. The discussions through the night had weighed heavy on his heart. With every detail Marius wrung from the recesses of human history, the world seemed a little darker, a little crueller.

It was still the early hours of the morning, so it was with some relief that he found his friends asleep. He tried not to think about what it meant when he saw his cot had returned to its original position, a shelf dividing it from Amber's.

'Back, are you?' Amber's voice came through the shelving as he settled down onto the lumpy, straw-filled cot.

Cade lay silent for a moment. 'I had to sell the expedition to Marius,' he whispered back.

Silence. Then:

'You couldn't have waited till morning?'

Cade winced, the question cutting through his deception.

'I . . . I knew I wouldn't be able to sleep until I'd dealt with it,' he replied lamely.

Even through the shelving, he heard her snort with derision.

'I'm sorry,' he whispered.

There was no reply.

He woke to Quintus's face, and the boy's thin hands shaking his shoulders.

'What?' Cade groaned, then caught Quintus's expression and instantly sobered from the drunkenness of sleep.

'They are preparing an . . . expedition,' Quintus hissed.

Cade rolled from his bed and followed the young Roman, who was already almost out the door. They emerged from the keep, yet Quintus ran on, down the tunnel through the mountain.

When Cade emerged, huffing and puffing, from the darkness of the tunnel, he found Amber there, with Quintus beside her. Ahead, a crowd of Romans had surrounded Marius, who was standing atop a log, speaking rapidly.

'Your little chat with Marius sure lit a fire under him,' Amber snapped. 'So much for our plan.'

Cade winced; he had no time to explain himself. Only to wade into the crowd, shoving and worming his way through.

'Who will go?' Marius bellowed.

Cade nearly fell to his knees as the onlookers jostled him, jumping high and raising their hands to volunteer. Whatever speech he had just missed, it had been a doozy.

'Marius,' Cade said, finally elbowing his way to the front. 'What are you doing?'

The commander grinned at Cade and tugged at his arm, pulling him onto the log beside him.

'And we have our little mascot to thank for this revelation,' Marius cried, even as the Codex whispered a translation in Cade's ear. 'Once again, he brings weapons of another age to aid us. But this . . . this will win us the war. This will bring us home!'

The men cheered again, and it was all Cade could do to hiss in his ear.

'You should have spoken to me first,' he said, and Marius grasped his arm, raising it in forced triumph and pulling Cade close.

'I am the commander here,' Marius replied through a grit-toothed smile. 'You should thank me for even giving you credit.'

There was a mad excitement in his eyes, and Cade saw the corruption of desire there. And it was he who had planted it.

Marius had always seemed to Cade a man on the brink between benevolence and despotism. Teetering between a good person and bad. Cade had fed the worst of his desires, and this was the result.

Cade gave a final wave, then descended the stump, leaving Marius to revel in his men's excitement. Now, the men let him through, thumping him on the back as he passed.

Finally, he stumbled to his friends, who had been joined by the others.

'What the—' Scott began.

But Cade cut him off with a finger to his lips, then motioned for them to follow him, leaving the yammering Romans behind them.

He led them to the waterfall, until they were standing close enough to feel the spray of the crashing waters. Cade sat down on a stump, clenching his fists with fury. For a moment he fumed, letting the roar of the waterfall wash around him.

'So . . . this is good, right?' Yoshi said.

Cade looked up at him, feeling his brows knit together.

'What?' Yoshi asked, raising his palms. 'They're gonna take all the risk, right? Go get what we need?'

'Yeah,' Amber said dully. 'But it's like sending a caveman to do brain surgery. Sure, we won't have to do it, but it's not exactly going to go well, is it?'

Cade chuckled despite himself. 'OK,' he said, rubbing his temples. 'We know that they need the Codex, and me to work it, right? So that means at least I have to go.'

'You think we're going to let you go alone?' Yoshi asked. 'They won't have your back like we would.'

'And we need to decide *together* what we spend the treasure on,' Grace said.

Cade sighed.

'We won't get a word in edgeways until later – he's too excited right now.'

The conversation had only just cottoned him to the fact that Marius's actions could work in his favour. If he was alone with the Romans, he wouldn't have to convince his friends of the need for the nuclear bomb. They were already sold on it.

'We have to talk to him,' Amber snapped.

'There's nothing we can do,' Cade said, even as his stomach twisted with guilt. 'At least one of us is going.'

THIRTY-SEVEN

Marius would not meet with them. Not that Cade tried very hard – the man would have seen him if he insisted. But instead he asked the guards if the commander was free, knowing full well that he was busy planning the expedition.

So it was no surprise to Cade when he was summoned to Marius's room the following morning after a fitful night of sleep. The others, despite their protests, were not allowed past the stairs.

It was a somewhat worrying precedent that Marius did not allow them to the third floor. The commander was establishing the contenders' place in the keep's hierarchy early. Cade would almost be impressed, were he not one of the ones being sidelined.

When he entered the room, Marius stood with his back to him, gazing out the window at the cobbles below. There, Cade had already seen men stacking amphorae, food, bandages and more.

'How are the preparations going?' Cade asked, trying to

begin the meeting on a peaceful note.

Marius turned to him, his jaw set. Cade saw the man was prepared for an argument, and sat down in the chair, hoping to remind him of their conversation the night before last.

'My men will need the Codex from you,' Marius said, his voice firm as stone.

Cade sat up a little straighter, shocked at the request. 'Didn't we already have this conversation?'

'That was before my soldiers needed it,' he said. 'We don't have the luxury of your stubbornness now.'

Cade gritted his teeth. 'I'll go with them,' he said.

Marius paused, and to Cade's surprise, he realised that the idea had clearly not crossed the commander's mind.

'And if you die?' he asked. 'The Codex will return to one of your contenders, leaving my men stranded.'

Cade rubbed his eyes. He was too tired for this. 'Let's say your men took the Codex,' Cade said. 'Say they come across a machine, or a gun out there. How will they know what it is?'

Marius waved his hand. 'The Codex will tell them.'

Cade let out a soft laugh. 'What would *you* do if you found a hellfire air-to-ground missile, fired using a Predator UAV? Would you haul it back?'

As Marius stared at him, the many hours Cade had spent playing *Call of Duty* had finally come in handy.

'Yes . . .' he said with some hesitance. 'A weapon is a weapon.'

Cade shook his head. 'They're shot from something similar to a *plane*. You know what planes are, right?'

Marius shook his head.

'Yeah, those weren't around in Louis Le Prince's time. It's a flying machine. A giant metal bird that uses fires burning inside it to move a spinning fan. You would never be able to use that weapon without one. The best you could do is set it off yourselves accidentally while you carry it, and kill yourselves.'

Marius grimaced, but at the same time searched Cade's eyes to see if he was telling the truth.

'Of course, it's much more complicated than that,' Cade went on, meeting Marius's gaze with as much confidence as he could muster. 'I could tell you about *drones* and *pilots*, *radio waves*, *control systems*. But that's the best I can explain it. And of course, the Codex won't explain it that way, will it? You have no idea how complicated the machines of the future are. Even I don't understand how they work exactly. How can you expect your men to?'

Marius sat upon the side of the bed, steepling his fingers and letting out a long sigh. 'So what would you have me do, Cade?' he said, and for a moment Cade saw the flickers of the other man. The good man, who had helped them so much before.

'Send two of us,' he said. 'If I die out there, another of my contenders will be ready to take my place.'

He regretted his words almost as soon as he had said them. Perhaps he should have pushed to go alone, but he had forgotten himself in that moment. Forgotten he was tricking his friends into summoning an atomic bomb to the keep.

'Fine,' Marius said in a low voice, avoiding Cade's

eyes. 'But you must do something for me in exchange. Trust for trust.'

Cade nodded slowly. 'What do you need?'

Marius looked up at him, and Cade could not read his expression.

'Keep the Codex. But if you die. And your friends die. What happens then?'

'We won't,' Cade said. 'Most of us will stay here.'

'Even so,' Marius said, 'it is an unnecessary risk to take. There is no reason why my men should not become contenders as well.'

Cade swallowed. Marius knew there *was* a reason Cade was keeping the Codex to himself. It was because Marius could easily get control of the Codex if he and the other Romans were contenders. All that stood in his way were the beating hearts of Cade and his friends. The Codex would pass down the chain to them. That was how it worked.

Now, Marius was daring Cade to voice it. To say he feared Marius's ambition. That he feared the Romans would kill them.

Cade's silence stretched between them, as Marius's eyes bore into his own. He could not read the man.

But in the end, it did not matter. In the short term, Marius needed them. Without them, there would be nobody to guide him with the weapons of the future. And while it was true Marius might kill them once their use ran out, Cade had no intention of being here that long.

As soon as he returned to the keep with the bomb, he planned to set off the EMP. Then have the Romans load the

223

bomb into the ship. Initiate the autopilot. And end the game once and for all.

'Deal,' Cade said, holding out his hand.

Marius looked at it in surprise, then took Cade's hand in his own.

They shook, once, then Marius dropped his hand.

'Are we done?' he asked.

Cade leaned back in his chair.

'Start bringing your men here,' Cade said. 'It's time to make them contenders.'

THIRTY-EIGHT

It took until the afternoon to induct all the Romans. They came in groups and declared their consent to become contenders to the Codex in a short Latin phrase Marius asked them to repeat. Cade did not leave until every Roman had visited, even the men working in the orchards above. He wanted Marius to trust him. And to think he had won.

As the last of the Romans left the room, he could hear his friends demanding what was going on in the stairwell, the guards still refusing them entry.

'Can I go now?' Cade asked, standing to leave.

'Of course,' Marius said. 'You can come and go as you please.'

Cade looked back at him. 'We both know that's not true.'

Marius cleared his throat as Cade stepped to the door. 'Do not bring your lover with you,' he said. 'Or any other of the women for that matter.'

Cade turned, shocked. 'Why not?'

Marius looked unashamed, despite Cade's glare. 'Women

and battle do not mix,' he said. 'They are bad luck.'

Cade held up a finger. 'I choose who goes with me on the expedition. *I* choose.'

Marius held up his hands, even looking a little surprised at Cade's outburst. 'Fine,' he said. 'On your head be it. Clearly you are not thinking with it.'

The words stung Cade, but he did not let his resolve waiver.

'You've got a lot to learn about the future, Marius,' Cade said, holding back the angrier words he wanted to say. 'Don't forget, it was those *women* who cracked open the Grey stronghold for you. I'd take one of them over ten of yours any day.'

He stalked out, raging.

'Cade!' Marius called.

His friends were still on the stairs, and he hurried to them, silencing their questions with a finger to his lips.

'Come on,' Cade said. 'We have a lot to talk about.'

'There you go again,' Grace growled. 'Making decisions for us.'

Cade closed his eyes and let his head knock against the wall. They were back in the storage room, and the others were not happy. They sat in a circle, but it felt like they were all facing Cade.

'I did my best,' Cade said. 'And he wouldn't see anyone but me. Trust me, I don't *want* to speak for you. But I had to.'

'You made them *contenders*,' Yoshi said. 'Do you realise what that makes us? Just a group of teenagers. We're expendable now.'

'They need us,' Cade said. 'Only we can understand modern weapons, modern tools.'

'For now,' Amber said.

It was the first time she had spoken for a while, and now she avoided Cade's gaze.

'I think we need some ground rules,' Yoshi said, looking guilty even as he spoke. 'It's nothing against you, Cade. You're trying your best, I know that. But you can't keep making decisions like this without talking to us.'

'You think I want to make these decisions?' Cade snapped. 'I hate it, OK? I *hate* it. Every time I make one, the people I care about might die. People I love.'

Amber looked up at him, almost startled.

'Ever since New Rome, you've been making choices for us. Do you know how powerless that makes us feel?' Scott said, unusually sober. 'You think it's bad enough being Abaddon's puppet? It's worse when we're yours too.'

'That's not fair, Scott,' Cade said. 'I didn't ask for *any* of this. I swear, I wish we could make decisions together. But I keep being put in situations where I'm the one who has to make them.'

Grace threw her hands up. 'Maybe it would have been difficult to get Marius to let us in,' she said. 'But you're not our *leader* any more. We're a democracy now, yeah?'

Cade looked to the others, but they only stared at their feet.

'I will follow you,' Quintus said. 'I do not care what the others do. I am still here. We are all still here. Because of you.'

Grace ignored him. 'You talk to Marius only when one of us is also present,' she said. 'And Quintus doesn't count.'

'Say that again,' Quintus said, standing up. 'You think I do not deserve a vote?'

'Not when you're Cade's lapdog,' Grace snapped back.

'Guys,' Amber said, tugging at Quintus's hand until he sat down again. 'This is exactly what Abaddon wants. What Marius wants. For us to turn on each other. Cade is doing his best. We're just asking him to do things a different way, right?'

Grace set her jaw and turned away before grunting a reluctant, 'Yes.'

'So we have a decision to make,' Amber said. 'One of us needs to go with Cade. And I think it should be one of the boys.'

'What?' Grace demanded, incensed again. 'Why?'

'Because things have moved on since our time,' Amber said. 'There might be something out there that's more modern than us. Something we won't understand.'

'Yeah, but Marius doesn't know that. And what are the chances of Cade *actually* dying?' Grace caught herself and looked ashamed for a moment. 'Sorry, but you know what I mean.'

Amber shrugged. 'If you want to go, be my guest. Bea, Trix, do either of you have a burning desire to head into the jungles?'

'Not a chance,' Bea said, followed by a silent head shake from Trix.

'And I don't feel safe out there with those Romans,' Amber

228

said. 'Here, there's some semblance of law and order. Out there . . . I don't trust them.'

She let the words hang in the air, and Cade felt ashamed he had not even considered the implications of being a woman alone with so many strange, uncivilised soldiers.

Grace crossed her arms and gave a curt nod. 'Well, if we're out because we aren't *modern* enough, so is Quintus,' Bea said. 'So it's either Scott or Yoshi, right?'

Yoshi paled and lifted his chin to meet Cade's gaze. 'I may have asthma, but I'll go if you need me,' he said.

Scott lay a hand on Yoshi's shoulder. 'As funny as it might be to watch you wheezing while you're chased by a *T. rex*, I think you're out of the running, man. No pun intended.'

Yoshi reddened and inclined his head.

'I've been hankering for a stroll through the woods anyway,' Scott said, forcing a smile. 'Plus, it'll be a relief to get out of this windowless room. Especially after Quintus had fish for dinner, am I right?'

He pinched his nose theatrically, even as the others laughed. The tension dissipated like a dark cloud on the wind, though the scowl on Grace's face was not entirely gone.

Cade let it go. There were bigger things to worry about.

THIRTY-NINE

They were woken at the break of dawn. There was no time for breakfast, only to gather their weapons and stagger down the tunnel, out to the edge of the jungles.

Cade had thought they would have a few days yet before the expedition left, but apparently Marius had wasted no time. Backpacks were shoved into Scott's and Cade's hands, and they had but a few moments to say their goodbyes.

Ten men were gathered at the edge of the jungle. To Cade's dismay, these were not the best of the Roman troops. These were the youngest of them, scrawny youths hardly older than Cade.

But worst of all was their leader. Cade had not imagined he would see Atticus again. The man had been out of sight since his arrival, and Cade had wondered where they were keeping him.

Now he was back. Standing at the edge of the jungle, his lips pursed tight as the original contenders approached.

Marius and a contingent of Romans stood apart, and

Cade hurried over to him, hardly able to believe what he was seeing. Atticus must hate Marius. Yet here Atticus was, leading the men who had, hardly more than six months ago, been loyal to him.

It was an affront Cade could not bear.

'Why is Atticus here?' Cade demanded, squaring up to Marius.

'He's . . . expendable,' Marius replied curtly. 'And we're down to less than a hundred soldiers. Did you expect me to keep him fed and guarded forever? I need every man to earn their keep. And it's time you started earning yours.'

Cade stared at him in disbelief. 'You think he'll treat me any differently from what he did before?' he demanded. 'It's suicide to go out there with him. He'll shove me off a cliff first chance he gets.'

Cade could feel the eyes of the men upon him and realised he had made a mistake. To challenge Marius was one thing. To do so in front of his men . . . there was no chance the commander would back down now.

Marius stepped closer to him, leaning his face into Cade's own until Cade could smell his breath.

'Atticus believed you were a liar,' Marius growled. 'An enemy. That was why he hated you. But you've proven him wrong, haven't you? So what grudge could he have against you now?'

Cade knew this battle was lost, but he knew he could not let this stand. 'That's not how people like him work,' he said, trying to keep his tone civil. 'He'll blame me for losing command.'

Marius shoved Cade and stabbed a finger at the ten men waiting at the edge of the forest.

'You'll do as you are ordered,' Marius said. 'Remember who's in charge here, boy. These are my men. This is my keep. You're just a guest.'

'I'm about to risk my life for you,' Cade growled. 'I've killed for you. I got you out of that hellhole you'd been in for years. You wouldn't even be *legatus* without me.'

Marius glared at Cade, mulling his words.

'Aren't we on the same team?' Cade asked. 'Why do you treat me like an enemy?'

Marius sighed and pulled Cade further away from the men. He leaned in close, but the man's anger seemed to have dissipated.

'Atticus still has men loyal to him. Not as many as are loyal to me, but enough to risk another . . . leadership change. I cannot keep him as a prisoner – he has done no crime, after all. In fact, it is I who have.'

Cade met his gaze and saw the hesitation in the man's face. It was strange to see someone oscillate between virtue and tyranny. The mantle of leadership had fallen upon this young man's shoulders, yet his only example over the last years had been Atticus himself.

'I cannot change my mind. His followers accept that he was wrong to doubt you, but they have not turned against him. Allowing him to lead these men has allowed me to placate them. To go back on my word will weaken my position. And I am sure you do not want Atticus to return to power.'

Cade knew he had no choice. He and Scott would just

have to deal with it. He could only hope that Atticus would let bygones be bygones. But at the back of his mind, he knew he would never forget the sight of Quintus's beaten body hanging on the rack in Jomsborg.

'All right,' Cade said, even as Marius tutted his impatience. 'But you have to promise you'll take care of my friends. Keep them safe from the others. Treat them with respect, as an example to your men.'

Marius nodded and clasped his shoulder. 'I will. You do your duty. Find us weapons.'

Cade inclined his head.

'Are we going to wait all day?' Atticus called, his Latin harsh in Cade's ears.

Marius turned his back, ignoring the show of disrespect.

'Go,' he muttered. 'Before this gets any worse.'

Cade hurried away, only to find Grace frowning at him.

'Another private parlay?' she asked, raising a brow.

'I think we can all agree we don't want Atticus leading the mission,' Cade said. 'But Marius won't back down. We'll just have to make it work.'

Grace grunted, then gave him a quick, unfeeling hug. 'Good luck,' she said.

The others crowded in, passing on their well wishes. Scott, apparently, had already said his goodbyes.

Quintus took the longest, hugging Cade close.

'If you do not come back,' he whispered, 'I will find you.'

Cade smiled and gripped his friend by the shoulders. 'I'll be back, my friend. You just protect the others while I'm away. I know they'll be safe with you.'

Quintus wiped a tear from his eye and nodded.

'Cade,' Amber said. 'Can we talk?'

Cade felt a flash of anxiety. She had not been exactly cold to him the past few days, but she had not shown him any warmth either. Now, she took his hand, and after a few steps, drew him close.

Her lips brushed his own before parting. It was enough to flood Cade with relief. Even now, with so much at stake, he found the greatest weight on his heart had been wondering if she still cared for him.

Amber grasped his arms and looked up at him, her eyes shining with tears.

'You're different since the battle,' she said. 'God knows you've been through so much. But . . .'

She struggled to find the words, then hugged him close.

'Just don't forget who you are,' she whispered into his chest. 'Stay my Cade.'

Cade took her chin in his hand, staring into her brown eyes. He kissed her deeply, drawing her close.

'I'm yours,' he said as they parted. 'Now and forever.'

'Stay safe, Cade,' she said.

In that moment, she looked so fragile. He saw the care in her eyes and felt his heart twist with the knowledge he had lied to her. And would do so again.

Then, before he could say another word, she walked back to the others.

'They're leaving without us,' Scott called.

Cade shouldered his bag and gave the others a final wave. Then he was running, following the Romans into the jungles.

FORTY

If Cade had expected some showdown with Atticus, he was much mistaken. The Romans moved at a blazing pace, and it was hard enough to keep up, let alone strategise how to deal with the ex-commander.

Cade and Scott trailed the group, glad that this part of the jungles, populated primarily by monolithic sequoia trees, was sparse enough to see any incoming predators.

It was like walking through an enormous, green-roofed atrium, one held up by rough-hewn pillars of wood. The ground was carpeted with moss and broad-leafed ferns, the only plants that could thrive in the dappled light that filtered through the leaves above.

The earthy air was already filled with the trilling calls of the animals that lived in the trees, and the flitting of pterosaurs and other flying beasts could be seen above. Cade wondered if Zeeb had once glided through these very trees. He missed him.

'They sure . . . can . . . run . . . can't they,' Scott choked, his chest heaving as they jogged behind the Romans. 'Glad . . . Yoshi . . . isn't here.'

Cade couldn't help but agree. It amazed him how fast they were moving, for the Romans were running in full armour, the clatter of metal making them easy to follow. He had left his own at the keep, knowing the tight-fitting suit would only chafe and slow him down.

Instead, he and Scott wore the padded clothing from their time in New Rome, with the metal-capped shoulders, elbows, forearms, knees and shins. The only difference was, Cade's had a second layer of golden spider silk, still there from his battle with the alpha.

As for weapons, both carried only their swords, with Cade's Honjō Masamune digging uncomfortably into his back beneath the rucksack. He did not dare stop to rearrange it, for fear of losing the group.

He had underestimated these young legionaries, for they carried their heavy shields as well. Years of hard marching must have acclimatised them to such athleticism, leaving the modern boys in the dust. Had the Romans not been so encumbered, Cade had no doubt he and Scott would have been left far behind.

It was some relief then when the sequoias began to thin out and were replaced by the heavy bush and branching trees of the jungles. Forced to cut a path ahead, the legionaries slowed, allowing Cade and Scott to catch up.

For a while they breathed heavily, hands on their knees. Cade ignored the pitying, if a little derisive, looks from the legionaries and jogged to fall in line behind them.

'We stick out like flies on a wedding cake here,' Scott muttered after a few minutes of trudging through the bushes.

It was true. The legionary metal clanked with each step they took and glinted in the mottled light of the sun.

Cade wondered if the segmented *lorica* armour would stand up against a carnosaur's teeth. If a hyena could munch down a steel saucepan, as he had once learned on YouTube, he'd bet the armour was little better than the foil wrapper around a KitKat.

Cade knew he would have to talk to Atticus about this, no matter the consequence. Without the armour, they would move faster, more quietly, and most importantly, less visibly. Best to do it now, while they could still stash the armour close to the keep.

'Hey!' Cade increased his pace and shouldered his way through the ten legionaries. 'Atticus!'

The man was close to the front, directing two legionaries to hack through the vegetation with their gladiuses. Atticus turned at his name, and Cade almost staggered back at the look of pure hatred across his face. Yet it was gone as soon as it had come and replaced by a haughty sneer.

'Yes, pup,' Atticus said, the Codex translating in his ear. 'What has you yapping?'

'Translate back,' Cade instructed the Codex.

There was no need to hide the Codex's presence now, and it translated his next words in its robotic voice.

'This armour will be useless against most of the predators here. It only slows us down and draws attention.'

237

Atticus raised his brows, and to Cade's surprise, considered his words.

'Do you expect us to leave it in the muck?' he asked, raising his voice for the others to hear. 'Armour we have carefully maintained for so many years. Armour that has protected us from the blades of the Tritons? Armour that will protect us again when the next round begins?'

There was murmuring from the men, and Atticus spread his arms wide, then clapped his hands against his breastplate.

'The pup feels naked without armour of his own. He wants us to be equally vulnerable.'

'The noise will attract predators,' Cade said, speaking over Atticus's final words. 'I know you've heard of them. They're like dragons, large enough to swallow you whole, and fast enough to catch you.'

'. . . leave it in the dirt to rust,' Atticus went on, talking through Cade's speech.

Cade had already considered this conundrum. He held up his hands in peace. 'We're only a few hours away from our first camp – the prison ship.'

Cade instructed the Codex to open the map and traced their route with his finger. Its appearance closed Atticus's mouth – it was the first time he had seen it. He had been following a copied, hand-drawn map.

'We can hide the armour there and collect it on the way back,' Cade went on, pointing to the blue dot.

Atticus's eyes bulged, and Cade remembered how he had lied to the man's face about not having the Codex.

'Would you oust me as leader of this group too?' Atticus

238

hissed. 'You are as Brutus, the usurper. Treacherous to your core.'

Cade knew this could not continue. He had to find a way to work together with Atticus. So he did something that took the greatest of effort. He knelt.

'Consider me a guide. That's all.' Cade lowered his head in supplication. 'I promise you. I'm only trying to win this game and get us all home.'

He turned his head, speaking with as much feeling as he could muster.

'Have I not fought beside you this whole time? What else do I have to do to prove I'm telling the truth?'

More murmuring, too quiet or too garbled for the Codex to translate. But Atticus knew he had lost the argument. The legionaries, at least for now, were on Cade's side.

'March on,' Atticus called, leaving the decision hanging in the air. 'We must reach the ship by nightfall.'

FORTY-ONE

The ship was an empty hulk, one impaled through the trunk of a tree, leaving a gaping entrance in its side. They reached it as the sun set, following a desperate effort in the dusk light for fear of being stranded in the darkness.

Their arrival was marred by the discovery of bones scattered about the ship's exterior, and a gaping, empty skull at the entrance – the remains of men long dead, scavenged by the beasts of the forest.

Now Cade huddled with Scott at the back of the ship, disgusted by the rusted chains upon the walls. Some shackles still held human remains, and finger bones were strewn about the ground like game pieces. Cade tried not to think of the fate of the men who had been abandoned here.

Tried . . . and failed. He saw it in his mind's eye. Men chained to a wall and left to die of thirst, or be savaged, helpless, by whichever beast came across them. It reminded him of his time upon Ishak's ship, and the memory made him shudder. But it was either that or the cold.

The small campfire Atticus had allowed them to light was little comfort as the temperature dropped lower than Cade remembered it had on that long night in the slavers' captivity, all that time ago.

Their makeshift hearth was within the ship itself, its smoke drifting between the broken spars of the boards above, giving off meagre light. It was too dark to see if there was anything worth salvaging – a musket perhaps, or some gunpowder.

But Cade already knew it was unlikely the ship would house anything of value. The chains were rusted through – the vessel had likely been left here a century ago or more.

'Pup,' Atticus called from the deepest recess of the ship. His face was illuminated by a tallow-fat candle, the only light other than the campfire, and that of the red moon above.

'Don't,' Scott muttered, clutching Cade's arm.

Cade pulled his fingers away gently, hushing Scott. In this dark, damp, lonely place, his friend had been drained of all his usual mirth.

'We need to make peace with him,' Cade whispered. 'If he's planning revenge, he's not exactly going to do it in front of his men, is he?'

Scott sniffed, but there was no reply. Hunched, Cade crab-walked around the fire, down towards Atticus. He was suddenly acutely aware of the sword on his back and was glad of its presence. Regardless of what he had told Scott, he was scared of Atticus.

This was a man who had kept his men alive for years, scratching out an existence on an alien planet, behind enemy lines. Cruel and paranoid as he was, there was no underestimating the man.

'Atticus,' Cade said, crouching on his haunches.

He did not come too close, for the man's hand was hovering just above his hilt. Atticus had fallen far and must be desperate to volunteer for a mission like this. Desperate men were capable of anything.

Atticus did not speak for a while, instead observing Cade in the wan light of the flickering candle. He steepled his fingers and leaned towards him.

'We will not remove our armour tomorrow,' he said, then held up a finger as Cade began to argue. 'We will not remove it, because the men are scared. Fear, pup, is our greatest enemy out here. A panicked man will run blindly, without thinking. And at the first sight of one of those beasts, they will panic.'

Cade, to his surprise, saw the sense in the man's words. False courage, though, was a fickle friend.

'I have spoken with the men who ventured into this place,' Atticus whispered.

He noted Cade's surprised expression and smiled. 'Oh yes. Not the men who have ventured as far as this. After all, only one man returned from the first expedition, and he died soon after. As for the second . . . well, they never came back at all. Now, we follow in their footsteps, and I am loath to repeat history.'

'So who did you speak to?' Cade asked, the Codex translating his words over his shoulder.

'The hunters. The men who bring in meat. They do not

242

venture as far as we have. But they have seen enough. And of course, we've all heard the stories. I did not come out here with my eyes closed. I am not such an incompetent as you may believe.'

Cade sat back on his haunches as he gained an understanding of the man. Still, these were just words. But he had seen Marius's actions.

'At Jomsborg you had your men form up even though they were injured and bleeding. That didn't seem like good command to me.'

Atticus sucked his teeth. 'Discipline kept my men alive. Do you know how many succumbed to madness in that first year? Men killing one another over morsels of rotten insect. Others who would just stare and waste away, refusing to eat. You were not there in those dark days. There was no hope in that place. So I gave them fear instead.'

'You had to be cruel to be kind?' Cade asked, then realised the Codex would not capture his sarcastic tone.

'Correct. Do not mistake me. I know I was wrong about your weapon. But I was right that you lied to us, yes? That Codex was with you the whole time.'

Cade conceded the point with an inclination of his head.

'And Quintus?' Cade asked.

Atticus shrugged. 'I have done a lot worse for a lot less. If there was one chance that he could give us the Codex, I could not afford to miss it. And I was right about that too. It was the Codex that allowed you to make your *gunpowder*, was it not?'

Cade bit his lip. There was guile in this man's words. Yet

243

there was a sick logic to his decisions too. What he had done to Quintus was unforgivable. Now though, Cade could understand why he had done it.

'I am not perfect,' Atticus pressed on. 'I have made mistakes. But it was the steel in my spine that kept us alive. It is easy to drag down those who stand strong above, holding back the darkness. Much harder to take their place, as Marius will soon learn. Do we have an understanding, pup?'

He extended his hand, and Cade stared at it. Finch had held his hand out to him, back in New Rome, just like this. Then he tried to kill him.

Cade took his hand.

'Call me Cade,' he said.

FORTY-TWO

They woke to the sounds of the jungle. Hoots, screeches and deep lowing echoed through the hollow of the ship; a dawn chorus that greeted the broken sunlight of the morning.

The soldiers were already outside, formed in a neat square of nine, with Atticus at the helm. But as Scott and Cade emerged from their shelter, they saw the legionaries looked quite different from how they had looked before.

'Our guide, Cade, made an excellent observation yesterday about our armour,' Atticus announced. 'So we have taken steps to correct that.'

Their armour was smeared with mud so that the bright sheen was gone. Stranger still, the armour itself looked different, somehow bulkier, with patches of cloth poking from some of the gaps.

'Sacking,' Atticus said, noting Cade's confused expression. 'Stuffed where the metal scrapes, to silence its noise.'

Cade was impressed. Atticus had saved both his own and Cade's face – while simultaneously demonstrating his willingness to listen to reason, something he had failed to do in Jomsborg.

He couldn't say Atticus did not learn from his mistakes.

'So, *Cade*' – Atticus emphasised his name, though not unkindly – 'are you ready to depart?'

Cade shouldered his pack.

'Let's go,' he said.

They found a trail at midday. A deer trail, as Scott described it – though it was much more than that. The thoroughfare was as wide as a motorway, pounded to mud by the feet of a thousand animals.

It did not follow their intended direction exactly, curving instead by the path of least resistance, worming its way between slopes and copses of trees. But it was the same general direction, and they made more progress in an hour than they had that entire day.

Atticus was the one who had made the decision to follow it. Cade did not resist the choice. In part because he was already exhausted, his legs aching from the walking. Too tired to continue through the heavy bush, and too tired to argue with the ex-commander.

It was strange, but his legs still ached from his time in the land of the Tritons. Months had passed for the others, yet for Cade it had been a few days. He was fortunate that his wrist seemed to be healing swiftly, now only hurting when he touched the livid, pink-scarred skin, rather than each time he moved his arm.

With each step, Cade examined the footprints, making

sure that the trail was safe. Or as safe as you could be with herbivores out there – certainly he wouldn't describe an elephant in the wild as safe, and the herbivores here were equipped with far more than tusks.

A stegosaurus alone could use its tail spikes to punch through a stone wall if it was so inclined, and the snap of a sauropod's tail would knock one of the sequoias toppling. Not to mention the ceratopsians, with their spiked, shield-like heads and horns like a bull on steroids.

Still, Cade's initial impressions were good, the ground mostly engraved with the great, round indents of long-necked sauropods and the chicken-like hopscotch of small, birdlike dinosaurs. The latter, he guessed, were the Compsognathus-type dinosaurs that Quintus had lived off at Hueitapalan.

As for creatures, they hardly saw anything at all. Only the flitting of flying beasts high above, and the rustle of leaves in the undergrowth.

For though the legionaries had tried to dampen the clanking of their armour and the shine of the metal, the tramp of their feet, coughs, snorts and swears meant they made more noise than a school canteen.

Any animals that were predated upon would be giving the approaching sound a wide berth. Unfortunately it wasn't these animals Cade was concerned about.

And then, he saw it. A muddy print, almost lost in the mud, trodden into near oblivion by the boots of the legionaries in front of him.

But the three-pronged print was unmistakable. A

theropod. Large enough to fit a car tyre within it. He didn't know how old it was, nor what beast had made it, just that it was definitely a carnosaur. And he only knew that much because he had seen one just like it in the sands of the arena.

'Atticus!' Cade called.

The man at the front stopped, a frown of annoyance on his face as he stalked back to Cade. Yet to his credit, he crouched to observe the footprint. Even measured it with the span of his hand, giving a low whistle between his teeth.

'We should get off the trail,' Scott muttered, though the Codex did not translate his words.

Cade grimaced, staring at the thick brush on either side of them. He whispered to the Codex, and the map of the caldera appeared once more.

'We're here,' Cade said, pointing to the blue dot that represented their group. 'And you can just about make out the path from the indent in the canopy. If we stay on this route another hour, we'll come close enough to reach Leifsbudir by nightfall. Leave now . . . we'll be working by torchlight. That's as much a risk as staying on this trail.'

Atticus nodded but said nothing, while Scott groaned and threw his hands up in the air.

'Do you not see the size of that thing?' he demanded.

'Better the devil you know than the devil you don't,' Cade said.

'That's a pretty big-ass devil if you ask me,' Scott said. 'It doesn't get much worse than that.'

Cade rubbed his chin as Atticus took a few steps away and drew his gladius. Curious, Cade saw him digging in a

248

small mound of dirt. Atticus stuck his fingers in and removed a long white object. A bone.

He sniffed it and wrinkled his nose.

'Meat eater,' he said, the Codex translating in Cade's ear. 'Fresh too.'

Only now did Cade realise it was dung. Atticus sniffed again, this time pensively.

'What say you, guide?' he asked. 'Have you met a beast of this size here before?'

'Not here,' he said.

Atticus hummed under his breath and looked up the trail.

'We walk half an hour more,' he said. 'Split the risk.'

Cade shook his head. 'We do that, we double the risk of getting lost in darkness *and* coming across one of these beasts.'

Atticus cocked his head. 'We run the half hour,' he said. 'Less time, less risk.'

Cade shook his head again, but Atticus had already stridden back, barking orders.

'I hope he's right,' he whispered to Scott, shouldering his pack.

FORTY-THREE

The darkness was near absolute. Torches were reluctantly lit, a pair held high at the front of the column, as men took turns to chop back the hoary undergrowth.

It had been like this for hours. The deeper into the jungles they went, the thicker the vegetation had become. Every move was made harder in darkness, men swinging their blades in dim light and those at the back blundering forwards, tangling in the low-hanging branches the rushed hacking had missed.

They were close though. So close, the blue dots were virtually on top of each other. Caution had been thrown to the wind now, as the rustling of the jungles around them grew louder and louder.

The jungles had come alive at night. Such as they had not seen or heard, in the cocoon of comfort back at their last camp.

Whether attracted by the light, the noise, or their very scent, glowing eyes watched them from the darkness, reflecting the flickering lights of their torches. Circling them, darting back and forth, yet staying shrouded in shadow.

Were they raptors, or something else? Cade didn't want to find out. The men had huddled into a formation of shield and sword, with two pairs at the front, continuing their frantic hacking at the barrier of branches, thorns and leaves.

Every few minutes, Atticus barked an order, and four men would cycle, two holding torches, the others swinging their blades. It was as efficient as they could be, and both Cade and Scott had taken their fair share of turns, their sword blades dulled from the constant grind of bark, liana and fibre.

'Lights ahead,' came a call from the front.

Cade didn't need the Codex to know what the man had said. It was ahead of them, filtering through the trees. A glow.

For a moment, Cade thought it was the moon, hanging low in the sky. But as he stared, craning his neck over the shorter Romans, he knew. It had to be Leifsbudir. And it was occupied.

Atticus shouldered his way to the front, and Cade followed, unable to resist an involuntary shudder as the undergrowth rustled at the movement.

The ex-commander gripped one of the torches, pushing his way forwards. There were only a few feet to go before the forest opened into a clearing of sorts, and following him Cade could soon make out a wooden palisade, one at least ten feet tall and made of solid wood. Whatever light it gave off was coming from the inside, lighting the low-hanging branches of the trees above. But what scared him most were the gates.

He had seen gates just like it before. All those months ago, when he had been captured by the slavers.

'We need to leave,' Cade hissed. 'Now.'

Atticus laughed. 'These are humans,' he said. 'Allies! Why, they could help us. What a success it would be to bring more men to bolster our army.'

Cade hushed him, his heart pounding. Behind him, the Romans crowded forwards, eager to be out of the undergrowth.

'These are slavers,' Cade hissed. 'You ever heard of them? Because I've been taken captive by them twice.'

Atticus spat. 'We've heard the rumours. But who is to say it is them?'

Cade stared at the gates, struggling to convey what he knew to be true in as few words as possible.

'The slavers have outposts like this across the jungles. Places to sleep while they hunt for us, and other remnants, out in the jungles. They must have repurposed Leifsbudir.'

Atticus crouched in the dirt, eyeing the gates, which now Cade saw must have been barred from the inside.

'Then we take it from them,' he hissed, drawing his gladius. 'We take them by surprise.'

Cade shook his head. 'There's nothing to gain. And who knows how many of them are there?'

'You would have us pass the night out here?' Atticus growled, stabbing with his blade into the still-rustling undergrowth.

Cade grimaced at the thought. 'We have no other choice.'

Atticus snorted derisively. 'I will scout their position,' he said, already moving.

Cade snatched at his skirts, but the man tugged free,

crab-walking up the slight slope of underbrush to the gates of the settlement.

Behind, the crackling of branches grew louder. No longer the sly movements of beasts following them in the darkness. This was louder, as if coming from further away.

'Atticus!' Cade hissed. 'There's something coming.'

Atticus shook his head, as if the fact did not matter; he instead pressed his face to the slim gap in the swinging doors and then tested his blade between, sliding it carefully through.

He withdrew it and turned, a scowl upon his face. To Cade's relief, he padded back to them.

'Chained,' he growled.

The noise from the jungle was growing louder. Almost as one, the men turned to meet it, already huddling together, shields twitching up into a makeshift shield wall.

Cade's eyes widened. There were flames flickering in the trees, but further away than the source of the sounds. Bobbing up and down, as if those carrying them were running.

Yet whatever was coming was almost on top of them. Footsteps, and the hoarse panting of ragged breaths.

'Ready, men,' Atticus called. 'We stand here.'

A dark figure emerged from the darkness. Her face, even terrified in its expression, was still set Cade's heart on fire.

Amber.

'Wh—' Cade began, but she stumbled into him, reeling from exhaustion. Behind her, Quintus staggered into view, a pair of torches held in his hands.

Amber choked out a single word.

'*Slavers.*'

FORTY-FOUR

They ran. Ran with wild abandon, all fear of the flora and fauna of the jungles gone.

Quintus led the way, the pair of torches in hand, and the rest followed, ripping through the thorns and tangled branches like beasts in the night.

By the time they stopped, their faces were bloodied, bodies bruised and filthy from their falls and collisions with trees in the darkness. It seemed to Cade they had reached some miraculous clearing, until he spotted the hole in the canopy above, and the crumpled remains of the plane at its centre.

They had arrived at the nuclear bomb. Or rather, the plane that it was contained in. Regardless, Cade muttered a question to the Codex. He had to be sure.

'What is it?'

'*Remnant is an A-4E Skyhawk attack aircraft, loaded with a B43 nuclear weapon, that fell from the deck of the* USS Ticonderoga *in 1965. Pilot, plane and weapon were never found.*'

Cade looked back, but men were still catching up,

emerging through the trees. He'd seen Amber and Quintus just moments ago, so he knew at least they were safe.

He staggered towards the plane, his legs giving way as he did so. He was beyond exhausted, yet he crawled through the mulch and tangled vines upon the ground until he came to its side.

It was, to Cade's relief, not the rusted, ruined hulk he had feared. Rather, the plane was virtually intact, with hardly any rust at all. However long it had sat in this forest, it hadn't been here for half a century. More likely, Abaddon had removed it from stasis more recently.

As Cade took in the aircraft, running his hands along its pitted hull, he realised the bomb was attached to its undercarriage, and it was as enormous as the Codex had described it.

Longer than two men were tall, and wide enough to hardly get his arms around it, there was no way they would ever be able to haul it back through the jungles. Especially with the slavers hunting for them.

It had to be slavers. Dinosaurs would not be carrying torches.

It was with these thoughts that Cade turned to survey the legionaries. Counted them. Realised one was missing. Caught by the slavers . . . or lost.

But that didn't matter. Not when he saw Amber and Quintus, bedraggled, weary, and in worse condition than even the legionaries were.

'Cade,' Amber said, falling to her knees in front of him. 'You're OK.'

Cade drew her close, wrapping her in his arms. She had been the last to emerge from the jungles, staggering in just as he'd turned away from the craft.

'We followed you,' Amber whispered. 'Quintus and I. His squad came too but . . .'

She shook her head.

'Why?' Cade asked, brushing mud from her cheek. 'Why come?'

'We saw the slavers from the orchards,' she whispered. 'So many of them, ship after ship.'

Her voice was halting as she caught her breath. 'We made a show of force outside the tunnel. They thought it would just be us teenagers, but they didn't expect the Romans. So they turned back. Decided to hunt in the jungles like they always do. We knew they'd follow you. So Quintus and I disobeyed Marius and came after you to warn you. We've been on your trail ever since. As have the slavers. At least a hundred of them. We were lucky to reach you before they did.'

'And Quintus's men?' Cade asked.

'Captured,' she said. 'Quintus and I were lucky to escape – if he didn't know the jungles so well I'd be captured too.'

'Thank you, my love,' Cade whispered. 'If you and Quintus hadn't followed us . . . I don't know what might have happened.'

She took a deep breath, taking a hold of herself.

'The slavers at the keep offered Marius the world – food, weapons, armour. In exchange for us. The old contenders. The slavers said the emperor is offering a reward for our

256

capture. But Marius wouldn't take any of it, and the slavers decided to follow the tracks of your expedition instead. The men chasing us won't give up easily.'

Amber stood, though shaky on her feet. 'We need to move,' she announced. 'The slavers will be right behind us.'

The Codex did not translate for her, but her meaning was plain. Soldiers, tired though they were, levered themselves back onto their feet, gratitude stamped across their faces.

'Where would you have us go?' Atticus growled, pointing to the moons above. 'I have already lost one man to the darkness.'

Cade stood beside Amber, presenting a united front. 'If we push ourselves, we can be at the tombs by morning,' he said.

'What then?' Atticus asked. 'Say we find the remnants we are looking for. Are we to race them all the way back to the keep, overloaded with your so-called weapons of the future? We should scatter and make our way back to safety. They cannot track us all.'

Cade blinked tears from his eyes. They were tears of frustration and exhaustion. That, and the relief of having Amber with him once more. He had thought he could do this alone. But here he was, at the bomb itself. And they had no hope of bringing it with them.

His plan, as it stood, felt like a Hail Mary. Some last, desperate plan concocted by another being from another world, driven mad from solitude and an anger that transcended logic and reason.

And he had been taken in by it. Betrayed his friends, lied to them, manipulated them. For what? A thin sliver of hope that would end in his own death.

'We have two hopes of survival,' Cade said.

Atticus crossed his arms, already wary.

'We will find one of two things in the tombs,' Cade said, speaking loud for the benefit of the men. 'Treasure or useful remnants. We'll use that to either get ourselves and whatever we find teleported back to the keep – or buy ourselves weapons to use against the slavers.'

His words sounded weak, and poorly explained. But the legionaries held on to his every word. They needed hope, just as he had. And though they understood the rules of the game not a jot, if one of the contenders from the future said it . . . well, it must have some truth to it.

Atticus saw it too. He made one last attempt to discredit Cade's plan.

'If they catch up to us while we're inside the tombs, we will have no way to escape,' he said. 'We'll be trapped like rats.'

Cade shouldered his backpack and gave a last look at the plane.

It was so close. The fifteen of them could have lifted the bomb. Dragged it back on a sled.

Instead, he turned his back on it. Pushed the plan from his mind. He would risk his own life for this. But not those of his friends.

'It's a risk we'll have to take,' Cade said. 'It's the only way we're getting out of this alive.'

FORTY-FIVE

The sun was blushing the horizon when the blue dots merged on Cade's map. It had been their main source of light when the torches ran out, and a source of encouragement as they neared their destination during the tortuous journey.

Their night had been a miserable affair, made all the more exhausting by the torrent of rain that had begun almost immediately after they had set out. The canopy had given them some protection, but they had to constantly stop to switch torches, cursing as they held the damp bundles beneath outstretched cloaks, striking flint upon steel with desperate abandon to light their way once more.

Now, they staggered on in the new light, the Romans calling out praise to their gods as the warmth of the dawn began to take hold.

Cade knew they had been lucky not to be set upon by predators. They had made no secret of their travels, crashing through the jungles without a care for the noise and light they gave off.

They had covered a lot of ground that night, their speed only increased with their desperation and in the knowledge that their enemies would not be far behind. Gone was the careful chopping of a path; instead they battled thorns as they had done earlier, ripping at the tangled undergrowth, careless of injury.

The rain was both a blessing and a curse. Their footprints were easily read in the muddied ground behind them, but at the same time Cade wondered if the slavers would brave the rain, knowing that their quarry would be so easily tracked come daytime.

Cade almost missed the tomb entrance. Might have missed it entirely had he not stumbled upon the ledge of stone that announced its presence.

'Stop,' Cade managed, gripping Quintus's shoulder.

The legionary was glad to do so, and seemingly as one, the men collapsed onto the muddied ground.

It seemed a miracle that they had not lost another man. All were accounted for, haggard-faced and broken though they appeared.

'What is it, Cade?' Amber called, bringing up the rear. 'Did we make it?'

'It's here,' Cade called back.

It was not the grand façade that Cade had expected. No statues flanked the steps, nor were there monumental pillars framing cavernous stone doors.

Rather, it was a square frame of dirty marbled stone, flat against the ground. Large enough to admit two men at a time and seemingly blocked by a pile of rubble, deadwood and rotting leaves.

'Help me,' Cade asked to nobody in particular, leaning down and pulling at the detritus with thorn-torn hands.

'Here!' called Scott. 'There's a hole.'

Cade let the rocks fall from his hands and stumbled back, ripping his way through the overgrowth. Scott was pointing deeper into the trees, an area strangely barren of flora. Beyond that, Cade could see a ragged tear in the earth, dank and dark as a vixen's lair.

And a lair it was. As Cade pushed closer, the others following, he could see the mud, trodden to a thick paste outside the cavern. Bones littered the outside, coupled with ragged scraps of fur.

The top of the cave was a straight line, the fallen-in edge of what must have once been a portion of the temple. Now, it had become the den of some unknown predator – a warm, dry shelter from the wind and rain.

The cavernous maw could fit an elephant riding on another's back with ease. And the bones were troubling – ribs the size of whalebones stood like spars of a great ship in the dirt. Cade dared not think of what sort of creature could drag something that size here, especially through the underbrush.

It was no wonder the Roman expedition had passed by this place.

A string of expletives disturbed Cade's thoughts. Scott had unleashed his fury upon the world, cursing bitterly beneath his breath.

'It's a goddamn death trap,' he growled finally as the

others crowded at the edge of the clearing. None dared to set foot out of the underbrush.

None but Quintus. The young legionary stepped into the mud, kneeling and inspecting the ground.

'They are not here,' Quintus said in both Latin and then English for everyone's benefit.

'How do you know?' Atticus hissed from the trees.

Quintus grinned and spread his fingers into what looked like the Vulcan salute from *Star Trek*, and Cade could not help but chuckle at it, for Quintus had no idea of its significance. Then the legionary slotted his hand into the footprint on the ground, where Cade could now make out the three-toed tracks of a predator heading away from the cave.

It was like one of those patterned illusions where you crossed your eyes and could suddenly see the shapes. Now, the mud was littered with them. Dozens of the things, like chicken feet in flour. But far, far larger.

'They moved after the rain,' Quintus said, sweeping his hand in the direction of the tracks. 'Nothing comes back.'

It was true enough. But his friend's words brought him little relief. Even if these were day hunters that would only return back to the cave at night, they had seven tombs to search before the creatures' return. And that didn't account for the slavers, hot on their heels.

'We have no choice,' Amber said. 'These slavers aren't the only ones hunting us. There was a whole armada of them racing here to get you when we left. If we split up and run back to the keep in the state we're in, none of us will make it back.'

Amber kissed Cade on the cheek, her cracked lips rough upon his skin, and stepped out into the mud beside Quintus.

She drew her blade and stalked to the cave mouth, staring into the darkness.

'Come on!' she yelled. 'Sooner we're in, sooner we're out.'

FORTY-SIX

If the outside of the tomb had shown signs of habitation, the interior left no doubt. The stench of the place was almost unbearable, so heavy they could almost taste it.

The floors were thick with bones, many splintered to fragments by the occupants' jaws to get at the jellylike marrow within. Cade did not want to think of the bite strength needed to do that.

Animal faeces, dried and full of fur, coated the ground almost an inch deep. This was no temporary shelter from wind and rain. This was a den.

'There are torches here,' Atticus called.

They were ensconced in the walls themselves, as if this tomb had been visited by family members at one time or another. These were soon lit, crackling to life despite the many years this place had been here.

Under the new orange glow, men crowded closer, as if the light would protect them from whatever lurked in the darkness.

Only Atticus had the courage to move further into the

cave. As he strode into the gloom with a torch held high, the true scale of their surroundings was revealed.

The floor space they were standing upon was just a ledge of limestone above a broad, dark staircase – one that descended ever deeper into the maw of the tomb. Enormous pillars held up the ceiling, with further plinths embedded in the steps as the stair receded into darkness.

To their left, the true entrance of the temple was packed with rubble and debris, and Cade realised it would have taken them hours to clear it had they not found the collapsed wall.

But it was not this that drew the eye. Rather, it was the enormous statue at the top of the stone staircase. A bearded man, seated with an intricately carved cape over his head and an unrolled papyrus in his hands.

As for the walls, they were decorated with scenes of life and surrounded by colourful hieroglyphics. Men gathered reeds from the swollen banks of a great river, while others dragged enormous square blocks. Both the writing and the art style were undoubtably Egyptian.

'Whose tomb is this?' Scott asked.

The Codex was swift to respond.

'*Imhotep died in 2950 BC. He was the greatest architect of his time and was the first builder in history to use stone, as well as pioneering the use of pillars. As the high priest of Ra and Egypt's vizier, he was ruler beneath the pharaoh in all but name. So great were his achievements that he was deified as a god himself and would be worshipped by cults for thousands of years. His remains and the grand tomb he was buried in have never been found.*'

'Damn,' Scott said after a moment's silence. 'Dude was badass.'

Cade chuckled and stepped closer to the stair's edge.

'Come on,' he said. 'If we're lucky, the animals that live here don't go down there.'

His words were hollow though, for he could see well-worn claw marks running down its centre.

Still, they had no choice but to go deeper. Cade began the slow descent into darkness.

It was only after a full minute of descending that he began to understand the true scale of the tomb. Not only was the ceiling so high above them that they could no longer see it, but when they approached the bottom he could see that there were other stairs, leading back up, opposite them and to each side.

He stopped, staring.

'What is it?' Amber asked. 'Do you hear something?'

'It's a pyramid,' Cade whispered.

'What?' Scott said, confused. 'Do you even know what a pyramid *is*?'

Cade shook his head and pointed.

'It's an inverted pyramid,' he said. 'It's genius.'

'Nerd,' Scott said, nudging him good naturedly.

They went on, edging deeper into the darkness, until they reached the very bottom. There, a square of flat ground marked the nadir of the pyramid's stair, with a large square coffin at its centre.

A bearded man was depicted upon it in an intricate wood carving, painted in gold filigree and studded with coloured stones: jet, jade and lapis lazuli.

'Was this guy a giant or something?' Scott asked. 'It's huge.'

The entire thing was almost as long as a school bus and as tall as Cade's chest.

Cade cast around, looking for some other doorway or hole in the ground. There was nothing.

'What now?' Amber asked, sidling closer. 'I thought there was supposed to be treasure here. And where are the other tombs?'

Cade cursed under his breath and brought up the map of the Codex.

But no, the cluster of tombs was tightly packed together, looking as if they were *inside* Imhotep's tomb. It seemed impossible, unless they were somehow built into the steps on either side of them – but there was no sign of any entrance.

'Let's open the sarcophagus,' Cade said, struggling for ideas. 'See what's inside. Sometimes they had more of them, like a Russian doll. If one of them is made of solid gold or something . . .'

There was a wet thudding sound. Then another, and another. Cade turned in its direction, his heart in his mouth. An object tumbled down the steps, rolling to stop at their feet as legionaries scattered out of the way.

Amber choked with horror as a tongue lolled and vacant, half-closed eyes stared up at them. It was a head. The head of their lost legionary.

'How kind of you to trap yourselves for us,' called a voice from above.

It spoke in heavily accented English, but Cade knew who it was. The slavers.

Already, the legionaries were rushing to form a wall, but there was no thunder of enemies charging down the stairs. The voice was distant, coming from the very top of the stairs.

'Your friend there was *very* forthcoming when we caught up to him,' the voice went on, echoing eerily in the vast space. 'Why, he even told us what language you contenders speak. I *am* speaking with Cade, am I not?'

There were no lights in the darkness, but Cade could hear the scraping of metal as armoured men moved above.

'You have no chance,' the voice went on. 'We have the high ground. No deals. Surrender, or die.'

'Move the sarcophagus,' Cade hissed.

Quintus caught his meaning and whispered instructions to the men. Within seconds, a score of hands began to heave on the heavy wooden lid, scraping it back inch by slow inch.

'So kind of you to prepare your coffin for us,' the voice laughed. 'But you presume too much. We will take you from here in chains.'

Still the coffin lid scraped, and Cade edged closer, letting his eyes stray casually over its contents. But it looked empty.

'Surrender, and live,' the voice called, now tinged with impatience. 'You won the tournament once. Perhaps you can win again.'

'Fight, you coward!' a legionary shouted, his Latin words shrill in the emptiness of the tomb.

A thin laugh echoed back.

The coffin lid crashed to the ground, the sound reverberating around them. Amber nudged Cade.

'We need to get in the coffin,' she whispered.

268

'Are you nuts?' Cade muttered back. 'We'll be penned in.'

'Trust me,' she whispered. 'Give the order.'

Every instinct in Cade's mind told him they had to fight. To run up the stairs opposite the way they had come, to take the high ground back and fight. Instead, he pointed into the darkness above and spoke.

'Scan them, Codex!'

The drone shot into the gloom, and Cade roared for his men to follow him. He caught a glimpse of flashing blue, saw dark figures rushing down the steps.

He vaulted over the coffin's rim, only to feel a rush of horror as his feet met nothing. He fell, but only for a second before he crashed into a heap. Armoured men fell around him, torches pinwheeling as they were knocked askew.

A stairway lay in front of him, carved into the very rock itself. The coffin had not been empty after all.

'*Action prohibited. Individuals are not remnants. They do not originate from Earth,*' the Codex intoned, descending from the opening above.

Cade staggered to his feet, backing away as more legionaries scrambled down the steps, pushing into the antechamber he had fallen into, massing at the stairs' bottom.

Already, Quintus was shoving men into line, five men abreast and two men deep. Atticus stood behind them, his torch held aloft, as they stared into the gloom above.

They could hear the rush of feet and the echoing battle cries of men coming to kill. Cade, still dazed, pulled his blade free, looking in dizzy confusion at the room they were defending.

It was no bigger than a tennis court, with another coffin at its centre. This one was far smaller, but Cade's eyes were drawn elsewhere. Rather, he was staring at the crumpled figures scattered about the room. Four of them, wearing dark clothing, in stark contrast to the yellow-white skulls atop their bodies.

And then he saw it. A pistol. It was holstered at the nearest body's hip. And beside it, tucked into a tight pocket loop . . . was a grenade.

Cade did not hesitate. He stumbled to the corpse's side and yanked both free, turning as the first slavers vaulted down the steps.

He lifted the gun, pulled the trigger, and cursed as it did not fire. More men filled the stairway with axes lifted, preparing to charge.

Cade yanked the pin from the grenade and hurled it over the legionaries' heads. It was a poor throw, one that bounced off the wall before disappearing behind the advancing men.

One second passed.

Two seconds.

Boom.

FORTY-SEVEN

Dust billowed in the wake of the thunderclap, pulverised rock pelting Cade's face before the cloud of white blinded him.

Rocks rumbled, and men screamed in agony, fear and shock. There was the crash and crack of stone upon stone. Then . . . silence.

Torches glowed sickly orange in the light, fallen from nerveless fingers and sputtering on the ground. Men groaned, coughing dust from their lungs.

Cade had fallen, though he did not remember doing so, and blood filled his mouth with its metallic taste where his face had hit the floor.

He struggled to his knees, watching dazed figures wander the room, zombielike in their movements. His ears rang, a constant whine and static like a TV with a bad signal.

His hand found his blade, and he crawled to the stairwell, ready to fight the men who would soon follow. But he found only rubble, the stairs hardly visible beneath the mass of rock.

The ceiling had collapsed entirely, and the high walls on either side of the stairs had caved in.

They were safe. For now.

He could hear the screams of dying men, along with barked orders and demands for light and water. The sound was muffled, and Cade knew that behind the barrier of fallen stone, the slavers would be in total darkness.

Now Cade and his group were trapped down here. With little air and an small army baying for their blood outside.

'What the hell was that?' groaned Scott, staggering to his feet.

His voice was tinny in Cade's shellshocked ears, but he had time now to see most of the Roman soldiers had survived the explosion with just a few bruises, though a couple were limping or nursing broken arms.

'A grenade,' Cade replied, the question finally filtering through his addled mind.

He spotted Amber and Quintus huddled against a wall, pawing at their eyes where dust had gritted them closed.

'Hold still,' he said as he unstopped his flask, letting water trickle onto their faces, careful to not waste it. Who knew how long they would be down here?

Even if they *did* find treasure, or the slavers gave up their chase, they might spend days digging their way out.

And of course, that didn't account for the journey back. So much to think about. But one problem at a time.

'Are you guys OK?' Cade asked as Amber looked up at him through red-rimmed eyes.

'We're OK,' she whispered. 'Quintus?'

The boy pointed at his ears, shaking his head. Then nodded regardless after patting himself down.

Cade stood, pushing through the groups of legionaries huddled around the three torches that had survived the explosion. He crouched beside one of the corpses, hoping for more modern weapons. Enough to turn the tide in the next round.

But to Cade's disappointment, he found no further weapons on the body, only empty holsters and straps. He found nothing on the others either. Only the pistol, which he scooped up from where he had dropped it in the corner.

The bodies had clearly been there for a long time, if the state of their decomposition was anything to go on. In the dry, sheltered environment there was still skin and hair hanging from the yellowed skulls, and sinew keeping them attached to the heads.

Strangest of all though was their clothing. The men were wearing wet suits, and fins on their feet. Like they had been scuba diving, only without the tanks.

'Is that it, Abaddon?' he muttered. 'Stripped them of their weapons, left us with hardly anything?'

'Seems like it,' Amber said, crouching beside him.

There was no other response, but the Codex floated close by. As if it wanted him to ask it something.

'Who are these guys, Codex?' Cade asked.

'*Remnants are the remains of four members of SEAL Team Six from 1983. They were on a failed regime-change mission, Operation Urgent Fury, following a communist revolution in Grenada. They were last seen when their transport plane veered off course in a storm and they parachuted into the ocean. Overloaded with equipment, they were assumed drowned – their bodies were never recovered.'*

Cade sighed and sat back on his haunches.

Amber wiped at her face, then settled on the floor beside him. 'So what now?' she asked.

Cade bit his lip and stared around the room. By now, his eyes had adjusted to the darkness and the worst of the dust had settled. Beyond the plain, stone-carved coffin, the only features were six enormous metal doors at equal intervals around the room.

'Abaddon left these guys here as a reward for whoever ventured this deep into the tomb,' Cade said. 'There might be more beyond those doors. We just have to pick one and hope we find something that can help us defeat the slavers.'

He motioned at the six metal doors. It seemed Abaddon had been doing some construction of his own, for they were uniform and plain.

A string of curses erupted from behind him, and Cade turned to see Atticus being lifted to his feet. His head was bloodied, and his eyes were wild with anger.

'You had that weapon the whole time?' he demanded.

Cade held up his hands, too tired to get to his feet. 'I found the explosive on a body. And this,' he said, lifting the gun. 'How many bullets does this kind of gun hold, Codex?'

The Codex responded once it had finished translating his words. *'Remnant is a Sig Sauer P226 produced in 1980. It holds ten 9mm rounds.'*

Cade held it like it was a snake. He had handled weapons

aplenty since he had arrived on Acies, but never a gun. The weapon felt . . . *wrong*. To hold so much power in something so small. To be able to point it at someone and just . . . end them.

An involuntary shudder ran through him, but he kept his grip on the gun, finding the small nub on its side and clicking it through to the other side to release the safety. That was why he had not fired it before.

After a moment's pause, he clicked it back. Better safe than sorry.

'Ten what?' Atticus asked.

Cade considered the question. 'Think of them like small metal arrows, but far more accurate and powerful. They can go through just about any kind of armour. You simply point . . . and pull the trigger.'

He demonstrated, miming the act of firing a gun.

Atticus waited for the translation, then muttered a curse under his breath.

'Not enough to even the odds,' he growled.

Cade shrugged. 'They don't know we only have ten bullets,' he said. 'It might encourage them to back off.'

Atticus inclined his head. 'Fine,' he said. 'But whether they tunnel in or we tunnel out, our mission is not complete. Your . . . *Sigsore* is not going to win us another round. What do you propose we do now?'

Cade motioned to the doors with his free hand.

'We go deeper,' he said.

FORTY-EIGHT

Behind the doors, each entrance was different, most a simple stairway into the ground or a mausoleum-style entrance complete with a stone plaque blocking the way. The Codex confirmed what each one was.

They split into three teams of one or two of his friends with a handful of Romans. Cade was loath to separate, but he knew they were running out of time.

Already, he could hear the sounds of the slavers working to clear the blocked passage behind them. As they gathered outside their respective tombs, Cade considered his choices, recalling the research he had done the night before the expedition.

Boudicca, the queen of the Iceni who had slaughtered so many Romans in her British rebellion, was for Scott's crew. It was Quintus who was most curious about her burial place, for she had a history with his legion, having virtually destroyed it in the Battle of Camulodunum some fifty years before Quintus had joined it. Cade had no doubt her tomb would be small, and Quintus could swiftly gather what treasures he could before moving on to the next.

Alexander the Great was left for later, for Cade knew his burial place had been moved several times before its location was forgotten, making it unlikely any of the original valuables were still there. In fact, Cleopatra, occupant of the tomb directly next to it, had pillaged his tomb to fund her war several hundred years later, and four Roman emperors had raided it for valuables too. No, there would be nothing left there.

Anthony and Cleopatra's tomb had been built by Octavian, the man who had defeated her, and though he would have been respectful, it was doubtful he would let it be filled with valuables. But Cade had Amber go in anyway, for one reason alone: Cleopatra was Caesarion's mother. The emperor of New Rome had questioned Cade on his own history, and Cade knew it was likely something the man obsessed over. Possession of his mother's body was a bargaining chip he could not pass up, should they come to a confrontation with the slavers once more.

That left Cade a choice: Genghis Khan, Attila the Hun, or Atahuallpa.

Atahuallpa was the last emperor of the Incas, a civilisation legendary for their wealth and known for burying their mummified dead with their possessions to take with them into the afterlife.

Cade had been excited at first, as the Codex had told him Atahuallpa had paid a ransom to conquistadors by filling his prison cell with gold and another two with silver to secure his release. Enough to summon a legion of Cade's own, had he wished to.

But sadly, his tomb was easy to dismiss, for the conquistadors had baptised, garrotted and burned him anyway, and then given him a Christian burial. No gold or jewels to be had there.

That left the two famous emperors of the steppes. Men who had conquered most of Europe in their times, though they had lived seven centuries apart.

But there was no doubt in Cade's mind which would bear the most fruit. Genghis Khan. A man so virile, one percent of the world's population was descended from him. He was the ruler of the largest empire that the world ever saw, one that would stretch from the Sea of Japan to Poland and contained over a quarter of the world's population – having killed one tenth of it to conquer them. He was responsible for more deaths than Hitler and Stalin combined. The planet had literally cooled after he was done killing.

His burial had been so secret that an army had slaughtered anyone they saw on their journey to the tomb, as well as the two thousand servants who helped bury him. They rode a thousand horses over his final resting place to trample the earth and even diverted a river over its top. That first army had then been ambushed by another to silence them, and legend told the second army had died by suicide after that battle, so that no man alive would know its location.

So Cade assumed it was a safe bet there was something worth hiding there. Attila's could wait.

A crash of stone on stone pulled Cade from his thoughts,

and he hurried over to view the open sarcophagus's contents. To his disappointment, there was only a mummy within, bereft of jewelry of any kind. There was, however, a cleaner patch of cloth, the outline of where a pendant had once sat upon the man's chest.

'Worthless,' Atticus spat.

Cade was disappointed but not surprised. 'I bet this place was robbed before Abaddon transported it here,' Cade said, rubbing the back of his neck.

'Damn,' Amber said. 'Let's hope the others haven't been robbed too.'

'What, you mean these places were dug up in the past to rob them?' Scott asked.

Cade nodded. 'Mostly around the same time they were built, but there was a lot of tomb robbing by Europeans in the past few centuries too. You know why there are so few intact mummies around?'

Scott shook his head.

'Because Europeans used to eat them all. For medicine, aphrodisiacs. You know, people were still eating mummies in the roaring twenties.'

Scott looked down at the mummy and retched.

'And on that lovely note, shall we get on with it?' Amber asked.

Cade turned and gripped his torch. 'All right,' he said, staring into the dark confines of Genghis's tomb. 'Let's raid some tombs.'

FORTY-NINE

Cade was the first to enter Genghis's tomb, torch held in one hand, gun in the other.

He was the first person to enter this place in centuries, and it still amazed him that it was possible. To walk where men had walked so long before. To see the lost grave of a man who had shaped the history of the world.

What took him by surprise was the simplicity of the room he had entered. It was a round antechamber with yellowing white walls.

Paintings, peeling though they were, were layered over the top of the walls, inscribed directly onto the crumbling plaster. Yet despite their apparent age, the colours remained vivid.

They were Chinese in style, and this was no surprise to Cade. The Mongols had pillaged China, such that even the poorest Mongol was clothed in silk and Chinese finery. The best minds of China had been put to work for the empire, acting as their engineers, scientists, academics and administrators. It was likely skilled Chinese slaves who had built this place.

As Cade lifted his torch higher, he saw they were in a domed room, not unlike the roof of a Mongol-style tent. And beneath him . . . was gold.

Great earthen pots of it, heaped in piles of coins. Glittering jewels filled others, and weaponry lay along the walls, propped like garden tools in an old shed. Bows, swords, lances – it was a veritable armoury.

Stranger still were the bodies. Twelve in all, six on either side. They were not mummified; rather they were each seated on a throne, resplendent in feminine, multilayered garb. Skulls leered at Cade from these seats, in stark contrast to the beauty of their robes.

'Wives and concubines,' Cade said. 'Buried with him. You have to hope they had already died from natural causes when they were left here . . . but somehow I doubt it.'

'And his horse,' Amber said, standing beside him.

Indeed, the full skeleton of a horse was laid out in battle armour at the foot of a large coffin. The coffin was finely carved from wood, covered in engravings of horses and war.

There was more to be seen – fine statues carved from jade, bundles of rich cloth, and fine china and crockery piled haphazardly throughout the room.

Cade could hardly imagine the loyalty one must have needed to lock away so many riches, knowing they would never be used or seen again. Genghis, even in death, exerted complete control of his people.

Legionaries piled in behind Cade, wandering through the riches with awe upon their faces.

'What do we do with it?' Atticus asked. 'Even *this* is too much to carry back with us.'

Cade rubbed his eyes, then handed the torch to the nearest legionary. 'I need to speak with Abaddon.'

There was a moment's silence, then: 'Fine. We shall check on the others.'

Cade waited until the Romans had left the room. He sat upon the stairs down into the chamber and laid the gun beside him. He waited for the footsteps to recede, then spoke.

'Well? I know you're watching.'

The little girl poked her head out from behind the coffin, a simpering smile stamped across her features. 'I see you have been busy.'

Cade grunted in acknowledgment.

She skipped closer, though her feet left no impression on the sandy floor. 'I assume you wish to barter?'

'I want to know how it works first,' Cade said, gesturing at the treasures in the room. 'What's this worth to us?'

'It depends.' The girl giggled. 'Are you beside the treasure, or far away from it? Is the remnant you wish to purchase one that has already been discovered, or is it one yet to be released onto Acies?'

Cade rubbed his eyes again. For the past few hours, he had given up on ever getting the bomb to the keep. Now, suddenly, it was back on the table.

'How much to transport the nuclear bomb to the keep?' Cade asked.

Abaddon wagged the girl's finger. 'Not so fast, my eager little friend. You must transport the whole remnant – no picking and choosing. The plane comes too, and for that, you'll have to pay.'

Cade said nothing, waiting for her to continue.

'Let me see,' she said after a reproachful tut at Cade's silence. 'You've already discovered the bomb after all, so it will cost you less. But . . . well . . . what *good* is it to you, Cade? I say this as your greatest supporter, you understand.'

Cade let out a bitter laugh, hoping it would mask the sudden increase in his heart rate. 'I'd say the greatest weapon known to man is worth something.'

Abaddon pouted and took a ghostly seat atop the lap of the nearest mummy. 'Well, it's not much good if you can't set it off remotely. I thought you were smarter than this, Cade.'

The girl's voice was sweet and simpering, but it belied an air of suspicion beneath the surface.

'I thought maybe we could put it on top of a pyre of wood, light a fuse, and run for it,' Cade said, shrugging. 'But I didn't plan on using it in an attack. Only in defence.'

'Oh?' Abaddon asked.

'Let's say some alien race attacks us and we're down to the last man. The keep is about to be taken over. So we set off the nuke and blow everything to hell. Any enemies would be wiped out along with us. Call it a deterrent.'

The little girl clapped her hands and giggled. 'Oh, *very* clever. But wrong. Very wrong. These bombs are not set off by fire and are not live unless a complex series of triggers are set off electronically. Lucky for you, I am willing to provide you with a remote detonator. One with a timer. For a price.'

Cade knew he did not need the timer. Knew he would set off the bomb while he was standing right next to it, using the Grey's toy. But Abaddon didn't know that. Logically, he needed to barter for this detonator.

'What's your price?' Cade asked.

'Well, you find yourself in quite a predicament,' Abaddon said, gesturing behind him. 'Slavers and dinosaurs and mummies, oh my!'

Cade shrugged. 'I have my gun,' he said, brandishing the pistol. 'And a plan.'

The little girl rolled her eyes as Cade laid the gun beside him. 'I'll make you an offer,' she said. 'All the treasures in the tomb for the plane and its bomb, the remote detonator, and instant teleportation for your soldiers and anything they can carry back to the keep. I need you there soon anyway for the next round.'

'Done,' Cade said.

Abaddon wagged a pudgy finger. 'Not so fast!' she said. 'This deal requires *all* the treasure to be left in one place. Every gem, every coin, every trinket. Bring it all here, to this room.'

Cade thought for a moment, then nodded.

'OK,' he said. 'Deal.'

Abaddon's avatar receded into the gloom.

'Be quick, Cade,' the girl whispered. 'And . . . good luck with *that*.'

She pointed, and Cade spun.

And saw the pistol, aimed at his face.

FIFTY

'What are you doing, Atticus?' Cade whispered.

The man held the gun awkwardly, with one hand on the grip, the other slotting its fingers into the trigger guard. But it was pointed right at Cade.

'Killing you,' he hissed back.

The Codex translated his words in the silence, its strange, monotone voice echoing through the chamber.

'That gun will make a loud noise,' Cade said. 'Like the cannons. My friends will come running.'

Atticus grinned. 'I'm counting on it. I can deal with them too.'

'Wasting four bullets, and four fighters,' Cade said, shaking his head. 'You're dumber than I thought.'

Atticus chuckled and took a step closer. 'I don't need either. I am sure that this *Abaddon* will strike the same deal with me – I heard everything. And with you out of the way, I will get all the credit. And with this . . . *gun*, Marius's reign will be over before it has even begun.'

'I thought you were different, Atticus.' Cade shook his head. 'You had me fooled.'

Atticus cocked his head to the side. 'It's nothing personal. I am simply a pragmatic man.' He chuckled. 'Well, I confess to taking some pleasure in this act. But I have also misjudged you. Even in the face of death, you are as calm as any man I've seen. Perhaps you would have amounted to something someday. A shame.'

'Last chance,' Cade said, pulling his blade free from its scabbard on his shoulder.

Atticus laughed. 'Goodbye, Cade.'

He pulled the trigger.

But the only sound was Cade's blade as it thrummed through the air, taking Atticus through the throat. The gun clattered to the ground, and Cade released his sword as it stuck the man. Atticus staggered back, clutching at the blade. Cade snatched up the pistol, disgusted by it.

Only a weapon like this would have tempted betrayal. There was something insidious in its power.

'You didn't have to do this,' Cade said. 'We were so close to . . . so close.'

The man only stared at him as he backed into the wall, his eyes wide with shock.

Cade turned the gun sideways and clicked back the safety catch. He had seen it was on when he'd tried to fire the gun earlier. When he struck with his blade, he'd only hoped the gun would not fire. But he hadn't been sure until now.

Atticus sank slowly to the ground, his attempts to speak blocked by the blade in his gullet.

Cade told himself that Atticus deserved this.

He had threatened his friends. Threatened Amber.

Cade lifted the pistol, pointing it at Atticus's chest. Then he lowered it and yanked the blade free in a spray of blood.

'I won't waste a bullet on you,' he said, averting his eyes.

The man gurgled, clutching at his throat, even as blood poured between his fingers. As Atticus's life twitched away, Cade turned away, unable to watch.

'Atticus is dead,' Cade announced.

The legionaries in Imhotep's chamber who were hauling Cleopatra's embalmed body through stopped in their tracks.

The men stared at Cade, shocked, and only now did Cade notice the blood that had stained his sword arm and chest.

'Why?' one of the legionaries asked simply, his single word translated by the Codex.

'He attacked me,' Cade replied back.

His sword was still drawn, with the pistol in the other hand, but there was no aggression from the legionaries.

Even so, Amber darted to Cade's side, her own sword drawn.

'Shit,' was all she said.

The men looked at them dully, and Cade saw the exhaustion in their eyes. In that moment, he realised just how hard this must be for them. Men, traumatised by their time on the Grey realm, outnumbered, hunted, and bereft of hope for years.

And now, thrown into monstrous jungles, marching through the night, their destination unknown, with almost no understanding of what they were there for.

These men just wanted to survive. When they returned . . . Cade knew he had to tell them. Let them know they were not subject to the whims of gods but of creatures from another planet. That their fates were not foregone, that their lives were not already forfeit.

For now, they needed one thing. Hope.

Now the other legionaries arrived, and the knowledge of Atticus's death rippled through them in a mess of whispered conversation.

'I have a way to get us out of this,' Cade said as every eye in the chamber turned towards him. 'Follow me, as you did at the Triton fortress, and I promise we will survive this.'

The men looked resigned. There was no outrage. These men were broken, living moment to moment. None had the energy to challenge his leadership.

'What's going on?' Scott asked, having just entered the tomb, oblivious to the latest turn of events. 'We've got some treasure here.'

Cade stepped forwards, and the legionaries parted to reveal Scott festooned with gold. It was rudimentary in design, a pile of torques, amulets, rings and brooches. Boudicca, Queen of the Iceni, had been buried well.

Scott clinked his way forwards and gave a little twirl, breaking the tension of the cavern. He even elicited smiles as he curtsied to Amber.

Behind him, Quintus carried a large staff topped with a trumpet, a horn Cade knew to be a carynx. It was gold too, and again Cade marvelled at the dedication of these leaders' followers to leave them with so much wealth. That, and a healthy appreciation for the afterlife.

'Right,' Cade said, motioning to his men to follow. 'Amber and Quintus, dump all of that in Genghis's tomb and move on to Attila's. Scott, you search Atahuallpa's. I'll do Alexander's.'

'What's going on, Cade?' Amber said as the others rushed off. 'Why are we piling it there? We need to negotiate with Abaddon soon.'

Cade winced and turned on his heel. 'He came to me already,' he said. 'Before Atticus attacked. He'll transport us all back, alive, in exchange for all the treasure here.'

Amber's face fell. 'That's it?' she asked. 'We did this for nothing?'

Cade paused. He knew her feelings about the bomb. Knew in another life, where he had never met Song, he might have negotiated for something different.

Amber stared at him, seeing his hesitation, her expression darkening.

'What did you do, Cade?' she asked, her voice a low whisper.

'I . . .'

A rumble of shifting rock from the stairs turned their heads. Voices called from beyond the rubble, and Cade could see the orange glow of torches. It looked like the slavers had found light.

'Hurry,' Cade said. 'We're almost out of time.'

FIFTY-ONE

Cade ran into Alexander's tomb, his three legionaries close behind, and took in the sight of the strange place in a few hurried glances.

This tomb had also been buried in Egypt. Alexandria, to be exact, named for and founded by the very man whose grave he was about to rob.

Still, the room was distinctly different from what Cade had expected, for it was a mess of conflicting cultures. The floors were covered in mosaics, rich in colour despite the dust that coated them. Here, a curly-haired man riding a horse was depicted, spear raised in defiance. Stranger still were the men he charged at: bearded soldiers riding chariots, and behind them, elephants.

These were the Persians and Indians whom Alexander had conquered, and Cade took some small pride in his heritage, knowing that it was in India that Alexander's rampage across the world had finally been halted.

As in Imhotep's tomb, the walls here were decorated

in two-dimensional figures, but here the figures had hawks for heads, and hieroglyphics surrounded them. Clearly, Alexander's tomb had begun its life as an Egyptian temple.

In the room's very centre lay a pale, smooth marble coffin, complete with engravings of Greek lettering.

And behind it, a naked man, youthful, contorted in an almost erotic pose, stood in white stone. It was a statue of the great man himself.

There was little in the way of treasure here. Cade knew that Alexander's tomb had been a place of worship for many years, visited by pilgrims and tourists alike. Anything of value would have been long gone.

Still, few would have had the audacity to open the coffin itself, and Cade motioned with his hands for his men to remove its top.

The coffin lid crashed to the ground, and Cade lunged forwards to see inside.

To Cade's surprise, there was not one but two bodies within. One was covered with time-eroded rags and seemed to stare back at him through hollow sockets.

The other, fresher body was adorned with clothes intact, and so fresh that the remains of a bushy white beard could still be seen, even if the head was a half-mummified mess of skin and bone.

'What the hell is this . . .' Cade breathed.

Abaddon had left him a surprise. Or at least, for whoever stumbled across this place. A further reward for the seeker's curiosity.

The man's clothing was formal. It almost looked like a

tuxedo, with an upturned collar, gloves, even a top hat.

'Codex,' Cade breathed. 'Who is this?'

'*Remnant is William Cantelo, a gun inventor who disappeared in 1880. He claimed to have invented the first machine gun, and went missing along with his prototype from his home in Southampton, England. Four years later, Hiram Maxim invented the Maxim gun, and made a fortune from the patent during the First World War. So similar were the two men in appearance, some believed he and William Cantelo were the same man.*'

Cade stared at the body beneath him, and his eyes slowly drifted up to the shadows behind the coffin. There, at the feet of the statue, was a large black box.

'Jackpot,' Cade whispered.

Behind him, he heard a yell. Then another, and the clash of metal upon metal.

'Grab that,' Cade ordered, pointing at the box. He was already moving before the Codex began its translation, racing back to Imhotep's chamber.

He took in the scene at a glance.

Legionaries surrounded a hole in the stairwell's rubble, their shields shoving against a tide of metal-clad men. Mailed hands and shoulders shoved to get in, pushing through a gap hardly large enough for a man to fit. Gladiuses clattered against the steel armour, and Cade saw one snap at the base, its rusted blade spinning away as the desperate legionary hammered down with the hilted stump.

'Get back!' Cade yelled, shoving a legionary aside. A helmeted head pushed through the rubble, and in the slit at its front Cade saw raging eyes.

He raised the gun, pressed it close . . . and fired.

The shot rang out like a thunderclap, knocking the man back with its force and near jarring the gun from Cade's hands. The body hung limp in the entrance, blocking it, while legionaries spun away at the noise, covering their ears with their hands.

Cade's own eardrums ached from the sound, and he could hardly hear himself as he screamed at the slavers a single word, over and over.

'*Tractate!*' he cried. '*Tractate!*'

Negotiate.

FIFTY-TWO

The body withdrew slowly, pulled back inch by inch. Behind the rubble, men grunted and cursed, clearly packed into the stairwell like sardines. Soon enough though, it was gone, and as Cade peered through, he saw that the slavers had retreated halfway up the stairwell.

Cade's wrist ached where the recoil had almost fractured it, and he sheathed his blade, taking it in two hands. He felt sick as he saw the pool of blood at his feet, congealing in the dust.

Another life he'd taken.

'Hello?' Cade called. 'Are you there?'

More cursing followed, then a voice called from the other side.

'You wish to surrender?' a man asked.

His voice was fuzzy in Cade's ears, and he shook his head, trying to focus. In the small, echoey chamber, the sound of the gun had almost made his ears bleed. The Codex's translation was not helping matters, for it blasted it out at a near-deafening volume.

'No surrender,' Cade called. 'A trade.'

Silence. Then:

'If you wish to trade, then your gun has not the bullets to kill all of us,' the voice said.

'It does,' Cade allowed. 'But I'd rather not waste them on your worthless lives.'

'We'll see,' the voice called back. 'We've faced men with guns before, and won. Soldiers from your Great War commanded high prices in the slave market. Not as much as you will though – even with your tongue ripped out.'

Cade grimaced and turned his head.

By now, all the legionaries had gathered, and Cade could see Amber hauling a sackful of what must have been treasure into Genghis's chamber. Scott, on the other hand, was empty-handed.

'So tell me of your trade,' the man called, impatient. 'Treasure? Remnants?'

Cade bit his lip, considering his next words. His head was swimming, exhaustion catching up to him.

'Would you consider a remnant?' Cade asked. 'I know Caesarion has quite a collection. He would pay a high price for the one I have in my possession.'

The man laughed. 'We will take it from you after we're done,' he said. 'That, and any treasures this tomb might contain. Fool child. There is nothing you could offer that we cannot have regardless.'

Cade smiled. The slaver had played right into his hands.

'Oh, but there is,' Cade said, speaking loudly for all to hear. 'I have in my possession something Caesarion would give half his kingdom for. And let me tell you, if he hears you had the chance to get it and didn't, it's not just your tongue he would rip out.'

The slaver was not so quick to retort now, and his silence stretched out. Cade took the opportunity to turn, and saw Amber and Scott had returned.

'Pick that up,' Cade said, pointing at the black box the legionaries had left beside Alexander's tomb. 'Quickly.'

He waited for them to do so, then whispered, 'Abaddon.'

There was no response, and Cade tried again.

'Abaddon, we're ready. Take us to the keep.'

The Codex hovered closer, and Cade heard the little girl's sardonic voice in his ear.

'*Every. Last. Piece.*'

Cade's eyes widened. 'We've missed something,' he gasped. 'Quintus, hold the box, and do not take your hands off it. Amber, Scott, there's something else here somewhere!'

They moved with speed, even as the slaver ventured a reply.

'What is it, then? And why can we not take it from you?'

Cade spoke with as much confidence as he could. 'This remnant has been drying out for millennia. One spark and it'll burn up. And don't think I won't do it if you attack us. It's worthless to me, and worth everything to the emperor.'

The slaver muttered under his breath. Then:

'The lies of a desperate man. What chances are there

that you would have such a thing in the very moment you need it most?'

'It's the whole reason why we came here,' Cade said. 'Treasure means nothing to us. We need weapons, food, clothing. We came here because we knew that Caesarion would give us anything for it.'

'More lies,' the slaver drawled. But Cade could sense the curiosity in his voice. And the doubt.

Cade did not reply. He was buying time. Every second he wasted was another that Amber and Scott had to find the missing trinket. Some coin that had rolled into a corner. A dull gem, fallen from its setting. Even the jewels on the coffins might count.

He could see Amber and Scott returning from Boudicca's tomb, an elaborate sword belt in tow, though one without precious metal.

'Abaddon, take us as soon as you have what you need,' Cade hissed.

'What was that?' the slaver called out. 'I lose patience. The beasts that call this place home will be returning soon. We'd rather not be here to watch them feast on you.'

Cade gritted his teeth, hearing the increasing rattle of metal as the men behind grew restless. He had hoped that he would not have to give them what they wanted. Especially since there was no guarantee they wouldn't attack anyway.

'Do you know who Caesarion is?' Cade asked.

The rattle of metal slowed.

'Yes,' the slaver replied simply.

'Who is his father?' Cade asked.

'Julius Caesar.'

The reply came quickly, and Cade was glad of it.

'And . . . his *mother*?' Cade asked. 'His *Egyptian* mother.'

There was a sharp intake of breath. 'Cleopatra,' the slaver said, intoning each syllable slowly.

Cade allowed himself a smile.

'Damn right,' he said.

FIFTY-THREE

The slaver was silent.

'We came for her body,' Cade pressed. 'She's buried here with Mark Anthony. Her son – your emperor – loved her with all his heart. He may not care much for history, but he does care about *his* history. So tell me, what would he do if he found out you let us burn his long-lost mother's body?'

Behind him, Cade could hear the frantic patter of feet and the frustrated cries of Amber and Scott as they roamed from room to room, searching frantically.

'Say I believe you,' the slaver called. 'Say you do have it. What do you propose we do? And how do we prove it is Cleopatra to Caesarion?'

Cade had not thought that far ahead. The exchange was practically a hostage situation now.

'Jens, we need to hurry,' a low voice muttered in another language, a Viking language of some kind, but the Codex translated it in Cade's ears regardless, and that gave Cade an idea.

'We have a machine from the gods. It can tell you anything about Earth. Caesarion has one just like it. He uses it to communicate with the gods, as we do.'

There was silence once more.

'Show us!' Jens called.

'Codex, scan Cleopatra's body and then reveal yourself to the slavers and give your answer,' Cade instructed loudly.

There was a flash of blue and a rush of air as the Codex whipped past Cade's head, and then a gasp as the Codex revealed itself.

'Remnant is Cleopatra, last queen of the Ptolemaic Dynasty in Egypt. She was embalmed and entombed with her lover, Mark Anthony, in 30 BC.'

'It can't lie,' Cade said as the slavers erupted into discussion. 'Ask it to inspect any remnant. It'll tell you exactly what it is.'

'It . . . Caesarion has one of these?' Jens asked.

'Yes,' Cade said. 'And he'll use it when he's alone with the body. There's all the proof you need.'

'Oracle, tell me what this object is,' Jens said.

Cade could not see what he had offered up, but the Codex soon gave him his answer.

'Remnant is the first ever bowie knife, developed by famed knife fighter James Bowie in 1830. The design was later popularised for use by soldiers and hunters and still survives in the modern day. The knife was lost by James Bowie in the Battle of the Alamo in 1836 and was never seen again.'

Jens took a sharp breath at the Codex's words.

'Give her body to me,' he ordered. 'You have a deal.'

Cade hesitated. 'Retreat your men up the stairs,' he said. 'Keep a few with you down here. Then we'll know you're serious.'

Jens laughed aloud. 'I could just bring them back down after. Or ambush you on your way out.'

'Do it,' Cade said. 'Or I burn the body.'

Jens muttered under his breath, but barked out orders to his men.

'You five, with me. The rest of you, return to the entrance.'

Cade listened as the Codex translated, and the stomp of nailed boots receded. Still, Amber and Scott continued their search, shouting at each other in anger.

What could they have overlooked?

'Abaddon,' Cade whispered. 'What's left?'

The little girl's voice giggled in his ear. 'What, and miss all the fun? Not likely, my child.'

Cade felt a bead of sweat trickle down his back, despite the cool confines of the chamber.

'Hurry,' Jens snapped. 'Pass her through.'

Cade racked his brains for a way to further delay, but nothing came to him. The slaver's patience would be wearing thin by now, and there was the chance that Jens wouldn't keep his end of the bargain.

'Pass through the body,' Cade instructed.

Legionaries rushed to the corpse's side, passing forwards the cloth-wrapped figure. It was almost childlike in its size, and Cade caught a glimpse of mailed hands cupping the ancient queen's head, before her body withdrew through the hole and disappeared into the darkness.

Cade waited, the gun's grip slippery in his hand. Jens would summon his men back if he intended to betray Cade. That, or attempt to breach the hole with the element of surprise after pretending to leave.

Cade could only hope that he attempted an ambush outside. That was what he would do in Jens's shoes. If he was a sadistic madman, that was.

Time seemed to stretch as Jens remained silent. Cade heard only the ripping of cloth as the slaver inspected the body.

'Oracle,' Jens said. 'What remnant is this?'

The Codex remained silent, but Cade repeated Jens's question under his breath. The answer came again, repeating what it had said to Cade earlier. Before it had finished, Cade heard the clatter of metal as the slavers began to move.

FIFTY-FOUR

Cade heard the screams moments later.

At first, they were words, instructions too garbled to hear through the mess of voices, intermingling through the echoing tomb.

But soon they turned into nonsensical, drawn-out screeches of fear. Men's cries came in chorus, and Jens's voice called up in confusion.

'They're back,' Cade whispered in horror. 'The beasts are back.' He looked at the hole, his mind racing. 'Block it up, quickly!' he called.

Even as the legionaries moved, he heard the sound of slavers running above. And screams. Screams of terror, some long, others cut short in an instant. No gurgles, no cries of pain. Just gone.

These were no raptors. It was far too quick for that.

'Come on!' Cade yelled.

They shoved Imhotep's tomb, inch by inch, closer to the blocked stairwell. The lid came ahead, leaned against the hole, just as Cade glimpsed the sight of mailed feet skidding down the stairs.

There was the thud of a mailed fist upon the stone, then a frantic *crack, crack, crack* of metal on rock as the man turned his axe on the thin barrier. Already fissures were forming, but Cade was shoved aside as men rammed the coffin over the top, sealing the men out.

'Let us in!' Jens's voice called, this time in Latin. 'We'll leave our weapons! There are Jörmungandar here!'

The Codex translated into Cade's ear, but he ignored the plea. Jens had sealed his own fate.

'Amber, Scott, any luck?' Cade bellowed.

'No!' Amber's voice drifted back, this time from Boudicca's tomb. 'We've started carrying the furniture through.'

Cade turned to the legionaries, who were standing in a semicircle, staring at the stairwell. The sound of axe blows had stopped, and Cade imagined Jens was hiding in the darkness.

'Go back to the tombs,' Cade ordered. 'Find any treasure you've overlooked. I want every stone, every fancy piece of furniture. Everything! Bring it to that chamber, and the gods will transport us back to the keep.'

The men moved with speed, leaving Quintus struggling to hold the box that had belonged to William Cantelo.

For a moment, Cade was tempted to set up the machine gun, but they could be teleported away at any moment, leaving the precious remnant behind. 'Come on, come on,' Cade whispered under his breath. Despite the silence beyond the rubble, he could see the sarcophagus lid shifting back and forth. Then, a gauntleted hand worming through the gap, bracing against the stone floor as whoever was on the other side heaved with his shoulder.

But it was no use – the sarcophagus itself was holding the lid in place, and it had taken nearly ten men to scrape it into position.

Then . . . he heard it. Almost felt it, so great was the thud above. Dust filtered down from the ceiling. At first, Cade thought a statue had fallen, until he heard the scrape of claws, rasping along the stone.

He could only hope the ceiling could bear the weight as another thud shook more dust free.

The hand grew more frantic, and now Cade saw the sweaty forehead of a man press through the gap. And then, Jens's face, contorted in a rictus of terror and pain, appeared as he scraped his nose bloody pushing his head through the gap.

Behind him, a man screamed. Then another, and the very ceiling seemed to shudder as the predators above moved onto the central platform.

Jens pushed further, but his breastplate would not budge. His face strained red as he scrabbled at his neck, trying to force the lid back a little more.

'Help,' he choked.

Then he was yanked away, his neck bones crackling as an extreme force pulled him awkwardly through the small gap.

Cade covered his mouth, horrified. Behind him, all was silent, the legionaries smart enough to keep their mouths shut. A pair strained with a heavy, ornate coffin, then shuffled on, crab-walking their way towards Genghis's tomb.

Cade crouched beside the narrow gap, his gun ready in his hand. He heard the crunch of teeth against metal. Heard it crumple like tinfoil.

And then, a snort. One that blew the dust through the gap. A snout, heavy and thick, nosed at the entrance. It was armoured with dark, horny scales and had two massive nostrils flared like a horse's.

A long, wet tongue flopped from the mouth, lapping at the pool of blood from the slaver Cade had shot. Cade held up his gun, the heavy weight trembling in his hands.

The creature was far larger than anything he had expected to see. It was like a raptor, scaled up to twice its size.

Another snort sprayed blood across Cade's feet, and he shuddered. Outside, he could hear more outsized thuds as the beasts roamed the floor above them.

Cade knew there would be plenty of dead men on the other side of the rubble. But there was no sound of crunching metal. Or feeding. This attack was not due to hunger.

This was their territory. And Cade and his friends had trespassed.

The lid of the coffin shifted as the beast pressed its muzzle into the gap once more. Cade knew it could smell him, smell the fear permeating the room like a cold mist.

Slowly Cade backed away. Turned, only to see Scott and Amber motioning at him with their hands. Their meaning was clear. There was nothing left to find.

Cade shut his eyes, even as there was the scrape of stone on stone. The snout pressed forwards another inch, and now

Cade could see the teeth, jutting over drawn lips. Massive yellow fangs, long as butchers' knives.

It was a theropod all right. What Cade called a carnosaur.

Cade gestured with his arm, sweeping the others into the confines of Genghis's tomb. They moved, reluctantly at first, but faster when Cade frantically waved his arms.

The legionaries retreated deep, but Amber, Quintus and Scott remained at the entrance, watching. Cade motioned for them to close the door, but they refused obstinately, rather closing it halfway so they could still see him.

It was as good as Cade was going to get, and now he saw the beady orange eye of the carnosaur, its pupil contracting in the new light of the room, where a crackling torch had been abandoned by the legionaries on the ground.

'Abaddon,' Cade hissed.

The carnosaur let out a choked breath, scrabbling forwards at the sight and sound of Cade. The tomb scraped once again.

Only now did he see the horns on its head, sticking out like those of a bull. He knew what it was now. A *Carnotaurus*.

'Where is the missing treasure?' he demanded.

The little girl's voice tickled his ear, so quiet Cade barely heard it.

'Trade me,' she whispered. 'Remnants for information.'

'What do you want?' Cade asked, stepping deeper into the chamber as the beast's neck squeezed a few inches deeper.

'Cantelo's gun.'

Cade shook his head. He shouldn't be bargaining, he knew. But that gun would keep his friends safe if he failed to find the treasure. They could use it to fight their way out of the tomb.

'You don't want that,' Cade said as casually as he could. 'You've been dying to see that in action. First machine gun ever? What a waste.'

The Codex twitched in the air.

By now, the carnosaur had eased its arms through the gap, and it clawed at the ground for purchase as it pushed deeper into the chamber.

T. rex-like in its form, it was monstrous in size. So large, it was struggling to fit through the hole the slavers had dug. But with every wriggle, rubble tumbled and shifted, and it eased in an inch more.

Cade considered shooting the creature there and then. But he did not want to waste a bullet.

'Have my blade and my armour,' Cade said. 'Take the pistol too.'

'No deal,' Abaddon said, louder this time.

And with his words, the girl materialised, just in front of the *Carnotaurus*. She mimed patting it on its horned head, and the beast's movements became more frantic as it snapped at the diminutive hologram's hand.

'What else?' Cade demanded.

He lifted the gun, trembling. The beast became more agitated by his movement, its front claws scratching furrows into the stone.

'The next round,' the little girl replied, her voice raised to be heard over the snarling of the beast in front of her. 'We start it. Within minutes of your return to the keep.'

Cade froze, calculating the odds. But he couldn't think it through. What would it mean for his plan? There were too many unknowns.

'Are we attacking or defending?'

'Deal is on the table for ten seconds, Cade. That's the only countdown you're going to get. Hell, I might just start it immediately anyway.'

The dinosaur wriggled again, and Cade heard the rumble of rubble.

'Deal,' Cade snapped. 'Where is the missing treasure?'

'Atahuallpa's tomb.'

FIFTY-FIVE

Cade ran, snatching the torch up as he did so. He skirted around the snapping carnosaur, and his stomach twisted as he smelled the bloodied breath of the monster and its heavy, animal stench.

He rushed through the door to the Inca emperor's tomb and almost ran into a wall. There were no steps down; rather it seemed the emperor had been buried within a crack inside a cave.

The cave was barren of anything beyond a pile of stones, beneath which the emperor must have been buried. Certainly, the Spaniards who buried him had not left any riches there. Only hidden away the body, so none of his followers would find him.

Scott and his legionaries had uncovered his body, one that had not been embalmed as so many of the others had. It was a skeleton with rags of charred clothing on its body.

'Where?' Cade hissed under his breath.

Behind him, he heard more rockfall, and a keening screech

that set his teeth on edge. Not the roar he had been expecting, but somehow the unfamiliar sound was far more terrifying.

The cave was shallow, and even now Cade could see there was nothing but deadwood and animal bones surrounding the rocks.

Then something caught his eye as he turned his gaze back to the rock pile. It was the skeleton itself. What looked like a brown thread dangling from its neck.

Holding his torch close, Cade pulled on it, only to find it was a thin chain, one near-rusted through. And at its end, hanging between the man's ribs . . . was a small silver cross.

Perhaps Atahuallpa had worn it to convince the men of his Christianity. Perhaps some priest had taken pity on the forlorn body as he had given him his last rites. At that moment, Cade didn't care.

Cade snatched it and spun, racing back to the crack in the cave wall. And as he eased himself through the crack . . . he saw it. The *Carnotaurus*, shaking itself free of dust like a wet dog, its horns scraping the tomb's ceiling. It had come through, and he could see its shadowy figure in the gloom of the chamber.

Behind that, Cade could see another sniffing at the hole the predator had left, but by some luck, the rubble had partly blocked the entry point once more. It was already pushing its way in too.

But the carnosaur was not looking at Cade. It was following its nose. Sniffing, it seemed, in the direction of his friends. Cade's only solace was that their door was now closed.

He needed to get the cross to Genghis's tomb.

311

Past the *Carnotaurus*.

He had to use his gun. He should have used it earlier, while the beast was pinioned, fired the rest of the magazine into the beast's head.

And as he pushed his shoulders against the crack, Cade realised he still could. He flicked the safety off on the gun.

'Hey!' Cade yelled. 'Over here! Come on, you big brute!'

The dinosaur froze, cocking its head and turning slowly.

'That's right, over here!'

Cade waved the torch through the crack. The beast faced him now, snorting in excitement.

It took a step, then another, and another. Still Cade remained in the crack, waving his torch from side to side.

'Come on!' he bellowed.

On it came, closer and closer, its great steps echoing through the chamber. He held his nerve, holding the torch high to see the approaching figure growing ever brighter.

Only when it reached the door to Cade's own tomb did he leap back. It was not a moment too soon.

The great teeth snapped closed in front of him, and then the head was pushing through the crack as he fell away, worming and straining to get at him.

Eyes, bright orange and full of fury, blinked in the torchlight. The great maw opened and closed, taking small bites at the air in front of him, inching closer with every lunge.

Cade raised his gun, the weight unfamiliar in his hands. Shaking, he aimed as best he could. And pulled the trigger.

There was a click. Barely audible over the *Carnotaurus*'s slavering breaths.

Cade pulled the trigger again, but still, nothing.

'No,' Cade whispered, scrambling back as the beast rammed itself forwards once more, crumbling the entrance's edges as earth and rock came away under its onslaught.

The gun's magazine had capacity for ten bullets. But it had only held one.

Cade was trapped.

'Shit,' Cade whispered in horror. 'Shit. Shit!'

Excited by the noise, the beast lunged forwards again, its entire upper chest breaching the cave.

Cade hurled the gun at the beast as it snapped at him. It swallowed it whole, the black pistol disappearing into its gullet as if it were an apple core.

With no other option, Cade drew his blade. In seconds, he would be trapped in a small space with a ravenous monster. He had to kill it. Now.

He whipped his sword forwards, slashing at the beast's snout. His blade cut shallow, jarring against bone and eliciting a screech of pain. The skin of the beast was crocodilian, almost like armoured scales.

Cade pulled the blade free, chopping down again and again, casting blood in scarlet slashes across his face, clothing, and the cave walls.

But his efforts only renewed the beast's own. It did not pull away, rather rammed itself towards the blade, chomping at it as if it were a stinging insect.

Cade had to back away, stumbling deeper into the cave, until just the beast's wide hindquarters remained trapped in the cave's narrow entrance.

He had to change tack, and drew the blade back, feeling cruel as he stabbed at its eyes. Once, twice, three times he managed to spear it there, and the creature roared in agony, jerking itself away before he could push the blade into its brain.

By now, he had chopped the *Carnotaurus*'s head into a bloody mess of furrows, yet he was no closer to escape. Blinded opponent or not, he had no way out. And if he didn't move quickly, there would be another predator in the chamber beyond.

The blade would never penetrate into the brain. So Cade rammed the blade deep into the monster's maw, up into the roof of its mouth.

The monster chomped down and screeched as this move drove the blade deeper, catching on bone, preventing it from closing its mouth.

As the blind animal yawped in pain and fury, Cade did the only thing he could do. He leaped onto the beast's neck, using its horns to throw himself forwards.

The beast bucked like a bronco, but its horns allowed him to cling on and scrabble forwards, his chest scraping painfully over the bony spines along its back, even as he used them as handholds beneath the shuddering monster.

There was space between its body and the top of the cave entrance, and Cade lunged for it, sliding down its back and collapsing to the ground. The tail, long and thick, whipped back and forth like an anaconda.

It caught him along his thighs as he dived beyond its range, throwing him to the side. It was like being hit with a baseball bat.

Hissing with agony, Cade struggled to his feet, limping towards Genghis's tomb. And there, standing between him and the door . . . was another *Carnotaurus*.

It was smaller than the last one, with shorter horns; its smaller size had allowed it to more easily wriggle through the gap.

Now, it sniffed, its exhalations misting the air. Its muzzle was red with blood – it had already killed that day.

'Amber,' Cade called. 'Open the door!'

The dinosaur snapped its head towards him, and Cade gripped the cross so hard in his palm it almost cut the skin.

Beyond, the door swung open, creaking quietly. Amber's eyes widened as her face peered around the door's edge. The *Carnotaurus* in front of her did not notice the movement.

'I have a crucifix in my hand,' Cade called. 'I will throw it to you. Get it in the tomb as soon as possible.'

The door opened a little wider, and Cade jabbed the torch at the beast's face.

The dinosaur lunged just as Cade hurled the cross between its legs. Then he was running.

He turned into Alexander's tomb, leaping down the stairs and tripping as he landed. He felt the hot breath of the beast as its jaws snapped behind him, and hurled the torch in its direction.

He rolled, and an enormous head smashed into the floor beside him, mosaics showering the air. He dived deeper, this time scrambling behind the coffin, between the statue's legs.

It was not a moment too soon, as the monster's head slammed the emperor's legs. Cade crawled further into the tomb, even as he heard the snap of breaking stone.

He saw the statue topple, falling towards him. Then . . . darkness.

FIFTY-SIX

'Are we dead?' Scott asked aloud.

Cade listened to the rushing water as his eyes adjusted to the gloom where he lay.

He sat up, taking in the baths of the keep. All of them were there, including Quintus, who let Cantelo's box fall with a thud and a relieved sigh.

He was not as relieved as Cade, though. Yet with that relief came a fresh wave of panic. For the darkness was suddenly lit with blue light, and Cade spotted the timer.

00:14:55
00:14:54
00:14:53

'Codex,' Cade croaked. 'Is that the timer started for the next round?'

'*Yes*,' the Codex replied.

'What are the rules?' Cade asked.

'*Survive for an hour while remaining within a thousand feet of the keep.*'

'Come on,' Cade said, struggling to his feet. 'We've got fifteen minutes before the next round starts.'

'What did we buy, Cade?' Amber asked. 'What was all that for?'

Cade didn't have the heart to reply to her, though he was also wondering where the plane was . . . and his remote controller.

'Cade!' Amber shouted as he stumbled up the stairs.

He ignored her once more, knowing they were running out of time, and reached the atrium above. It was empty.

He was starting to panic, to worry something had happened, until a young soldier stumbled from the barracks corridor, rubbing sleep from his eyes.

'Where's Marius?' Cade demanded in broken Latin.

The boy pointed a finger in the direction of outside, and Cade hurried through the doors to the courtyard. Almost all the legionaries were milling about, their attention seemingly split between two things.

One was the plane that had apparently just appeared upon the cobblestones, resting awkwardly on one wing, the nuclear bomb still attached to its base.

The other was upon the walls. Or rather, beyond them.

Now he saw Marius on the ramparts, staring into the bone fields with his advisers close by. Cade wasted no time examining his prize, instead rushing for the stairs, ignoring the cry of outrage from Amber as she saw the plane.

He reached the man in a matter of seconds, waving aside

the onrush of surprised voices and faces.

'Cade,' Marius said, a shocked look upon his face. 'Our watchmen did not see your arrival. What—'

'We've got about ten minutes before we're attacked,' Cade cut in. 'We have to . . .'

He trailed off, staring into the bone fields, where a terrible sight awaited him.

The blue forcefield. Just like the one there had been when Cade had to fight the alpha. And beyond that . . . were insects.

Hundreds of them, identical in appearance, size and shape. They seemed to be like ants, humanoid, and standing upright.

From this distance, it was hard to see much more, but Cade wasted no time in summoning the leaderboard to get a closer look.

He saw humanity's own location on the board, now second from the top following their victory over the Greys.

But to his surprise, it did not appear that they were being attacked from below. Rather, they were being attacked by the very top. An ant-like carapace, complete with antennae and mandibles, was flashing, with a red arrow pointing down towards their own spot, represented by a human skull.

'What is this?' Cade demanded. 'Why are we being attacked from the top?'

The little girl's voice emerged from the Codex.

'Why, a little lesson,' Abaddon said. 'You traded poorly, Cade. Your bomb is no use here.'

Cade cursed under his breath. 'But why attack us?' he demanded. 'They'll stay in the same spot even if they win.'

319

'Your bomb, rather than protecting you, has precipitated this attack,' Abaddon replied with surprising viciousness. 'Should you have attacked them, you would have easily destroyed their hive and moved to the top. But if they attack preemptively . . .'

'Then we can't use our bomb,' Cade muttered, understanding dawning on him in a black wave of despair. 'We'd blow ourselves up.'

Marius cursed.

Only now did Cade see the rest of the original contenders had joined him, except for Quintus, who was dragging Cantelo's box out of the keep.

As they digested the Codex's words, they stared at him in horror and disappointment. And as he looked at them, awash with his own shock at the revelation, their disappointment turned to outrage.

'Cade . . . you didn't,' Amber whispered.

Her face was full of pain and betrayal, and as he looked her in the eye, she turned her face away.

He was suddenly intimately aware of his pack. And the Grey alien toy inside it. One press, and he could end this whole farce. Tell them *why* he had done what he'd done.

But he couldn't. Not with an enormous army ready to invade. Not when it was the very technology he was about to disable that held them at bay.

'It's your job to make the rounds fair,' Cade growled at Abaddon. 'We've got fewer than a hundred men. There's at least five times that number out there.'

The girl's voice giggled. 'I have agreed to open and close

the forcefield once, in half an hour. Two waves, the second larger than the first. That sounds fair to me, Cade.'

Now Cade knew he could not trigger the EMP, even if he wanted to. They'd all attack at once.

'Hey, don't look so glum,' Abaddon said. 'If you win, you'll switch places with them. You get to go home. All of you.'

Cade gritted his teeth and looked at the timer.

00:09:26
00:09:25
00:09:24

'Marius, we have to survive an hour. Is there somewhere we can survive that long without fighting them?'

Marius thumped the wall. 'We'll hold them at the wall,' he said. 'They've no weapons that I can see, only their mandibles.'

Cade rubbed his eyes. 'Ants can lift at least ten times their body weight, and they have a hardened carapace. Some have venomous stingers, some shoot acid. We don't know how similar these aliens are to ants, but they're at the top of the leaderboard for a reason.'

Marius growled but nodded his head. 'We hold the first wave at the wall, test their strength. Then, if we struggle to hold them in the first wave, we fall back to the keep, try to blockade the windows and door. Lastly, we retreat to the baths.'

Cade nodded. It was the same plan that he had followed when they had fought the vipers all that time ago.

'Men, defend the walls!' Marius bellowed to his legionaries, the Codex translating for the benefit of the others. 'Prepare for attack!'

They had no other choice, Cade knew. They could not hide out in the jungles, nor did the fields of stumps within the area present a strategic advantage, nor did the waterfall, or the orchards above.

But the tunnel. That perfectly round, narrow tunnel, bored through the mountain like a straw . . . that did present one advantage.

'We've got less than ten minutes to get that machine gun to work,' Cade said.

His friends stared at him.

'Aren't you going to address the fact that we're being attacked because of a choice you made without us?' Grace demanded.

'We can discuss it later,' Cade said.

'No,' Amber said. 'That's what you said last time, and now look what's happened. We're going to discuss it *now*.'

Cade stopped dead, even as legionaries rushed around him, arms full of javelins and heavy rocks.

'I did what I had to,' he said.

'I heard you,' Amber said. 'You sent us away, but I heard you negotiating with him.'

'That was to find out where the last trinket was,' Cade said. 'And I sent you away because we didn't all need to be out there risking our lives to find it.'

'You sent us away so we wouldn't have a chance to stop you,' Scott snapped.

322

His friend's face was a rictus of grief, and Cade had no words to defend himself.

'You've killed us, Cade,' Scott gasped, his face contorting as he tried to hold back his tears.

'Power went to your head,' Grace said. 'Did it make you feel good, playing god with our lives? You're no better than Abaddon. He's rubbed off on you.'

Cade blinked back tears and straightened his back. He had to get through this. If they survived . . . he would let them know why. For now, he would endure their hatred.

Only Quintus looked at him without fury in his eyes. But then, the Codex had no lips for the young legionary to read.

'They're attacking because of me,' Cade said to his best friend. 'I bought the bomb. They're attacking us so we can't use it against them.'

Quintus shook his head and clasped Cade's shoulder.

'If we win this,' Quintus whispered, 'it's over. We all go home.'

'We didn't ask for this,' Yoshi said. 'You've jeopardised more than our lives. Our planet is at stake. Our friends, our families. Our species.'

Cade lifted his chin and turned away. 'We have Cantelo's gun,' he said. 'Quintus, come with me. And anyone else who still believes in me.'

He pushed past his friends down the steps, where Quintus had brought the box. It was made of aged leather, and Cade knelt beside it to undo the straps that held it closed.

Only Quintus followed him.

Not even Amber left the ramparts, her back to him as

she wiped tears from her eyes. He did not know if it was their rejection or the pain he had caused them that hurt him the most.

FIFTY-SEVEN

Cade glanced at the timer, pushing his despair from his thoughts. He had a job to do.

00:06:12
00:06:11
00:06:10

The box lid eased open. Inside sat an ugly tube of black metal, alongside a large tripod and two metal boxes.

'Help me,' Cade said as he struggled to lift the heavy tripod, which unfolded creakily with a reluctant screech. There was a red dusting at the hinges, and Cade groaned at the sight.

He was about to pin the future of humanity on a rusted old prototype, one that had never been proven to work.

With the tripod set up, Cade and Quintus lifted out the gun. It was surprisingly basic, a cylinder with a barrel protruding from one end and a square block on the other. At the base of the cylinder were two openings, where Cade imagined the bullets were inserted and the casings were jettisoned out. The only other detail was a button at the back, likely the trigger.

It was a simple thing, and Cade was glad of it. Anything more complex and they would need far more than the five minutes they had remaining to work out how it worked.

He borrowed Quintus's gladius and levered open the top of one of the metal boxes, and was relieved to find bullets there, each connected in a long belt.

With quick calculation, he unspooled the belt, guessing there were two hundred rounds.

He'd learned from his mistake with the pistol, so he checked the other box and found an identical belt within. Four hundred bullets would wipe out most of the ant army.

'This could work,' Cade whispered.

'What could?' Quintus asked.

'This gun is like the pistol, but it will fire . . . well, I don't know how fast, but a lot of bullets. Our only problem is accuracy. Pointless firing four hundred shots if you only hit forty.'

Quintus pondered Cade's problem, but Cade already had an answer.

'The tunnel. They'll be funnelled right down the middle,' Cade said. 'We might even hit two with each bullet.'

Quintus grinned and nodded, but his eyes widened as he looked at the timer.

00:04:37
00:04:36
00:04:35

'Marius!' Cade called.

The man came quickly, having watched their activities from the walls even as he was giving orders. He came down with hopeful eyes.

'A cannon?' he asked.

'A machine gun – remember when I told you about those?'

Marius's eyes widened. 'Place it on the walls,' he said. 'We'll thin their numbers.'

Cade shook his head. 'We only have four hundred shots. Most will miss from the walls, or almost anywhere else for that matter.'

Marius spat. 'What use is it, then?'

'If we set up the gun at the tunnel, they'll be like rats in a barrel.'

Marius furrowed his brows, confused by the idiom, but bit his lip. 'You want me to abandon the walls?' he asked.

Cade closed his eyes, considering the question. 'Survive the first wave,' he said. 'Then retreat down the tunnel before the second wave hits. We'll fight them there.'

Marius looked skeptically at the machine. 'Does it work?' he asked.

Cade held up a finger and carefully fed the end of the bullet belt into the gun until he felt it stop.

He leaned the gun back until it pointed towards the mountainside, above the heads of the milling Romans.

Breathing a prayer, he gave the button at the back a hard tap.

Crack.

The gun jolted slightly but remained in its seat on the tripod. Halfway up the mountain, a puff of dust erupted outward. Cade gulped, noting that it was a fair way off from where he had pointed the gun.

Marius nodded grimly. 'The second wave, then,' he growled. He patted a whistle upon a string around his neck. 'Or whenever I sound the retreat.'

The timer ticked on, and Cade picked up the gun and dangling belt, leaving Quintus to take the tripod and box of remaining ammunition.

Together, they staggered into the tunnel.

'If we live,' Quintus said, stopping for a rest. 'And we attack the . . . ants . . . we will go home?'

Cade groaned and set down the weapon.

'Yes, Quintus,' he said.

Quintus bit his lip and stared vacantly, and Cade saw tears on his cheeks in the ethereal light of the Codex's timer.

'Will you . . .' Quintus began, struggling to find the words. 'I . . . I don't belong in your world.'

Cade stepped close and embraced his friend, pulling him tight to his chest. Tears, hot and bittersweet, burned a trail down Quintus's dust-streaked face.

'You don't belong in this one either,' Cade said. 'And you did pretty well here. You'll just come stay with me, OK?'

Quintus pulled away, a smile upon his face.

'My mum would love you,' Cade said. 'She'd pinch your

cheek and say you need fattening up.'

Quintus laughed and embraced Cade once more.

Cade could imagine it now. Quintus, eating dal and pakoras with his family for dinner. Watching his first movie. Playing his first video game.

But it was all a lie. Should he survive the next hour, and there was time to set off the EMP, he would condemn his friends to this world forever. Even now, he was betraying his friend's trust.

Quintus, who had stuck with him through it all. Who had saved his life more times than he could remember.

'Come on,' Cade whispered, releasing Quintus. 'Let's get this where it needs to go.'

FIFTY-EIGHT

Cade made it to the ramparts just in time, the timer ticking ever closer to the first release of ants.

00:00:56
00:00:55
00:00:54

All along the walls Romans bristled, javelins, slings and piled rocks at the ready. And in the heat of the moment, Cade realised he didn't have a sword. He had left his own in the mouth of a dinosaur, miles away.

'Thought you could use this,' came a voice to his left.

Scott gave him a half-smile, and passed Cade a blade. A Japanese sword. One of their spares.

'Thank you,' Cade whispered.

Scott shrugged.

'Not worth staying angry,' he said. 'We've got a chance to go home now.'

'And the others?' Cade asked.

'They'll come around.' Scott forced a smile. 'Just . . . you know. Make sure we all live through this.'

00:00:35
00:00:34
00:00:33

Cade looked down the rampart, where the contenders had gathered behind the Romans, their long blades poised above the legionaries' helmets.

Amber caught his eye, then turned away. Cade set his teeth and faced the enemy, blade sweaty in his palm. Behind, Quintus rattled up the stairs, having sloped off to put on some spare armour.

This was the unknown. There had been no time to prepare for this enemy. There was no knowledge of what they faced, for humans had never been high enough on the leaderboard to fight them.

What Cade did know was that this would be the greatest enemy they had ever met. Certainly their numbers dwarfed those of the vipers, all that time ago. But these insectile beings were not flesh and blood, but carapace and ichor. Would a blade, stuck through a thorax, stop them as it would a man?

00:00:10
00:00:09
00:00:08

'Get ready, men!' Marius screamed, mounting the ramparts and pointing a gladius down the field. 'One last battle. One more, and we're free of this cursed place!'

The legion roared and rattled their blades upon their shields. Cade felt a surge of pride. This was for humanity. And he was honoured to fight for it.

00:00:03
00:00:02
00:00:01

The forcefield disappeared, its blue glow washing away. Yet to Cade's surprise, the ants did not move. They continued milling about as if they had not been waiting for battle at all.

'Why aren't they attacking?' Scott whispered.

Cade leaned forwards, taking a closer look at the creatures now that the opaque forcefield no longer blocked his view.

They were strange things. Like red-black upright ants, true, but there was more to them than that. Their upper arms were like those of a crustacean, with two claws, one larger than the other. The carapaces were not dissimilar from a crab's either, with spines and jagged spikes covering their torsos.

As for their lower set of arms, these reminded him more of a mantis's, with two fingerlike appendages at the ends, clearly what they used to manipulate the world around them. That and the giant mandibles upon their heads, which emitted a stream of clicks and whistles, drifting across the fields towards them.

'What do we—' Scott began.

A new timer had appeared, counting down the hour.

00:59:59
00:59:58
00:59:57

At the same time, Cade felt a strange sprinkle of liquid, like a fine mist sprayed from above.

'What the hell is that?' Scott hissed.

'Pheromones,' Cade said, near gagging at the stench of it. 'To get them to attack.'

He cursed under his breath. Had he triggered the EMP, the ants might never have attacked at all. But it was too late to think about that now.

The ants seemed to turn as one, their antennae twitching. Mandibles chattered, the sound setting Cade's teeth on edge.

And then, as if by some hidden signal . . . they came.

The creatures were fast, swarming towards the keep in a wave of red-black bodies, running upright in a bowlegged sprint, their claws outstretched.

Yet as the frontrunners passed into the bone fields, the forcefield appeared again. One ant, caught halfway, was sliced in two, black ichor spurting as its momentum hurled its front half forwards.

'Hold!' Marius called as the first sling-stones were hurled towards the enemy. 'Hold!'

The stones pattered short, and the overeager men rushed to reload their slings. On the ants came, and now Cade could see the black pits of their insectile eyes. There were over a hundred in this first wave, more than one for every legionary.

Marius raised his arm.

'*Funditores!*' Slingers.

The stones whipped out, a hailstorm of stone bullets. There was a crackle as the projectiles hit home, ants thrown back or tumbling to the ground.

Men cheered at the sight. Yet even as they did so, ants returned to their feet. Their carapaces were cracked, and they followed slowly behind those that had not been hit, but they came on regardless. Few remained motionless on the ground.

'*Pila!*'

Now, the men pitched their javelins with all their might, a mass of dark poles whipping into the sky. They rose, rose, then tilted and fell, pattering like heavy rain on the oncoming horde.

Again, the sound of projectiles striking home, this time quieter than before. Yet to Cade's horror, few ants were knocked from their feet. Javelins glanced from their shells, or stuck and fell away, leaving shallow dents that seemed to hardly hurt at all.

'*Funditores iterum!*' Slingers, again.

More sling-stones buzzed across the field, but the ants were close now. Their insectile feet tripped and stumbled over the sharp spikes hidden in the ground, yet that was all they did – slow them.

As for the rows of stakes, their great pincers snapped them as easily as stalks of grass, mowing them aside before pushing through the stumps left behind.

Still the slingers worked, almost every soldier on the rampart. Only the old contenders did not take part, instead hurling spare javelins, though they did little good.

Now, the first ants reached the base of the wall, mandibles clattering as they looked up. But to Cade's horror, the beasts did not climb as he had expected. Instead, they began to pound at the walls, their crab-like claws scraping into the ancient concrete.

The first boulders were pushed from the ramparts, thudding into mud and ants in a deluge of rockfall. Marius bellowed at his men to hold back, but panic had set in to them, having seen the ineffectualness of their weapons.

Of the hundred or so ants that had crossed into the bone fields, only ten had fallen in their journey to the walls. Now, ants massed at the bottom, beating their mandibles and claws, corkscrewing them like drills as chips of mortar and stone dusted the bodies of those behind.

Rocks fell and fell again, punching great holes in the insectile mass beneath. These, it seemed, put the ants down for good, as prehensile limbs twitched and black ichor sprayed high at the impact.

And then, the second row of ants began to climb. They clambered over the diggers with ease, their claws finding purchase in the crumbling façade.

Men screamed, pushing the last of the boulders, the angle too tight to use their slings. By now, almost half the enemy's number was gone.

Beneath him, Cade saw the first opponent clamber just outside sword range, close enough for him to see the hexagons

335

of its eyes. It chattered its mandibles and scrambled towards him, pincers snapping.

Cade speared down, two handed, his blade slipping over the hard surface of its chitinous head and into a geometric eye. The beast froze, its claws deep in the wall. Then it plummeted to the ground.

'The eyes!' Cade yelled. 'Go for the eyes! *Oculi, oculi*!'

To his right, a legionary stabbed with his blade, only for the sword to be clasped within a pincer and yanked from his grip. He panicked, lashing out with a foot, and the ant took the man's boot in its mandibles, dangling its weight to pull him down. Cade swung his blade and cut it off at the head.

But it was too late, for as the ant fell away, the man teetered over the edge, Cade's snatched handful of cloth slipping from his fingers as the legionary tumbled to the ground.

Cade heard a single short scream before he disappeared into the mass of seething insects.

Another appeared beneath Cade, chattering its mandibles, a claw snapping in front of it in anticipation of his blade. But as Cade stabbed, the ground shifted beneath his feet, throwing his blow wide.

'Get off the wall!' Yoshi screamed.

The wall to Cade's right was swaying now, and Romans scrambled for the stairs, some leaping from halfway down the steps as the wall collapsed around them. The entire façade was buckling inward on itself, rocks falling loose from ancient mortar.

Many soldiers were not so lucky, and as Cade ran for it

himself, he saw men disappear into the mass of falling stone, tumbling down in an avalanche of rubble.

Cade jostled and pushed through a frantic mess of running soldiers, men who were retreating into the courtyard and forming a makeshift shield wall. With no shield, Cade hung at the back, his heart near-bursting with relief as his friends, one by one, came to join him.

The entire wall swayed before beginning the same slow collapse. Ants appeared on the ramparts, seemingly unaware of the swaying wall.

Then, in a sudden chain reaction, the wall collapsed in a great wave. Dust erupted in a haze, caustic in Cade's nose and mouth. Men dragged themselves, bloodied and broken, from the wreckage of the western wall, while the braver of the soldiers left the safety of the wall to gather the injured.

'Marius!' a man called in Latin. 'What do we do?'

FIFTY-NINE

Cade looked at the timer, feeling sick.

00:40:12
00:40:11
00:40:10

'We can't hold the keep.' Cade coughed, trying to clear the dust from his throat. 'They'll punch through it in minutes.'

'And a shield wall will be better?' Amber demanded.

Cade rubbed his gritty eyes, staring into the rubble.

A handful of ants crawled along its top, pincering their claws into dead and dying men. Beyond that, there didn't seem to be any ants alive at all.

'They killed themselves,' Cade whispered. 'The wall took them out completely.'

'Why would they do that?' Scott asked.

'Because they're a hive mind,' Cade said. 'They're not individuals. More like appendages of a greater intelligence.'

Marius bellowed with fury. He was screaming orders, pushing men into line. But as the pair of ants on the walls skewered a crawling man's back, he raised his sword.

'Retake the walls!' he bellowed.

The legionaries charged en masse, leaving Cade and his friends behind. They didn't need help anyway. The group of ants was soon swamped beneath a tumult of rising and falling swords.

'We've got ten minutes before the final wave hits,' Cade said. 'Less, actually.'

'Marius!' Cade called.

The commander turned, his face spattered with black ichor, and sanity seemed to descend upon him in a sudden shock.

'The tunnels,' Cade called. 'Hurry!'

He didn't wait to see if Marius would follow, nor even his friends. Instead, he sprinted to where he had laid the gun, his mind blanking as he tried to plan his next move.

The gun was where he had left it, ugly as sin, bathed in the light of the other end of the tunnel. It was a long tunnel, and he was out of breath when he emerged from its darkness on the other side.

Luckily, the Romans had placed torches at intervals along the borehole, though Cade had not stopped to light them. As he turned to sight the gun, careful not to place his finger on the trigger, he could see the torches being lit by the exhausted legionaries, each frantically striking their gladius with flint.

In this tunnel, seven men could stand abreast, though the soldiers at the outer edges would have to stand awkwardly on the curve. Marius had around seventy soldiers left, by

Cade's estimation. It was enough to make a shield wall that was ten men deep. In that, the ant numbers would stand for very little.

Marius arrived first, leading his men with hoarse shouts of encouragement. He leaned on his knees, panting, but asked the same question Cade had been pondering.

'What now?'

Cade considered his options. The ants would come fast, and he could not be sure at which range to shoot the gun. Too soon and he'd waste his ammunition. Too late and they'd overwhelm him before his clip was spent. He looked at the timer.

00:33:45
00:33:44
00:33:43

'We need a wall,' Cade whispered. 'A barrier to protect the gun.'

Marius lifted his head, looking at Cade as if he was mad.

'In three minutes?' he asked.

'They'll take some time to realise where we've gone. I'll make a shield wall for now. We can use the real wall you'll build for when they begin to overwhelm us. Something to fall back to.'

He *hoped* they had time for that. Marius looked doubtful, but Cade couldn't spare a moment to second-guess himself.

Instead, he pointed to the waterfall, some hundred feet away.

'Send half your men. Gather the boulders in the rock pool, dig up tree stumps if you have to, and create a semicircular barrier around the mouth of the cave. They'll be blinded by the light and surrounded.'

'And the rest?' Marius asked.

'Task them to follow me and Quintus. I'll fire into the tunnel.'

Marius nodded and gave the order.

'What can we do?' Scott asked.

The others were there. His friends . . . if he could still call them that. It was some relief to see that none were injured – it seemed the ants' sacrificial attack had meant there had been little hand-to-hand fighting so far.

'Can you help with the rocks?' Cade asked. 'You'll be no good in the shield wall.'

They did not look happy to take his orders, but moved to help the legionaries. Watching them go, Cade dragged the gun deeper into the cave. By now, he was exhausted.

But then, he *had* just been chased by two enormous dinosaurs less than an hour ago.

When the gun was finally in place and he had gone back for the ammunition, he was glad of the light of the timer, for the torchlight was dim. He counted down the seconds as the legionaries shuffled into position.

00:30:02
00:30:01
00:30:00

It was time. He could almost feel the forcefield on the other side of the tunnel descending. By his guess, some two hundred ants would be pouring into the tunnel, and there would be no rockfall to decimate them.

There were over thirty soldiers in the cave behind Cade, talking in panicked voices as Cade worked his futuristic magic.

Setting his teeth, Cade stared down the tunnel and set himself up at the machine gun. Peering down the corridor of perfectly smooth rock was like looking down the barrel of a gun, and Cade was tempted to fire a few shots to test the accuracy.

Instead, he waited. Better to do it when the ants were in the tunnel.

Cade centred the gun, balanced precariously on the tripod, and hoped he'd have the strength to hold it steady. As if his mind had been read, Quintus appeared at his side, crouching in front of the gun and letting Cade rest it upon his shoulder. Cade raised his shield and called out in a strong voice:

'*Testudo!*'

Cade did not turn, but he heard the clatter of men moving into position. The world darkened as a shield was lifted over his head, protecting him from who knew what. Men took their places on either side of him and Quintus, and Cade elbowed himself a little space so they would not jostle him.

Then . . . they waited.

SIXTY

Cade heard them first. That clicking sound, rattling down the tunnel like macabre maracas. Then the darkening of the tunnel mouth as figures criss-crossed in front of it.

Time ticked by, and with each second Cade rejoiced. There was a chance . . . a slim one, that they would not need to kill every ant to win. That the time would run out before the battle was over.

He didn't know what would happen then. If they would be immediately transported to Earth. If Abaddon would make a little speech before sending them on their way.

By Cade's estimation, he had to make a decision before the timer ran out, in case of immediate teleportation. And it *was* a decision; he didn't have to go through with Song's plan.

In the back of Cade's mind, he knew he could take the coward's way out. Go home. See his family again. Let some other poor souls pick up his mantle. Let humanity dance to Abaddon's tune until they could dance no more.

Perhaps they would dance forever.

He tried to tell himself it wasn't selfish. That he would save his friends. That he owed them it. And then Cade stopped agonising. Because the ants were coming again.

The tunnel seemed to shrink suddenly. And Cade saw the true horror of what they faced: the ants weren't just charging along the tunnel's bottom. They were on the walls, the roof. Crawling towards him in a great flood, blotting out the light beyond.

00:25:14
00:25:13
00:25:12

Quintus nudged Cade with his foot.

'Now,' he hissed.

'We need to wait,' Cade whispered. 'Make every shot count.'

Men whispered prayers around him, and the tunnel echoed the frantic chittering of the beasts approaching. As the swarm neared, each torch winked out, one by one, knocked to the ground by the mass of insectile monstrosities.

'Wait for it,' Cade whispered.

The noise grew thunderous, rattling around Cade's mind. He picked the nearest torch, some fifty feet away. Waited for it to blot out. And fired the gun.

A crash of gunfire erupted, strobing the dark tunnel with light. Dust and ichor plumed as black smoke belched from the gun throbbing in Cade's hand, half-obscuring his view.

Ants fell from ceilings and walls, trampled underfoot by the fearless horde. Insect bodies were hurled back, tangling and tripping the legs of those behind.

Yet still they came, for the winnowing of the swarm still left frontrunners, ants that had miraculously survived the hail of bullets. They crashed into the shield wall on either side of Cade. Men roared, both in fear and fury, as hand-to-hand combat began. Cade's only solace was that within the cone of accuracy directly in front of his gun, not a single ant survived.

Soon enough, there was a pile of insectile corpses choking the tunnel. But the ants swarmed over and around the mound as if it were no more than a feature of the landscape. They came on, and all the while the bullets spattered random death through the masses.

Then, just like that, the gun fell silent. Cade released the button and yanked the empty belt through the bottom of the gun. As he fumbled for the next belt, an ant dropped from the ceiling and slammed into Quintus's shield.

Cade tried. He really did. But the gun was heavy and his hands were slick with sweat. The space was too cramped and dark to see the gun teeter, and it fell from the tripod, landing on the ground with a clang. A death knell.

Ants poured forwards, the hail of gunfire no longer cutting down their numbers, and Cade could see them slashing their great claws into the front line's shields with abandon, splinters flying.

They were like machines. Methodical, precise and untiring. And seemingly ignorant of the swords that severed limbs and punctured their carapaces. Each fought until it fell, and another took its place.

Cade gripped the gun, slotting the belt into place with frantic fingers as he tried to lift it back to the tripod. Another blow from the front knocked Quintus back once more. The tripod fell, and Cade screamed above the furor, using his hand to pull Quintus away.

'Retreat!' he bellowed. 'Retreat!'

To their credit, the Romans did not break. They stepped backwards as one, grunting in unison. Once. Twice. Three times.

Thuds sounded from above as more ants dropped onto their formation. One fell on the shield above Cade's head, knocking the heavy wood into his head and pressing him into the ground.

Dazed, Cade could only push on, gripping Quintus and the gun with all the desperate strength he could muster as they slow-marched out of the tunnel.

The wall held, even as men cursed and pincers broke through shields and sliced away fingers, scissoring through metal and flesh.

Behind, a rattle of sling-stones gave blessed, brief relief, and the ants standing upon the roof of their testudo were knocked down, sliding along the edges or through to the floor below.

Step. Step. Step. Cade realised now that his blade lay forgotten, for he dragged the gun with one hand and held Quintus's shoulder and thumb-hooked loops of ammunition in the other.

Light, dim from the setting sun, was blessed relief, letting Cade know they had exited the tunnel. But suddenly the men stopped. Cade took a moment to turn, only to see his formation pressed against a low wall of river boulders, with their reinforcements crouched behind the wall, flailing slings as they hurled rocks above their allies' heads.

Cade's men were trapped by their own barrier, unable to find the time to retreat behind it.

And as the ants began to mass in front of their faltering shield wall, his men could not turn around to leap over it. Only crouch beneath the flailing claws, living by the grace of their disintegrating shields. Quintus fell to one knee, a claw slipping through his defence, snipping a deep wound into his thigh.

Cade set his jaw and blinked sweat from his eyes. If he didn't do something, they were all going to die. The men needed time.

'Come on!' he roared.

In one motion, he yanked Quintus back, straightening and stepping over him. He faced a wall of clicking and hissing ants. Cade lifted the gun in both hands, straining beneath the weight as the first of the ants lunged forwards.

He rammed it into his hip, depressing the trigger button. And the ant was blown away, spinning into oblivion.

It was like a holy wind had erupted in front of him, sweeping away insects in a hail of bullets. Limbs flew, and ichor spattered, tumbling their bodies back into the tunnel mouth. Cade swept the gun back and forth, his entire body juddering beneath the weight. He could not speak, only pour hellfire onto the creatures that wished his destruction.

Scores of ants were massed in the tunnel, slowed by the retreating testudo. At this close range, he could not miss.

And then, just like that, the gun fell silent again. His ammo was spent, and he could do no more. A hand pulled Cade back, tugging him towards the wall.

The gun fell from his nerveless fingers, and hands lifted him over the low barrier. In front of him, the pile of bodies twitched and quivered. And beyond that, the ants' chatters echoed down the tunnel.

They were still coming.

SIXTY-ONE

00:14:13
00:14:12
00:14:11

The ants did not come in a great wave, but trickled out in ones and twos, hurling themselves at the wall with suicidal abandon.

Many were missing limbs, or leaked ichor, as they limped and crawled over the dead. For every ant that reached the low wall, a higher magnitude of swords stabbed and slashed, overwhelming the hardy creatures by the fury of their onslaught alone.

Cade's gun had done its task. Enough to give them a fighting chance.

He stood on a nearby stump, watching Marius bellow orders and spread the exhausted survivors among the new wall's defenders. The barrier of river stones, hardly more than waist-high in places, was held up by gravity alone.

Looking into the tunnels, Cade could see the human bodies mixed in among the ants. Few and far between, but at least ten, with more hidden by the darkness within. They had made the ants pay dearly . . . but they too had taken losses.

More ants came, their antennae twitching, seemingly dazed as they emerged into the light. And to Cade's sudden relief, he noticed their condition. Hardly any of them were in one piece.

'We're going to make it,' Cade whispered.

His contenders were alive. His *friends* were alive. Bloodied, terrified, but alive.

They stood, unyielding, at the very centre of the wall, their long blades held high. He was proud at the sight of them. And ashamed.

Ashamed of the lies he had told them. Of the decisions he had made for them. The betrayal of their trust.

Now, he would ask much more of them. More than he had the right to. He would wait until the last vestiges of the ant army had emerged . . . and trigger the EMP.

He wished, more than anything, that he could ask them. Pose them some hypothetical. Ask if they would trade their lives for the Pantheon's. Live out their days in this place to ensure the safety of Earth.

Cade let his pack fall from his shoulder and reached deep within. He had wrapped Song's toy in sackcloth, and it was some relief when he took it out and saw it was intact.

He had purposefully not looked at it to avoid suspicion – for it was only supposed to be a memento, some reminder of his battle against the Greys.

Now, he held it in his hand, looking at it as if it had some deeper meaning to him. He had to be ready.

'Congratulations, Cade,' a voice said.

Cade spun, startled.

The timer still hung in the air, but it showed an entirely different number than what he had expected to see.

00:00:00
00:00:00
00:00:00

'What's going on?' Cade demanded.

Even as he spoke, he heard cheers from the Romans. He did not turn, instead staring at the Codex. Sure enough, the little girl appeared, replacing the timer.

'My opponent forfeited,' Abaddon said through his avatar. 'That is, the Pantheon member that leads the Formids, as I call them. He realised it was no use throwing his whole army away when you will all be returned to your planet once the battle is over regardless, and he will need them to defend now that he has lost his top place. In exchange for his forfeit, I have returned the remainder of his army, rather than let you fight it out. Don't say I never do anything for you.'

Cade glanced back and saw it was true. There were no living ants. Indeed, even the bodies had been teleported away. Only the black ichor and churned ground were evidence they had ever been there at all.

He stared at Abaddon. It was over. And at the same time . . . it was just beginning.

'So we get to go home?' Cade asked.

His fingers were sweaty as he ran them over the toy's eyes. Was it time? Every cowardly instinct told him to wait. Even as his heart told him that he had made his decision a long time ago. He was only delaying the inevitable.

Abaddon's avatar smiled sweetly at him. 'Well, yes. But first . . . I have another offer for you.'

Cade's finger froze. Was it a trick?

Before he could decide, the other contenders arrived around him.

'Cade,' Grace snapped. 'So nice of you to invite us to your little meeting.'

Cade knew their trust in him was the lowest it had ever been. If he pressed the button, would they believe him?

The little girl held up a finger.

'I have designated Cade as your leader. There is no *invitation*.'

Cade stepped down from the stump and went to stand with his friends. 'This time, Abaddon, we all choose. I'll decide once I hear what they've had to say.'

Abaddon clapped the little girl's hands. 'Oh, how exciting! This is going to be *delicious*. Decisions, decisions.'

'Spit it out, Abaddon,' Amber snapped.

The little girl rolled her wide eyes. 'All good things come to those who wait, isn't that what you humans say? But I suppose you have waited long enough. Here is your choice.'

The little girl paused for dramatic effect, then giggled at their stony faces. 'Oh, all right, then. You can go home now. Every one of you. I'll even leave you all at a place of your choosing, so long as nobody is there to see it. Say what you want to the world, if you can get them to believe you. That's choice number one. A good one, I grant you.'

She held up two fingers. 'But here's what's behind door number two. You stay. Fight on. Defend your place at the top of the leaderboard.'

The contenders stared at him, aghast.

'I know, I know,' Abaddon sighed. 'You miss your families. But I have grown so *fond* of you. I don't want to let you go. But I never lie, you know. Never.'

'There is no chance in hell that we'd stay,' Amber interrupted. 'You're insane if you think we'd do so voluntarily.'

Cade's heart twisted at her words. Would he be forced to choose this for them?

'Uh-ah,' the girl said, shaking her head dramatically. 'But you haven't heard what I offer in return.'

She gestured dramatically to her right, where the leaderboard materialised into thin air. Cade could not help but feel a little pride at seeing the human skull, now sitting at the top. Even if it was an achievement in as sick and twisted a game as this one.

Still, his finger twitched over the button. But a small flicker of hope played in the back of his mind. That somehow, Abaddon would offer him an advantage. Or some way of getting his friends back home.

'See this red line?' Abaddon said, pointing the little girl's finger at the line that bisected the leaderboard. 'When you fall below it, your world ends. What if I told you that red line didn't need to be there?'

353

The girl paused again and flashed them a bright smile.

'Keep talking,' Yoshi said.

The smile slowly turned into a grin. 'I knew you'd be interested. So if you all stayed, Romans included of course, we could remove the red line for . . . oh, I don't know. Ten thousand years?'

Silence.

By now, the Romans had gathered, standing some distance away. To them, the moderns were communing with the gods. Some had even knelt in awe. Marius, however, stood with his arms crossed, listening closely.

'So what do you say?' Abaddon said. 'Shall I leave you to discuss it?'

The little girl didn't wait for an answer. She disappeared, along with the leaderboard, leaving the Codex hanging in the air.

'Well . . . shit,' Scott said.

SIXTY-TWO

'We have to do it, right?' Yoshi said.

They were in the courtyard, sitting around the campfire. Marius was there too, joining them as soon as Abaddon left – nobody had asked him to leave.

'For the Earth's guaranteed safety?' Amber said. 'What are our lives, in the face of that? We might just live if we stayed here.'

'You can't be serious,' Grace snapped. 'You think we'd be dying in our sleep at a grand old age out here? We choose to stay, we'll be killed. Violently. And soon.'

Amber kicked at the fire, then shrugged. 'So be it,' she said.

'And how can we even trust Abaddon to keep his word?' Grace demanded.

'He's never lied to us before,' Cade said quietly.

'Well, I'd do it,' Bea said. 'I'd stay.'

Trix shook her head. 'No, Bea. We're going home.'

Grace threw up her arms. 'After all this, we're playing

right into his hands!' she said. 'Maybe he wouldn't destroy Earth anyway! Maybe it's just a lie to keep us fighting. Is he really willing to wipe us out and start all over again?'

'You think so?' Bea asked. 'There's a thought.'

Amber laughed bitterly. 'Say you're wrong,' she said. 'Say he *is* willing to destroy Earth. What happens when we go back home? Can you live your life knowing that some other poor souls will be out here, fighting to keep above that red line? Who knows if we'd even live a full life before they fail and we disappear in a flash of white light?'

'And say we're right?' Grace retorted. 'We have to choose to believe one way or another. Can't we choose to believe the one where we get to go *home*?'

'To what?' Amber asked. 'If my parents are alive, they'll be almost ninety years old. And can you imagine their reaction when their teenage daughter shows up? Would they even recognise me? People will think we're insane.'

Grace stood and stalked off. 'You're idiots!' she called over her shoulder. 'I vote home. That's it. Make the right choice.'

'Grace!' Scott called.

He groaned and followed her. Trix waited a few seconds, then went too.

Amber sighed, then looked over to Cade. 'You're awfully quiet,' she said.

Cade stared at the Grey toy, holding it in his hands. 'He'll destroy Earth if he has to,' he said. 'Don't you remember what happened to the Greys? They're not on the leaderboard any more. They're gone.'

His words were sobering.

'We'll stay,' Marius said.

Cade looked up and caught the grim look upon the man's face.

'Why?' Cade asked. 'You've been here longer than almost anyone.'

The man shrugged, staring into the flames. 'Go to a world full of your lot?' he asked, a half-smile on his face. 'No, thank you. I'm a relic. By rights, I should have died in Caledonia. So should all the men here. We're living on borrowed time.'

He tutted. 'I did wish I could have seen your world for a second though,' he said wistfully. 'See what the world's become. Knowing what we're fighting for. But meeting you, that's enough for me.'

Cade nodded respectfully. 'You're a good man, Marius,' he said. 'I had my doubts, I confess. Just stay that way. Don't lose your humanity in this place.'

'You speak like you're not staying with him,' Amber said.

Cade shrugged. 'Who knows how long I'll live. Once the world's safe . . . I won't know what I'm fighting for. I'm tired, Amber. I hope Abaddon picks another favourite, because you're right. I can't make decisions for us any more.'

He looked to the toy once more. Abaddon had made him a cruel offer. A way to live. Not to go home but . . . Earth would be safe. Who knew how long his planet would last, left in humanity's own hands? Perhaps in ten thousand years, the place would be a nuclear wasteland anyway.

'Cade,' Amber said.

She stood and walked over to him, taking her place beside him on the log.

'We were angry at you before. But look at what you did. We're all alive. And we're either saving Earth or going home.'

She took his hand and lifted his chin with the other, meeting his gaze.

'Either way, we both have something to fight for.'

She kissed him then. Softly, gently, and it was over all too quickly. But it was enough to set Cade's world on fire. And utterly break his heart.

Because now, Cade knew what he had to do.

'I have a solution,' Cade said. 'We don't all need to go.'

'What?' Amber asked.

'Why do you think Abaddon always talks to me?' Cade asked. 'It's because he likes me the most. God knows why, but he does. So I'll stay. Marius stays. Everyone else goes home.'

'Just like that?' Yoshi asked. 'You think he'll just let that happen?'

Amber held up a hand. 'Cade, I'm staying with you,' she said. 'We're both going or we're both staying. That's the deal.'

Cade smiled at her and squeezed her hand. 'It's me he wants,' he whispered. 'Let me negotiate with him. Just us two. Trust me one last time.'

The others looked at him, and only now did Cade see the tears on their faces.

'I'll stay too,' Quintus whispered.

Cade shook his head. 'You go to my family for me, Quintus,' Cade said. 'Tell them what happened to me. Tell them the stories I told you; they'll believe you. You deserve to enjoy our world. You've earned it. You all have.'

Amber sobbed. 'And you haven't?'

Cade smiled and wiped a tear from her face. 'I'll be fine,' he said. 'This is the way it has to be. Trust me. And I promise, whatever we agree . . . I'll only do it once you've all heard what deal he offers. OK?'

There was a chorus of agreement, though Amber and Quintus remained silent. Cade understood. He'd feel the same way in their position.

He stood and walked away.

'I know you're listening, Abaddon,' Cade said. 'Let's make a deal.'

SIXTY-THREE

Cade felt at peace as he and the little girl walked to the plane, some distance away from the fire, near the remains of the fallen wall.

It was strange to know exactly what he needed to do. That was an unfamiliar feeling in this world.

'Tell me something,' Cade said. 'Why me? Of all the people in the world. Why?'

The little girl paused and took his hand, like a daughter reaching to her father for comfort.

'I watch your world, Cade. It's an interesting place. With interesting people. But you . . . well . . . you were even more interesting. I could see in you the type of mind that was made to play my game the way I *wanted* it to be played. An inquisitive, problem-solving, lateral-thinking mind, plus a thousand other personality traits that suited my purposes. One that knew history, and appreciated it. And so young too – I could wring many years of entertainment from you. That's why, Cade. Of all the people in the world, you were the right age, with the right knowledge and just the right mindset and personality.'

Cade rubbed his eyes. He almost believed Abaddon. 'So I was special, was I?'

'You were a good *fit*,' Abaddon said. 'Don't be getting delusions of grandeur now.'

Cade shook his head, ignoring the alien. Perhaps he *did* have some innate traits that made him play the game well. Or maybe he was just lucky.

But Abaddon was going to regret choosing him. Because perhaps it was for the same reasons Abaddon chose him that Cade had made the choice he had.

'So you heard my proposal,' Cade said. 'What am I and the Romans worth to you?'

The girl skipped over to the plane and sat upon its wing, dangling her pudgy legs.

'A thousand years,' she said. 'And another five hundred for each one of your friends who decides to stay too.'

Cade crossed his arms. 'That's not what's on the table,' he said. 'Just me and the Romans. Everyone else, including Quintus, goes home.'

'Didn't you say earlier that you'd *all* choose? Can't go back on your word now. Like I said, honesty is *very* important to me.'

'Five hundred years,' Cade said.

The girl looked up at him, startled.

'Do the deal right now. Everyone goes home. I stay with the Romans.'

The girl furrowed her brow. 'Love does make humans do

crazy things,' she said. 'But I'm sorry, Cade. I've made up my mind.'

She dropped delicately off the plane, then paused and clicked her fingers.

A device appeared in her hand. It was a simple thing, a dial beneath a calculator-like screen, and a large button at the top.

'Tick up the dial. It goes up in five-minute intervals. When you want to set it, press the button,' Abaddon said. 'Simple enough. I assume you might need it, since you're going to be staying. Like I said. I *always* keep my promises.'

She pressed it into Cade's hands, then pranced away, heading for the others. By now Grace had returned, and she was scowling at Cade from across the fire. It was a shame that she would never know what Cade was about to do.

'Ladies and gentlemen, boys and girls, I do believe Cade and I have made a deal,' Abaddon's avatar announced, clapping her dainty hands. 'Cade and the Romans are staying, except for you of course, darling Quintus. That's bought Earth one thousand years of safety. For every one of you who stays with him, that's another five centuries on top. So, Grace and Trix are going home . . . who else?'

When no one moved or spoke, she tapped a tiny foot, her arms crossed.

'Hurry now,' she said. 'I may be immortal but I've got better things to do.'

Grace raised her hand, as if somehow Abaddon would forget she wanted to go home. Cade hardly blamed her. He might have made the same choice in her shoes.

Scott was the next to raise his hand. He looked at Cade apologetically, mouthing *sorry*. Cade simply inclined his head and smiled. This was what he wanted.

'Everyone is going, Abaddon,' Cade called out. 'Just—'

'Not one more word!' Abaddon snarled, turning the little girl's face towards Cade in a rictus of rage. 'Be silent, or there will be no deal at all.'

Cade held up his hands in peace but raised his eyebrows at the others. He wanted to beg them to go. Because there was no need for them to stay. The moment they were gone, Cade was going to press the button . . . and end the Pantheon for good.

'Is that all, then?' Abaddon said, turning back to the others.

'No!' Bea said, raising her hand. She grasped Trix's too, lifting it above the girl's head. Yoshi followed suit, avoiding Cade's eyes.

'Anyone else? Going, going . . .'

'Amber, you have to—' Cade begged, but was suddenly cut short.

His mouth had been seized by an invisible force, keeping it clamped closed.

He was not the only one who went silent. Quintus and Amber said nothing. Only stared into the flames, ignoring Abaddon's words.

'Very well, then,' Abaddon giggled, clapping her hands. 'I'll leave you all in the locations I first took you from, shall I?'

She didn't give them time to answer. Because in that

instant, they were gone. Like they had never been there at all. No goodbyes. No heartfelt words. Abaddon had stolen even that from them.

Cade's heart broke a second time that day. Of all his friends that could have stayed, Amber and Quintus were the ones he'd wanted to save the most. Now, they would live out their days on this planet if he succeeded. And face Abaddon's wrath if he failed.

Cade walked to the fire and sat down heavily. He laid his head on Amber's shoulder and pulled Quintus close.

'Thank you,' Cade said. 'For everything.'

They held him tight, and Cade allowed the tears to flow freely down his face. It was time.

'How very sweet,' Abaddon said, leaning in close for a better view. 'Such sentiment. But hey, look on the bright side. You bought Earth two thousand years of safety. And you get to stay here and play with *me*.'

Cade cleared his throat and patted his friends to let him go. He looked down at the timer in one hand and the toy in the other.

'I have one last thing to say to you, Abaddon,' Cade said, his voice shaking with anger.

'Oh yes?' Abaddon asked. 'What's that?'

Cade smiled through his tears and looked up into Abaddon's avatar's eyes.

'This,' he said.

And detonated the EMP.

SIXTY-FOUR

The girl crackled, then disappeared, followed by the thud of the Codex falling directly into the fire. Cade left it there and jumped to his feet.

'Listen to me very carefully,' he said forcefully. 'We have to do a lot of things very quickly. Otherwise we are all going to die. Follow me. Now!'

He ran towards the plane, his heart pounding near out of his chest. He was so used to a timer. Now, there was none. The Pantheon could come online in an hour, or ten minutes. All he knew was he had to get that bomb to the alien ship. And get the alien ship out of the water for that matter.

Marius, Amber, and Quintus had followed, but the other Romans were still milling about, having watched the disappearances in awe.

'Detach the bomb,' Cade shouted, pointing at the weapon. 'And carry it down the tunnel to the waterfall. Marius, call over your men, it's going to take at least a dozen of them to lift this thing. And be careful with it!'

'Cade, what the hell is happening?' Amber shouted.

'The Greys,' Cade said. 'I'm working with them. This bomb is going to destroy the Pantheon. Please, we don't have much time. The Pantheon got knocked out by an electromagnetic pulse, but they could come online at any minute.'

He grabbed Quintus and pulled him along.

'Come on,' Cade said. 'They'll catch up.'

He began to run, and shouted over his shoulder.

'As fast as you can!'

They sprinted down the tunnel, slipping and sliding over the gore left by the gun. It was dark there now, with no timer from the Codex, nor torches to light their way. But even in the dim darkness, he still tripped over pitted surfaces where the bullets had sprayed.

They emerged into the moonlight. It was dark that night, the small white satellite moon almost entirely hidden behind the larger red one.

Cade pressed the toy's left eye twice and muttered a silent prayer. Quintus watched him silently.

'What will happen if this does not work?' Quintus asked.

Cade closed his eyes. 'Then Abaddon will find out what I've been planning. He'll torture me for information. Rip me apart atom by atom. Maybe he'll kill you all in front of me as revenge.'

Quintus grinned. 'So we will . . . piss him off . . . right?' he asked.

Cade chuckled at Quintus's grin. 'Yeah, I guess we will.'

Quintus punched him on the shoulder. 'Worth it.'

They stared at the waterfall. Still, nothing happened.

'Maybe we can dig for it,' Cade whispered.

He hurried to the pool, praying that the ship would emerge. But still, nothing.

He stared into the water's inky depths. No movement. Not even a hint.

'Useless . . .' Cade whispered, lifting the toy and pressing the left eye twice again.

Instantly, the water lit up. He could see the rocks upon the bottom, white light glowing between the cracks.

'Oh . . . oh damn,' Cade said. 'Get back!'

They fell over themselves backing away as rocks and water exploded outwards, and an enormous, sleek black machine exited the water.

It was nothing like Cade had expected. A cigar-shaped craft, complete with what might have been a cockpit of dark glass at the front tip.

The ship spun slowly, before floating closer and settling on the grass alongside the lake. And in the moment it stopped, the back end opened up, splitting in two and widening.

Cade gaped at the sight, even as water poured out from the interior, nearly knocking Cade over. With it came an object. Once the deluge had stopped, Cade picked it up.

It was a helmet. Similar to what an astronaut might wear, complete with sun visor and what looked like flashlights on either side.

'You will fly in this?' Quintus asked as Cade stared at his reflection in the mirrored surface.

He hardly recognised himself. He appeared so much older now. His eyes ringed with deep black, his skin waxy and bloodless. His hair was a rat's nest, and his facial hair patchy. He might as well have been looking at a beggar.

'Cade?'

Cade glanced up and nodded. 'I think so. Just gotta get the bomb in there now.'

Even as he spoke, he could hear shouting coming from the tunnel. For a moment he was worried, then he saw the Romans emerge from the dark hole, yelling one another instructions on how to manoeuvre the bomb.

It was so much larger than Cade had expected. The thing was going to take up most of the ship.

'Go help them,' Cade said. 'I need to suit up.'

Quintus furrowed his brows, not sure what Cade meant, but went anyway. Cade leaped into the ship, which was floating two feet from the ground.

The inside was as much a surprise as the outside. The walls were perfectly smooth and round, almost like those of the tunnel. And at the end of that smooth, rounded room was a protruding console beneath a dome of black glass. Again, it was entirely smooth but for the lights that danced along its surface.

But most interesting of all was the single chair affixed to the floor. And its occupant. A humanoid figure, draped limply across it.

Cade edged closer and found himself looking at a skeleton in a space suit. One with an enormous round skull and giant pits for eyes. A Grey.

Cade could only wonder what had killed them, if the suit was still intact. It seemed, on closer inspection, that the pilot had drowned. Their helmet must have been out of reach when the ship flooded, and Cade could see the scratches where they had attempted to rip off the seatbelt and failed. It was jammed, and Cade had to fiddle with it before it came loose.

'Terrible way to go,' Cade whispered as he began to undress.

SIXTY-FIVE

He was almost fully dressed when the Romans arrived. They heaved the bomb onto the ship, its great rusted frame so long that it almost reached the cockpit.

'Amber?' Cade called.

She wasn't there. Only Marius, clambering into the ship and giving a low whistle.

'So this is what the Tritons had at their disposal,' he said. 'A wonder we beat them.'

Cade ignored him. 'Where's Amber?' he demanded.

'She took one look at this ship and went running back to the keep,' he said.

Cade groaned and instinctively looked for the Codex, before cursing the habit. He had no idea how long it had been since he'd pressed the EMP. Ten minutes? Twenty?

'Get off the ship,' Cade said. 'I need to take off soon, and there's only one of these suits.'

He pulled on the final glove as he did so, flexing his fingers. One of them had to be tucked into his palm, for the

370

Greys had one digit fewer than humans. But it was worth it if it kept him alive in space.

He didn't know how much oxygen the suit held, but he was sure it would last the hour. Now, it was time to leave. He hurried to the back of the ship and leaped down to join the others.

'Quintus,' Cade said. 'It's been an honour, my friend. My brother. Look after yourself while I'm gone. And look after Amber.'

'Cade!' Amber's voice called. 'Cade!'

Cade turned, only to see Amber sprinting towards him. She was holding something bulky in her arms.

She reached him, panting, and shoved something into his arms. He almost didn't recognise it. It looked like a green backpack. Why was she giving him a backpack?

'Put it on,' she said. 'Seriously, put it on.'

Cade didn't have time to argue, and spun, allowing her to put his arms through it.

'If you get shot down,' she said. 'You use this, OK?'

Cade stared at her, confused.

'It's a parachute. I took it from the pilot in the plane.'

She smiled at him and kissed him deeply. 'I know you're short of time but . . . I love you.'

Cade felt his stomach twist as he looked down at her. Despite the battle, the exhaustion, the dirt, sweat, ichor and blood, she had never looked more beautiful to him. He kissed her And time seemed to slow. He savoured every second her soft lips were pressed against his before she pushed him away.

'I lov—' Cade began.

371

'Tell me when you get back,' Amber said, looking down. 'Go on now. Go.'

Cade took one last second to hug his two friends close. Then he was on the ship and running for the chair.

He sat down and put on his helmet, swivelling it until he heard it lock into place. He grabbed the Grey figurine from the console and pressed the right eye three times. Then he closed his eyes as the ship's back door sealed shut. The world seemed to throb . . . and he shot into the sky.

Cade woke up. His stomach lurched, and the bones of the Grey alien clattered around the room. As did everything else, including the backpack, Abaddon's remote and the figurine, having fallen from his awkwardly gloved hand as the g-force rammed back his head, arms and legs.

When Song had programmed the autopilot instructions, he must have not accounted for Cade's humanity. Maybe Greys could withstand faster speeds. Or maybe he just wanted Cade to get there really fast. Either way, Cade had passed out.

As it was, Cade could already see the blue of the sky turning into black as they pierced the atmosphere, and he wished he could take another look at the planet he had come from. Instead, as the seconds ticked by, a shape began to form, red in the moonlight.

The Pantheon's ship.

It was every bit as impressive as Cade had imagined. A giant metal lump of machinery, all spires, antennae and protrusions. It seemed to approach slowly, yet Cade knew it was simply the sheer size of the thing that made it seem that way.

It expanded endlessly in his vision, virtually a small moon in its own right. Cade wondered what possible need there could be for something of such size when only twenty-one passengers – the entire Pantheon – lived within.

Was it the machines that powered their teleportation technology? A factory for Codexes? Or perhaps a massive, complex system of life support, keeping the immortal beings alive forever.

Regardless, he soon found the pressure lift from him and experienced a strange feeling of weightlessness. They had left the atmosphere, air hissing out from the hole in the Grey ship's windscreen.

Still they flew, closer and closer to the enormous ship. Soon, it was all Cade could see. The seconds ticked by, and Cade only knew that the Pantheon's power was still down by the fact he was still alive. There was no way of knowing how long he had.

The Grey ship was closing now, so fast that Cade threw up his arms, thinking they would collide. Instead, the ship stopped abruptly.

There was a hiss, and Cade turned to see the back of his ship opening. There was no sound at all, for sound did not travel in a vacuum. All he heard was the hoarse sounds of his breathing.

He took a few more gulps of air. All good. The suit was working fine.

Cade stood, only to find himself floating up to the ceiling.

He pushed himself back down and dry heaved, fighting a bout of nausea. He hadn't got his sea legs yet. Or his space legs.

Wary of the time, he gathered the Grey figurine and the remote, shoving them into his backpack and slinging it front ways across his chest for easy access. It wouldn't do to lose the figurine in space – let it float off into the night.

Still, it had only one instruction left. The bomb.

He decided to look at the Pantheon's ship itself. He edged by the bomb, which was gently twisting a few inches in the air, and looked down, to see he was directly beneath a hatch.

A hatch that was open.

'OK, Cade,' he said. 'Time to kill a god.'

SIXTY-SIX

Cade had not considered how he would carry the bomb into the ship, so trusting had he been of Song's plan. Now he realised it would be a piece of cake. Without gravity, the enormous thing was weightless.

All he had to do was manoeuvre it into position above the hole . . . and pull it in with him.

The hatch was wide as a lorry and had no lid – perhaps it was an exhaust or served some other futuristic function. Whatever its purpose, it was so deep and dark Cade could hardly see.

The inside of the hatch was a long circular corridor, one that seemed to stretch for miles, straight down into the ship. He might have been blind entirely when he got in were it not for the lights that had come on automatically on either side of his helmet.

Now it was time to figure out how to get the bomb down with him.

It was a brute of a thing to manoeuvre, and once it moved

it was hard to stop. Only after a lot of wrangling – and a few heart-stopping collisions with the Grey ship's back end – did he manage to get it floating in roughly the right position.

Cade wrapped two hands around the tip of the nuclear missile, nestling it in the soft outside of his backpack on his chest. Then, he placed two feet upon either side of the hatch, where a convenient rim was, and pushed off with all his might.

He flew. Grazing along walls, bumping them. He was lucky they were so smooth, a virtual borehole into the ship, almost as if some bullet or missile was supposed to be travelling *out* of it.

His vision soon became an endless blur, staring into the dark pupil of the tunnel, with the grey wall the iris surrounding it.

It was like that for almost two minutes, and Cade craned his neck, straining to see what was ahead. But all he saw was the endless tunnel, taking him ever deeper into the ship.

And then . . . he saw it. Lights, coming up fast. Cade extended his legs, scraping them against the smooth walls, trying to slow himself down.

It was in the nick of time, as he smashed into a dead end, knocking the wind out of him. The bomb near-broke his ribs, such was its momentum.

He choked, and threw up into his suit. But no time to heave more, no time to blink away the tears from his watering eyes.

This had to be it.

With trembling hands, Cade tugged open his backpack. Pulled out the Grey figurine.

And screamed in horror.

The toy was crushed.

Its head had come clean off, broken by the impact of the missile against his chest.

He cursed, and cursed again. Screamed into the silent oblivion. How could he have been so *stupid*?

His vision blurred as he cried bitter tears and looked around for something, anything to use to blow up the missile. He should have let it crash into the wall – perhaps that would have blown it up.

Only then did he truly see where he was. The lights he had noticed seemed like emergency lighting, flickering on and off, giving off a low electric glow.

There was a glass panel in front of him, though it had not cracked with the impact of his crash. But it was what was behind it that took his interest. There, floating in liquid . . . were the Pantheon.

It had to be, for he counted twenty-one of them. Living creatures, so deep inside their ship. They could be nothing else.

The sight sickened him.

In his mind's eye, he had imagined malevolent figures in black hooded robes, cackling on ancient stone thrones and rubbing their decrepit hands with glee.

These things . . . they might hardly count as alive at all. They were featureless. Like the torsos of deboned pigs – blobs of pink, semitranslucent flesh, hanging in liquid. Pickled meat, bereft of appendages or senses.

Each one was plugged into a mess of tube and wires, running into the walls of the ship. Metal antennae studded the walls, and the flesh twitched horribly as he swept his headlamps from one to the next.

Eons of time relying on machines had rotted away their limbs. Electric senses had robbed them of their corporeal ones. They were the ghosts in the machine. The ghosts of life.

As he pressed his hand against the wall, he felt something. A vibration. Not constant, but intensifying and ebbing. It was almost as if . . . he leaned his helmet against the glass.

'. . . will give you riches beyond your imagining. Immortality, should you want it. We can make you a member of the Pantheon. I never lie, Cade. I *never* lie. Do not do this—'

Cade had always wondered what Abaddon sounded like. And now he knew. It was the Codex's voice. The electric one. There was no humanity to be had. Nothing even close to it.

'Can you hear me, Abaddon?' Cade said.

The voice stopped. Then:

'I can send you home. You and your friends. We'll let the world know what you've done. Do not *do* this. You'll never survive the blast.'

'Your game ends here, Abaddon,' Cade whispered, tasting the bitter tears trickling down his cheeks. There was nothing he could do now. Nothing but give Abaddon the fright of his immortal life.

'You're right, Cade,' Abaddon wheedled. 'It's over. I see

that now. But think of what we could do for humanity. Life eternal. A whole universe to explore. I cannot *lie*, Cade. Make one last deal with me.'

Cade laughed, half in despair. Perhaps he *should* make a deal. After all, he was bluffing. There was no way to set off the bomb now.

'This is *my* game now, Abaddon,' he hissed, his anger hot in his belly. 'How does it feel to play?'

'Don't do this!' Abaddon shrieked, and now it was the little girl's voice, trembling and plaintive. 'Did I not hold my end of the bargain each and every time? Did I not give you the bomb and timer? You can trust me, Cade. We can both get what we want. You must want to make a deal if you're still here.'

And that was when Cade realised. He didn't need the figurine at all. Abaddon didn't even understand its importance.

Because the fool had already given him exactly what he needed: the timer.

Cade reached into his pack, giving a silent prayer. He grasped the timer Abaddon had given him, holding it up to the light. He closed his eyes . . . and pressed the button.

Nothing happened, and he pushed his head against the glass once more.

'There's no self-destruct, Cade,' Abaddon's voice came. 'The timer lasts five minutes at least, and by then we'll be back online. I'll rip you to shreds, Cade. You and your friends. Your family. Everyone you've ever loved. Every human. Every animal. Every blade of grass. An eternity of torture. Make a deal with me now, and you'll have everything. Ignore me and die. I *never* lie, Cade.'

Cade clicked the dial up, once. Saw the five minutes on the little screen.

'I'll take my chances,' Cade said.

He pressed the button.

SIXTY-SEVEN

Cade pushed off from the glass, gliding over the bomb and deep into the corridor. He had no plan. No inkling of what he would do next.

The corridor was an escape hatch – of that he was now certain. There could be no other reason for there to be a tunnel that led directly to the outside world. It seemed the Pantheon had detected the EMP and almost triggered their ejection in time, machinery within the ship slotting their little ecosystem into position. But the EMP had put a stop to their ejection sequence before it had completed.

It was all just a guess, and Cade wished there was some way of hijacking the system to get to safety, but he had no time to figure out how it worked. Better to return to the Grey ship and try to figure out how to make it fly. At the very least, he'd be outside the Pantheon's ship when the bomb blew.

His mind raced as he hurtled down the corridor, watching the timer on the remote in his hand. This was the first time he had willed a timer to go faster.

3:14
3:13
3:12

He had been plummeting for almost two minutes, and it was only by good fortune he spotted the hatch in time. He did everything in his power to slow down, kicking off one wall to rattle back and forth between the walls, scraping his hands against the smooth surface, the remote shoved back into his pack. He stopped a few feet from the hatch's entrance, after a Herculean effort. He was battered but alive. More alive than he'd ever been in his life.

Cade pushed himself out the hatch, knocking the ship gently in the process. The thing moved, drifting into space.

Panicking, Cade leaped after it, passing in through the back before it drifted out of reach. He slammed into the ceiling and set the thing spinning.

Dizzied, Cade shoved off the wall of the rotating ship, his fingertips hooking onto the chair. He managed to take a seat, looping his arms through the belt there.

The ship was dead. He knew it as soon as he sat down. The console in front of him was bereft of the dancing lights he had seen before, just plain black glass.

He tentatively pressed at it with his fingers, then his palms, then slammed his fists down in an attempt to do . . . something. Anything.

But instead, the ship drifted on. And shook.

Slowly at first, then more and more, until Cade's teeth rattled in his head. Was this to be his end? Drifting into oblivion until his oxygen ran out?

It almost didn't matter. All that mattered was that the timer hit zero. He sat there, one hand clutching the timer, another still prodding desperately along the console of the ship.

2:11
2:10
2:09

The ship shuddered, and Cade looked up. The spinning stopped, and the outside of the cockpit was flaring orange.

He had re-entered the atmosphere.

Flames erupted outside the ship, flaring along the dark glassy material of the cockpit. His body pressed into the seat, at first gently, then harder and harder. His vision was filled with fire outside the ship, and he could hear a roaring that reverberated in his chest.

The pressure ramped up higher and higher, until Cade could hardly breathe. He counted down from ten. And passed out at eight.

Cade woke up falling. Still strapped into his seat, the world spinning and flipping. Blue, then yellow, blue, then yellow.

The ship was flipping, over and over. Dropping, fast. By some miracle, the Grey ship's exterior had acted as a heat shield. He was alive. Half-dead, but alive.

But he wouldn't be if he crashed into the ground, and they were now in the atmosphere.

Cade looked up, if you could call it that, and saw the back

of the ship was still open. He undid the strap . . . and leaped.

There was pain as he slammed into a wall and slid down its surface. Then, he was out, into the bright light of the sky. Spinning into nothingness.

Far beneath him, he saw the patchwork quilt of Acies, and the ship seemed to tumble up and past him. And far above, he saw the flash.

Cade stared at the timer. Glimpsed the remote before it was snatched away by the wind.

00:00

He'd done it. The gods were dead . . . and Cade was finally free.

EPILOGUE

Cade fell and fell.

It felt like hours of falling. He threw out his arms and legs to catch as much friction as he could to slow him down.

Above him he had seen the pieces of the Pantheon ship falling through the atmosphere, blazing like meteorites before burning to nothingness. The streaking of the smaller pieces strobed out light, and great lumps of material left behind smoking trails, criss-crossing the sky as they burned slowly towards the planet's surface.

Whatever material the Grey ship had been made from, it was sturdier stuff than the Pantheon's.

He knew at some point he would need to open his parachute. But he needed to decide where he would land first.

He knew what he was looking for. It was just one patch among the hundreds spread across the world below him. A drop of blue, in a sea of green, within an ocean of desert.

Once he found it, he pulled the cord on his parachute.

Yanked the guide straps to take him left, take him right.

He drifted on the wind, breathing the suit's oxygen. There was no cold. No pain. The suit kept him safe.

The parachute spiralled, and Cade prayed he would land in the right place. Prayed he would survive the impact.

Fiery debris flamed past him. Dozens of metal shards, raining like a meteor shower around him.

He could do no more than stare at the canopy above him. That thin, ancient stretch of canvas, half-rotted by seawater and the jungle heat. Any second, a flaming ball of death could end him.

So it was with some surprise when he found himself circling above what he thought was the caldera, honing down into the square he had called home for so long. It was painstaking work, keeping himself centred, and twice he spiralled out of control, kicking at the rat's nest of strings tangling above him.

Somehow, they held.

He knew where the keep was. Had stared at the Codex's map for so long, he knew it as well as the freckles upon Amber's face.

Pulling the straps, he angled towards it. Past it, into the salt flats, then back. The ground was growing closer and closer now. Beyond him, he could see the entrance to the bone fields.

And tiny figures, streaming out from the keep.

Down he went, the wind whipping at him. He was going so fast. Too fast. He felt giddy, as if it couldn't be real.

He hit the ground, tumbling over and over, sinking into

the salt-sand crust. His legs screamed in agony, then his ribs, his back.

Cade smelled the air as he stared into the wide blue sky, marred by a fresh crack in his helmet. It smelled familiar. Smelled like home.

Yes. His new home. He watched the black trails of the Pantheon's wreckage, and the flashes of light. He had set the sky on fire.

Hands lifted him. Twisted off his helmet.

Amber and Quintus were there, clutching him close. He could hear his name, distantly.

'It's OK,' he whispered as Amber clutched him close. 'We're going to be OK.'

He lay back, letting them lift him. Let them carry him back to his home.

Back to a new world.

ACKNOWLEDGEMENTS

There have been a great many people who I owe a debt of gratitude for their contribution to the creation and publication of *The Champion*.

I would like to thank my agent, Juliet Mushens, for all her hard work, teaming up with many amazing publishers around the world. She has been my guiding light throughout the entire process, and my life would not be the same without her.

Thank you to the publishing teams at Hodder Children's and Feiwel and Friends for helping bring a beautiful book to as many readers as possible. They have done fantastic work and have stuck with me from start to finish. In particular, I would like to thank:

Naomi Greenwood, Michelle Brackenborough, James McParland, Lucy Clayton, Jennifer Hudson, Nic Goode, Kelly Llewellyn, Emma Roberts, Jean Feiwel, Emily Settle, Liz Szabla, Kim Waymer, Dawn Ryan, Ilana Worrell, Julia Gardiner, Mariel Dawson, Trisha Previte, Kathleen

Breitenfeld, Katie Quinn, Morgan Dubin, Katie Halata and Liza DeBlock.

I would like to thank my friends and family for their ongoing support, guidance, and patience. Vic James, Sasha Alsberg, Dominic Wong, Michael Miller, Brook Aspden, as well as Liege, Jay, Sindri and Raj Matharu, you guys rock.

Finally, thank you, the readers, for all you have done. Your comments, reviews, messages, and encouragement have meant the world to me. It is ultimately you who made me a success, and you who keep me writing. I will be forever astonished, honoured and grateful for your support.

Thank you.

Taran Matharu

TARAN MATHARU

was born in London in 1990 and found a passion
for reading at a very early age. His love for stories
developed into a desire to create his own, writing
his first book at nine years old.

At twenty-two, while taking time off to travel, Taran
began to write *Summoner: The Novice*, taking part in
NaNoWriMo 2013. Thanks to Wattpad.com and
updating daily, its popularity dramatically increased,
reaching over three million reads in less than six
months. After being featured by NBC News, Taran
decided to launch his professional writing career
and has never looked back.

The Summoner series is now published in fifteen
languages, and is a *New York Times* bestseller.

@TaranMatharu1
@taranmatharuauthor
authortaranmatharu.com

SUMMONER

— BY TARAN MATHARU —

'Influenced by Harry Potter, *The Lord of the Rings* and video games, it appeals to fans of all of these' *The Sunday Times*